Shoot
The Staff

Shoot
The Staff

CJ Houy

Published in the USA by:
CJ Houy

ISBN: 978-0-9992187-4-7 (paperback)
       978-0-9992187-5-4 (ebook)

Printed in the United States of America

Book & cover design by Darlene & Dan Swanson • www.van-garde.com

Chapter One

"Fred Hendricks?" A chubby, dark-haired woman in a clingy dress stared at him from behind a gleaming oak counter with a speckled laminate top. A large American flag hung on the wall behind her. She held a piece of paper with both hands.

Fred nodded and stood up from the padded folding chair along the glass wall. A sharp pain in his stomach jolted him. An acid eruption scalded his throat. He groaned and faked a cough to disguise the moan.

"That's me," he responded in a gravelly voice. He winced as his lower back sent a sciatic twinge down his leg. Forcing a smile, he approached the wooden barrier.

The woman pulled open a swinging half door adjacent to the counter and beckoned Fred to join her in the US Senate's disbursing office anteroom. The poorly named office handled payroll, among other things, including retirement counseling.

"I've seen you around for years. Now I can put a name with the face," she said.

"Yeah, you look familiar too." He followed the squat, middle-aged woman as she jiggled past a maze of cubicles, desks, and chairs. She peered over her shoulder several times, eyeing him. At the last cubicle, she plopped behind the desk and motioned for him to take a seat.

She tapped a few keys as he sat down. "So, you're retiring. It says here it's been almost forty years. Most of that on the Appropriations Committee. Wow! That's a long time in the pressure cooker, Mr. Hendricks. You must be under the old retirement plan . . . but you should've maxed out by now."

"Yeah, I did. They switched me over. I'm paying into the new system now. Don't your records show that?"

"I see. Yes, there it is. So, your annuity will be eighty percent of your highest three-years' average salary and a smidgen more under the current system. Not bad, if I may say so. But frankly, forty years in the Senate. There aren't many who do that. You must have put up with a lot of sh . . . stuff to last so long. I'd say you deserve it. Besides, you guys on appropriations are worth a lot more on the outside with your ties to the senators and the money. You're a 'secret society.' Appropriations is all gobbledygook to outsiders. I've been an accountant here for twenty years, and I struggle to follow what's going on in your world."

"That's what people always say. But look, I don't have a lot of time. What do I need to do to retire?"

"Really, not much. Does your boss know?"

"No. I told your counselor I'm not quitting till December. I'll even put it off if we haven't finished our bill by then."

"OK." She smiled and shook her head. "It's terrible the way things are working. Or, should I say, not working." She giggled. "How many years have you worked over the holidays now? It seems like it's been ten since we adjourned before Christmas."

"Yeah, pretty much. I don't mind, though. Keeps me busy. But forty years is long enough." He drummed his fingers on his knee.

"I should say so. I'm out the door when I turn sixty. Which subcommittee are you on? Or do you work for the full committee?"

"I just took over as Sam Jackson's clerk on the defense sub-committee." He squirmed in his seat and sighed.

"On defense! You guys have all the money. And you run the show, Mr. Hendricks. Wow!" She gave him an admiring head nod and winked.

He faked a smile and glanced at his watch. His eyes narrowed a bit. *What's taking her so long? Jesus Christ. This isn't a date. Just tell me what I need to do, lady.* "So, am I all set?" His voice sounded more like a Doberman's growl.

"Almost. Are you signing up for survivor benefits?"

"No," he grumbled.

"OK. But we like all our pending retirees to understand what the benefits are for your family before you make the final decision." She looked at him and smiled again.

"No need. No family."

"Oh, I see." Her expression shifted to a sympathetic grimace. "OK, sign here. We'll also need to tell the Office of Personnel Management where to send your annuity."

He sighed. "Just keep sending it to the Senate Credit Union." Resignation had overpowered his disgruntlement.

She nodded, tapped on her keyboard, and printed another form. "Sign here. Now, it's customary for your office to send in the retirement request."

"I don't plan on telling them until I'm ready to walk out the door," he snapped.

"OK. You're certainly eligible. I guess we can dispense with that." She clacked a few more keys. "You're all set. We've got your retirement date as December 1. If you decide to change that, you'll have to let us know two weeks before. And congratulations.

I know it's still more than six months out, but you'd be surprised. That time will pass in a flash." She winked.

Yeah, right. He'd have to get a defense bill marked up by the committee, get on and off the Senate floor, complete a conference with the House, and hope the idiot downtown signed the damn thing. As far as he was concerned, that "flash" was probably a bullet train's headlight racing straight at him and it'd keep getting bigger and brighter until it crushed his bones.

He forced a smile. "Thanks for your time. Send me an email if there's anything else I need to do. Enjoy the weekend."

He shook her hand and headed toward the door.

Chapter Two

"We will never give in to the *yanquis*!" hollered a dark-haired woman who stood atop a ladder in a nearly vacant warehouse. A crowd of five hundred men and women wearing tan overalls and blue jeans and surrounded by large crates looked up at her. They roared with approval.

Thousands of miles away, in a dark room, Hans Edison snarled at the television. "That's my fucking warehouse."

On the wall, the TV monitor showed Simona B. Corazon nodding and smiling at the wildly applauding throng.

She raised her hands for silence. "My friends, this factory will be completed. You'll produce electric automobiles, just as I promised." A smaller cheer erupted. She raised her hands again. "And this is very important. I want the whole world to hear." She stared directly into the reporter's camera. "Bolivia is not for sale! We'll do this on our own. We don't need the damn *yanquis* or their money!" She hollered at the top of her lungs and punched one fist skyward.

The crowd echoed her cry and raised their fists in collective solidarity.

An aide handed her a piece of paper.

Simona lifted it above her head. "I have the order right here.

Today, I'm nationalizing the lithium harvesting at Salar de Uyuni, and our battery-manufacturing facility here in La Paz."

A cheer echoed through the cavernous space.

"That's not all, my friends. Listen now. And this facility too. You will build cars right here. Beautiful, new electric cars. And we'll sell them throughout Latin America. And Hans Edison can rot in hell."

"Jesus Christ. What a clusterfuck." The TV switched off. Hans rubbed the gray stubble on his chin. "When was this?"

"Yesterday, boss," said Hans's executive assistant, his prominent Adam's apple bobbing as he swallowed. "Right after *Business Daily* dropped the bombshell that you now own a controlling interest of Daedalus Sunpower."

"God damn it. How'd that get out?"

"No idea, sir. But frankly, it was just a matter of time. The press guys had been tapping around for weeks. All Europe knew that D.S. needed a capital infusion. Sales in the Belgian solar-power business have been dropping for the last three years. Industry observers knew the *Belgiques* were in over their heads. No way they could develop the Bolivian lithium fields and fulfill their commitment to manufacture batteries.

"It's a shame, sir. You rescued them. You're one of the few people with the knowledge, skill, *and* capital to pull this off. You would've made the Belgian stockholders rich. You would've guaranteed Bolivia an up-and-running lithium capacity that rivaled anything else in the world. And opening an EV-manufacturing facility in La Paz would've given Bolivia a toehold—hell, a monopoly for all practical purposes—in South American automobile production. It was a win-win situation. Now, left on their own, what've the Bolivians got? Nada."

"Yeah, well, that leaves me with nothing, too. How do we fix this? That's my God-damned warehouse. She's trespassing."

"I guess you could say that. But she's the president, sir, and she nationalized it. In many respects, it's hers now."

"Oh yeah? We'll see about that. Get Parker on the phone. I'll teach her she can't fuck Hans Edison."

Chapter Three

"Jesus Christ, Fred." Roxy Fowler stood in the interior doorway between the boss's and staff offices. "Where've you been? I was about to have the police check out your cabin. It's nine forty-five. Marty's been calling for an hour. He said you weren't picking up your phone or responding to email."

Fred Hendricks let the door to the Dirksen Senate Office Building hallway swing closed behind him. He tossed his coat and briefcase on a chair and glanced at the tall, chestnut-haired woman dressed in a black pantsuit and light-blue blouse.

"Fred, are you OK?" Roxy's brow furrowed. "You're starting to worry me. Marty keeps calling."

"God damn it, Roxy." Fred growled. "Fuck Marty. Can't I come in a little late one day without the FBI starting an investigation? Forty years, Roxy. I've been here forty years—two-thirds of my life. I was working in this building when Marty was still wetting the bed. Before you were even in diapers. It's nobody's business where I was. And God damn it! It's recess. The chairman's at home in Spokane. It's not even seven in the morning there. I doubt he's awake."

He pulled his phone from his pocket and looked over at the thin, attractive young woman. She had blue eyes, rosy cheeks, and a worried frown.

"What's Marty want?"

"No idea," she said. "But he's agitated about something. He was squealing the last time I talked to him. *'Where's Fred? He's not picking up.'*" She did her best to mimic the full committee staff director's high-pitched voice.

Fred chuckled. "You do that pretty well."

She gave him a disarming look. "Hey, I know you don't need my advice. But you better call him. He's our boss now. He can make your life miserable."

"Yeah, yeah, I'll call him. Close the door on your way out."

Roxy squinted and cocked her head.

"You heard me. Get outta here." Fred laughed, dismissing her with a wave. After she closed the door, he opened the bottom drawer of his desk, pulled out a large bottle of Mylanta, and took a big gulp of antacid. *That's it. No more coffee. But boy, a jumbo would do my head a world of good.* He sighed.

OK, what did Marty Barons want now? He picked up his desk phone and hit the intercom button. "Marty, it's Fred. I heard you're looking for me."

"Fred. God damn it. Where've you been? Chairman Colbert is fit to be tied. He heard the House is putting a provision in the defense bill to ban the sale of cigarettes in commissaries. Why didn't you tell me?" His voice rose from second tenor to soprano.

"Well, Marty, because I didn't know. They don't go to markup till next week. How am I supposed to know they might include a ban on cigarettes?"

"Wait. Did you miss the part where I said the chairman knows?" Marty squealed into the phone.

Damn. Roxy's got that impression about perfect. He picked up a pencil and doodled a round face with a pig's ears and snout, curly black hair, and a thick, wiry beard.

Then he crumpled it up and threw it in the trash. "I heard you, Marty. But just because some tobacco road lobbyist is saying the House is gonna do something doesn't make it true." Fred paused. "I get that your North Carolina senator doesn't see the humor of a ban on cigarette sales. But even if the lobbyist is right, nothing I can do about it. Doesn't mean we'll stick it in our bill. Although I gotta tell you"—he hesitated for a second—"Sam Jackson's probably gonna like the sound of it. He's been anti-smoking for the last twenty years." He covered the receiver and stifled a chuckle.

"Oh yeah? Well, Jackson isn't chairman anymore. Francis J. Colbert is *the* committee chairman." That squeal was at an even higher pitch.

"I hear ya. But Jackson still chairs the defense subcommittee. I'm not saying he'd do it. But between you and me, it all comes down to who's got the votes. I'd bet you a week's pay the Democrats would side with Jackson if he picked it up. That's all it'd take."

"You better hope he doesn't." Marty's voice had dropped back to its normal tenor. "You may think you work for Jackson, but Chairman Colbert can fire your ass."

Like I give a rat's ass anyway. "I serve at the pleasure of the chair. Anything else I can do for you?"

"Just this. Try to know what's going on in the fucking defense world." Marty hung up, and the sound of the phone slamming down jolted through the line.

"Sure thing, you little shit," Fred muttered.

Chapter Four

"Mr. President, it's Hans Edison with Edison Electric. Thanks for taking my call." The voice boomed from the speakerphone.

"Of course, Hans. How are you? Car sales doing OK?" President James Parker sat in the Oval Office, staring at the phone on the *Resolute* desk.

Chief of Staff Steve Simpson stood at the president's side, clutching a briefing book in one hand and scrolling on his cell phone with the other. He looked over at his boss. Yeah, over the last two and a half years, the president's hair had gotten thinner than when he'd been a senator. But his broad shoulders didn't look worn down, and his square jaw still jutted out like he was ready for a fight.

"Cars are doing great, sir," Hans Edison continued. "But I've got a little problem and could use your help."

Parker looked over at Simpson, who shrugged. "OK. What's the problem?"

"Bolivia, sir."

"What the hell's wrong with Bolivia? And what's it got to do with you—or me—for that matter?"

"Mr. President, my company, Edison Electric, recently acquired fifty-one percent of a Belgian firm that's developing large deposits of lithium on a dry seabed in Bolivia. They, now we, contracted to harvest the lithium and build lithium batteries there. Eighty percent of the profits from battery sales would be used to clean up the air in and around the city of La Paz. You probably don't know this, Mr. President—"

Parker slouched in his chair, rolled his eyes, and sneered at the phone while Edison rambled.

"—but La Paz has some of the worst air pollution in the world. At twelve thousand feet, it has thirty percent less oxygen than cities at sea level. Bolivia's done some good things, like starting a cable car to reduce emissions. But, even so, cars have tripled in La Paz in the past ten years. President Corazon has vowed to clean up the environment. She's staking her reelection on it."

Parker twirled his finger in the air. Simpson jotted a note with two words, *New Mexico*, and handed it to him. Parker read it, scowled, crumpled it up, and threw it at his chief of staff.

"OK, Hans. That's enough background. I haven't got all day."

"Yes, sir. To make a long story short, Simona Corazon, Bolivia's president—"

"Yeah, I know. I've met the socialist princess."

"Yes, sir, Mr. President. Yesterday, President Corazon nationalized the lithium-harvesting and battery-manufacturing facilities."

"What? She can't do that." He glanced over at Steve Simpson, who hunched his shoulders and flopped his head back and forth as if to say he wasn't so sure about that.

"I'm glad to hear you say that, Mr. President. And to make matters worse—"

"No way we're going back to the 1950s." Parker's face got bright red, and he bolted from his chair and shouted at the phone. Veins bulged in his neck and temples. "My administration won't allow American companies to be blackmailed by some banana-republic dictator. I can tell you right now this won't stand!" He glared at his aide.

Steve Simpson tilted his head and frowned.

"Your comments are most welcome, Mr. President." Edison's voice rang out from the phone. "But it's worse. She's also nationalized my half-built factory to build electric cars in Bolivia. EVs would dramatically change the face of Latin America. We believe there's an enormous untapped market.

"While Bolivian labor rates aren't as favorable as Mexico's, they're a hell of a lot better than Detroit's. My plan was to produce cheap cars with my electric motors. Since I now control their lithium batteries, I could buy them at cost but sell them to my competitors at a huge markup. In short, Mr. President, I could crush the competition."

Parker chuckled. "That's pretty clever, Hans. I can see why you're worried."

"Well, Mr. President, you should be worried, too." The voice on the speakerphone took on a sharper tone. "American businessmen won't support our companies being nationalized by foreign powers. To be frank, sir, you need us as much as we need you.

"You may be able to win in Nevada without my help, but you're also going to need New Mexico. You can't count on Pennsylvania and Michigan this time. Manufacturing jobs are still down. That's going to make those states a tough sell. And your last campaign was based on Democratic corruption. The Chinese bribed that senator. You discovered it. That made you a star. But it's old news now.

"Listen, sir. I've got ten thousand workers in Las Cruces and Santa Fe. I can get them to the polls on Election Day. I can guarantee you New Mexico's five electoral votes. With that, plus

Florida and Ohio, you're a lock for reelection. But, you lose New Mexico and my ten thousand votes, you could be toast."

Simpson nodded with a grimace. *This could fuck us up.*

If the president lost American businessmen like Edison, plus New Mexico, that would be a disaster.

He released a long sigh. How had they gotten into this mess? Parker's whole career had been close to perfect. Star tailback at UNLV. Yeah, he'd lost his chance of going pro when he blew out his knee, but he'd landed on his feet working for the local Las Vegas Fox affiliate as a TV sportscaster.

Pretty soon he was a local star, and he turned to politics, spouting anti-liberal truisms that rural Nevadans loved. He'd run for Congress. With his name recognition, good looks, and natural charm, he'd steamrolled his opponent.

Then he'd campaigned immediately for the Senate against an old Democratic hack with a drinking problem. After releasing video of his opponent staggering in the halls of the Capitol, he'd practically stampeded into office.

I knew nothing could stop him when he uncovered that Chinese bribery plot. Even when they tried to turn the tables on him.

But after all that success, now this. Jesus Christ.

Parker shook his head and extended his middle finger toward the phone. Simpson scribbled another note and handed it to the president.

Parker took a quick look at it. "I'll tell you what, Hans. Let me get with my people and see what we can do. But you have my assurance. Nobody's going to be nationalizing American companies while Jim Parker's president."

"I knew I could count on you, Mr. President. Thanks so much, and thanks for taking my call."

Simpson reached over and hung up the phone. *Shit. Now I've got to give him the bad news.* "I hate to say it, sir, but that little prick is right. You might need New Mexico to reach two hundred seventy electoral votes. Early polling shows you can't count on the rust belt, like he said. And voter security is going to be a lot tighter this time around. The social media companies are trying to eliminate fake news from bots." He frowned. "It won't be like last time. Sadly, we might need that little asshole."

"So, what can we do? Should I call the socialist bitch and threaten her?"

"She might retaliate. Nationalize our oil refineries or something." Simpson cocked his head and nodded. "You know what, sir?" He looked down at the president. "I got an idea. Give me a little time, and I'll get you a proposal that could stop her in her tracks. She's got an election coming up. With a little luck, she could lose." He smiled widely.

Parker's frown slowly morphed into a grin, and he laughed uproariously. "That's right. She could lose. I like the way you think, Simpson."

Chapter Five

"Staff meeting at four thirty in the boss's office. He says bring your beverage of choice." Roxy repeated the call three times as she walked through the interconnected staff suites of the defense appropriations subcommittee.

Roy Peterson looked at his watch. *Shit, it's already four fifteen. I'm supposed to pick up Lester in thirty minutes. Julie's gonna kill me.*

He took a deep breath, picked up his cell, and hit the speed dial. "Hi, sweetie. I got some bad news. Fred just called a staff meeting. I can't pick up the kid. Can you get there before five thirty?"

He listened for a moment.

"Yes, it's recess. Yes, it's Friday. And yes, I know you've got a mani-pedi appointment. But I'm stuck. I'm sorry." He lowered his voice and spun his chair around to face the wall. "You know I can't give him reason to think I'm not a team player."

He paused.

"Thank you. Like I said, I'm sorry. I'll try to make it up to you this weekend." He stood up and headed through the office door to the Dirksen hallway.

◆ ◆ ◆

At the desk across from Roy's, Mindy Abrams sat facing her computer screen. She glanced over her shoulder as Roy left, crushed a Miller Lite can in her hand, and tossed it into the trash.

"Jackass," she muttered under her breath.

Roxy smiled as she walked back into the suite and retreated to her semiprivate cubicle by the window. "Where's he off to?"

"Got me. Probably got spook secrets to take care of before the meeting." Mindy glanced at the doorway to the adjoining suite, where a wide-eyed Judy Jameson was about to knock.

"Come on in, Judy. It's just Roxy and me." Mindy reached to open the small refrigerator next to her desk and pulled out another beer. "Want one?" She motioned to Judy.

"No, thanks. But that's what I wanted to ask about." She proceeded into the office and grinned at Roxy. "Can we bring alcohol to the meeting?"

"Bring whatever you want." Roxy smiled back at the young woman. "Mindy's got beer, of course. Roy's probably bringing a soda. Stevie Guy usually opens a bottle of white wine, and Fred's likely to pull out his secret stash of hard stuff. What's it called, Mindy? Fred's brew?"

"Maker's Mark."

"Oh, yeah. It's not bad. Anyway, bring whatever you want."

"So, it's OK if I drink wine?"

"You're twenty-one, right?" Roxy chuckled as she said it and glanced at Mindy. Mindy snorted in her beer.

Judy nodded, her curly black hair bouncing.

"Go for it," Roxy said. "Stevie Guy always shares. Now, if it's red wine you want, you better check with the minority staff. Don't worry about bringing a glass. Fred's got plenty in his bathroom cabinet. Hey, why don't you know this already? You've been here for what, three months?"

Judy nodded.

"Are you saying we haven't had an afternoon staff meeting since you got here?" Mindy asked.

"No, but I always drank water. I didn't want to assume. And Roy never drinks alcohol so . . ."

"You just think Rox and I are lushes. Is that what you're trying to say?"

"Jeepers, no. I didn't mean that at all!" Judy's voice rose to an anguished cry.

"Relax, Jameson. I'm just busting your chops." Mindy took a long swig from her new can of Miller Lite. "Listen, you're part of the A-Team, even though you're just an intern. I was one, too, not that long ago. And look how I turned out." She suppressed a belch.

Roxy laughed outright. "Right, Mindy. Now, Judy, there are role models, and then there are *role models*. But one thing you should know about Fred is he wants everyone to be comfortable."

"OK. Thanks. So, why doesn't Roy drink?" Judy asked.

Mindy cast a sidelong glance at Roxy, tilted her head, and raised her eyebrows.

"Mindy and I have asked ourselves the same thing a few times."

"Yeah, Roxy thinks he's afraid what he'd do with a few drinks in him. My bet is he's a mean drunk."

"Like I said, Fred wants everyone relaxed." Roxy shrugged. "He uses late-afternoon staff meetings as a way to brainstorm. We're only a few weeks out from markup. He wants to make sure everyone is focusing. Anyway, we better get in there. The guys with kids won't want to hang around any longer than they have to. The rest of us might make a night of it. You're welcome to stay or go. Take your cues from Roy and Leonard. They'll be clock-watching."

"What about you, Rox?" Mindy cocked her head. "I thought you had a racquetball date with what's-his-name."

"Oh, it's just Arnie. I told him we might be working late. Besides, if we're going to be imbibing, I'm not sure I want to play. I don't want to give him a chance to ruin my perfect record." She smiled.

"C'mon, guys," Roxy continued. "Let's go join the boys."

Chapter Six

"Mr. President, this is Lieutenant General McNeal." Steve Simpson motioned toward the six-foot-five army general at his side. "Mac is the Deputy Director of the National Security Agency and Acting Commander of the Army Intelligence and Security Command, INSCOM. I asked him to drive down from Fort Meade this afternoon and join us here in the Situation Room where we can speak freely about a highly classified project called SWEET REVENGE."

Parker chuckled. "Great name. My sentiments exactly."

"Yes, sir. Before Mac begins, let me give you some background." Simpson motioned for General McNeal to sit in a black leather chair at the long, wooden conference table, to the immediate right of the president. The general, dark-haired and dark-eyed with a ruddy complexion and square jaw, took his seat and scanned the president's basement command post. The Presidential Seal and several large television screens covered the beige walls.

"SWEET REVENGE is an offensive cybersecurity project," Parker's chief of staff explained. "It was mandated by Chairman Schmidt of the Senate Intelligence Committee during the last Congress—in her first, and only, term as chairman. The program's a retaliation for Russian meddling in the last election."

"That bitch," Parker grumbled.

"Yes, sir. But despite its origin, we think you're going to like what NSA has come up with," Simpson continued. "NSA has designed computer software that could conceivably swing any election toward candidates of our choosing."

"We can't do that, Steve. If word ever got out, they'd lynch me. Besides, I'm going to win next year, fair and square."

"Oh, no, sir. I don't mean your election. You're right. There's no way we could legally interfere in *your* reelection. And I would never counsel that. No, sir. We're talking about something else entirely.

"But there's a catch. To perfect the system, they need to do some beta testing. That is, we need to hack a real election to see if the system works as predicted."

"So, are you thinking a city council race or something?" Parker queried.

"Heavens, no, sir!" General McNeal stood up, towering over the room. "Mr. President, we can't interfere in any *American* election. No, sir." He shook his head vigorously, a horrified look on his face.

"We're thinking about an election in a small foreign nation," McNeal explained. "Maybe one of the so-called democracies in Africa where the UN says elections are rigged. But, Mr. President, we simply must test the system in a real-world environment."

"I see. So, how's it work?"

"Yes, sir. Let me explain it this way." General McNeal took a deep breath and sat back down. "Say country X is having an election. In most cases, about fifty percent of voters participate. If the ballots are electronic, and most are, we can adjust the totals to increase the percent voting. In theory, we could get to a hundred percent turnout. Now, practically, that wouldn't be smart. But like I said, we can have some of those who didn't show up vote for our candidate."

"What if they use paper ballots?" Parker asked.

"That's a little trickier. But we're pretty sure we can still adjust the results. Let's say a precinct reports a hundred votes for candidate Y and two hundred for candidate Z. When those numbers get entered into the database, we can reverse them so that candidate Y is recorded with two hundred votes and Z gets a hundred."

"That's fascinating." Parker yawned.

"Sir, we're also prepared to fill social media with our propaganda. We can vilify our opponent in the weeks before the election. That should improve our candidate's chances."

"Yes, sir." Steve Simpson leaned toward the president. "I'm not sure this is what the Senate had in mind when they started us down this path, but we're here now. So, the question for you, sir, is—whom should we target?" Simpson smiled widely.

"Aha! Very interesting, Steve. Very, very interesting. Thank you, General. And I've got to say, this is great stuff. Just great. You'll be looking at a fourth star soon, General."

McNeal beamed. "Thank you, Mr. President. And let me add, sir, what a great pleasure it is to meet a true patriot like you."

"Thanks." Parker turned toward his chief of staff. "Steve, why don't you escort the general out and then come back so we can discuss this further."

Chapter Seven

Roxy sat in the overstuffed brown leather armchair, her favorite perch in Fred's office.

It provided her a direct view of Fred, who sat behind his recently restored nineteenth-century mahogany partner desk, one of ninety-two desks originally manufactured and reserved for senators. A desk that Senate staff had conspired for generations to hide from the eyes of countless junior senators, who lusted after such a piece of history. It served as a stark reminder that the Senate's entrenched staff bureaucracy of woodworkers and painters believed the clerk of the defense subcommittee held a position at least as important as that of many junior senators. The clerk was responsible, after all, for overseeing a budget of seven hundred billion dollars and served a chairman whose position and seniority invariably cast him as a key power in the Senate.

Roxy scanned the room. Classic Winslow Homer nautical paintings, on loan from the Smithsonian, adorned the beige walls. On her left, Leonard and Roy positioned themselves on opposite ends of the brown leather sofa. Judy sat between them. To her right, within reach of the coffee table, Mindy Abrams chose a wooden armchair with a leather seat that matched the other furniture.

Stevie Guy opened a bottle of white wine and sat down in the companion chair to Mindy's.

"Roxy," Fred questioned in a soft voice, "where are Bernie and Dwayne?"

"Bernie's off today, sir, and Dwayne's on travel. You sent him to Groton, Connecticut, to the Electric Boat shipyard to talk about the replacement for the Trident submarine."

"Oh, yeah."

Roxy continued, "I checked with the minority. They're not around. It's recess, after all."

Roy and Leonard glanced at one another as if thinking, *We should be so lucky.*

Roxy smiled and looked around. Here they were. Mindy's *A-Team.*

Fred, the ancient mariner, kicked back at his desk. The deep wrinkles on his forehead looked like rows on a freshly plowed field. Below his silver-gray flat top haircut, eagle-talon crow's-feet surrounded his watery eyes.

Mindy slouched in her chair, wearing jeans and a navy blouse on her pudgy but athletic frame. Her round, pockmarked face and gray eyes already looked bored. She ran a hand through her short sandy hair.

Stevie Guy sat sipping white wine in his chinos and button-down. He was no taller than Mindy, but lean with hazel eyes and reddish-brown hair framing a pleasant face.

Judy, her eyes darting back and forth, wore a short black dress, showing shapely legs. She gulped wine a little faster than she probably should.

Skinny, blond Leonard, all legs and long arms in jeans and

a polo, nursed one of Mindy's beers. He eyed his watch every minute or so.

And Roy . . . Roxy took in his long-sleeved gray shirt, black slacks matching his jet-black hair, dark eyes, perfect complexion, perfect frame. He looked so frigging smug.

Roxy's smile turned to a frown.

"OK, let's get going." Fred leaned forward. "So, Ms. Abrams."

Mindy sat bolt upright and almost dropped her beer.

Fred continued, "My day started with a call from Marty, our dear full committee staff director." He looked around. "He wanted to know why I hadn't told him that the HAC is including a ban on cigarette sales. So, Mindy, why didn't we?"

"First I've heard of it, sir."

"Yeah, figured. Well, to put it mildly, he wasn't too pleased. Said something about 'do your effing job,' or some such bullshit."

"I'm sorry, sir. I talked to Louise Smathers, the House appropriations staffer, last week about where they're headed. She said zippo about cigs. I mean, two years ago we led the charge to raise tobacco prices in the military exchanges and commissaries. Patterson was subcommittee chairman. That is, until he died. But Marty must know about all that. Colbert wasn't committee chairman, obviously. But he didn't try to stop it. At least, not that I recall."

Mindy took a quick swig of beer and continued, "The House had a hearing on cigarettes with the head of the Defense Logistics Agency a couple months ago. I heard it was contentious, but nothing about a ban."

"Well, according to dear ol' Marty," said Fred, "some tobacco lobbyist told the big chairman—Colbert, I mean, not Chairman

Jackson—that the House is including a ban on the sale of cigarettes in all military shops, the commissaries and the exchanges. Hell, I'd bet the officer and enlisted clubs and golf courses, too—if they're still selling smokes there. Look, we all know that half the crap the industry talks about never happens. But it got me thinking. We haven't had a little soiree for a while. Figured maybe we ought to get together and share what we think they're up to—and at the same time, what we know about the authorizers, both Armed Services and Intelligence Committees. And speaking of that, intel authorization's coming up on the floor soon. Any news on SSCI, Roy?"

"Not much, sir. Chairman O'Shea's markup was pretty uneventful. They're hoping to call up the bill soon. Maybe next week, in wrap-up, at the end of the day with no amendments and no debate. Leadership's been calling members' offices to see if there are problems. So far, from what I hear, everything's OK.

"There's a couple of things I need to remind you about, but you'd have to clear the room for us to do that." Roy smirked at the other staffers around him.

Roxy frowned. *Asshole. Nothing he'd like better than to try and lick Fred's ass in private while the rest of us cool our heels outside.*

"OK, but not right now." Fred removed a tiny key from his pocket and reached down to unlock a small door on the side of his desk. He pulled a bottle of bourbon from the shelf and poured himself a couple of ounces. "Anybody want a splash?" He held up the bottle.

"I'll have a swallow." Roxy stood up, holding an empty glass tumbler, and took a couple steps in Fred's direction.

"That's funny. I heard you don't." Roy looked at Stevie Guy and back at Leonard, smirking. "Swallow, I mean."

Stevie's eyes widened.

"Hey, knock that shit off, Peterson." Fred growled. "No rough talk in the office."

"Don't worry, sir. Crap like that doesn't bother me." Roxy sighed and shook her head. "Mindy and I are used to his high school shit. If that's how he gets his rocks off, I say go for it. I just wish the attempt at humor was a tad more sophisticated. I mean, you did go to college, after all. Didn't you, Roy? What was it? Podunk State?"

"Enough of that. Both of you," Fred snapped and glared in their direction. Roxy reached out her empty glass, blocking the rest of the staff's view of the boss. He gave her a look that said, *Did you really need to do that?* She smiled widely in return.

He poured her a large shot and sighed. "I'll talk to you later, Roy."

Roxy suppressed a smirk as Roy jolted to attention in his seat.

Fred held up his hand. "About intel, I mean."

Roy relaxed and nodded.

"OK, what else?" Fred continued. "Roxy, what's the scuttle-butt on planes? Anything we need to worry about?"

"Not that I know of, sir." She slid into her seat. "We suspect they want to plus up the F-35 fighter again. The House, I mean. The authorizers are likely to fight about retiring the old A-10s. The House, HASC Chairman Boudreaux, won't see the humor of that, with them stationed at Barksdale and all. My guess is we'll see a little Ragin' Cajun action if the Senate authorizers don't back down. Losing his A-10s would be the kiss of death for Louisiana if there's ever another base-closure commission.

"Not much on ships, either. There's a rumor that the House—appropriators, I mean—might want to bail out a shipyard in

South Carolina, but I don't have any details." She took a little sip of her drink and sucked in some air.

Judy Jameson raised her hand. Roxy, Fred, and the others looked at her. Fred gave a head nod for her to speak up.

"Um, so you guys said something like, 'hack, hask, sask,' I think, and 'sissy.' Are those acronyms, maybe?"

"OK, yeah. Sorry." Fred sighed. "Let's see. HAC is the House Appropriations Committee, and the others are House Armed Services Committee, Senate Armed Services Committee, and Senate Select Committee on Intelligence—'Sissy.' What else?" Fred scanned the room. "Mindy, any news in O and M?"

Mindy took another sip of her beer. She pursed her lips and wrinkled her brow as if deep in thought for a second. "Same ol', same ol', sir. The senators don't really care about operations and maintenance. I mean, they care, sir. But unless we've got a readiness crisis and ships are tied up or planes are grounded, it just doesn't reach the level that gets members excited. Luckily, things are going pretty well. I mean, there's always shortfalls. If oil prices spike or something, we'll be in a world of hurt. But for now"—she rapped on her beer can a couple times—"knock on brew, all's good."

"Anybody else? Leonard? Health care? MILPERS?"

Leonard put down his beer and shook his head. He took a deep breath as if to calm his nerves. "I think, like Mindy said, sir, the members don't care about MILPERS. I mean, they care. The military family caucus cares about military personnel. And, of course, they're always pushing to increase pay more than inflation rates. But that's not our jurisdiction. The authorizers set pay levels. Same thing with bonuses and other special pays like hazardous duty and such. In those areas, we're like the accountants. We make sure the budget matches what's actually being spent.

"Members don't concern themselves with the cost of PCS." He glanced around at his colleagues, then nodded at Judy. "Permanent change of station—moving troops and families between bases. Or how much we spend on subsistence. As for health care, well, what the members mostly care about is how much we're going to spend on what I like to call *the disease of the month*. One year, the lobbyists push for a big increase in breast-cancer research. The next, it's lung cancer or childhood diabetes. Whichever wheel is the squeakiest.

"Jackson will have a fight with the SASC, specifically Chairman Brinkman, over health research; that's almost a guarantee. But it won't matter."

Leonard picked up his beer and took a small sip. "True-blue conservatives like Brinkman object to adding a billion or two of defense money to disease research. But when you count the votes, the disease supporters always win. From what I've seen, looking back over thirty years of history, it's always that way. Republicans are in charge. But that won't change a thing. And Jackson's well aware of it. Brinkman will stew and maybe spew a little, but end-game, he loses. I think even he knows it. So, short answer, nothing here."

"Stevie?"

"Not much, sir. One or two CIA and defense-intel things I need to talk to you about. But, like Roy, we'd have to discuss them in private. Not much in army or defense-wide research and development."

Fred nodded and looked around the room. "Judy, anything you want to add?"

Judy froze. She took a huge gulp of her third glass of wine and glanced at her lap. "No, sir."

"Yeah, OK. Just relax and watch what's going on. You'll learn a lot. And you might want to slow down on the wine. Unless you've got a hollow leg like Mindy, that stuff'll catch up to you pretty quick. Don't want to have to call a cab. We reserve those for days when we've got something to celebrate." He chuckled, a knowing gleam in his eye.

"OK, everyone, take the rest of the week off."

The staff got up in near unison. Stevie grabbed his nearly empty bottle of wine, and they started to walk out.

"Roxy, stick around a minute. I want to ask you something." Fred's sandpaper voice was curt.

She nodded.

"And close the door."

She pulled it shut.

Chapter Eight

Harris Ward, longtime congressional reporter for *Roll Call*, sat scanning news stories on his laptop. He rocked back on his red fiberglass-and-aluminum tube chair, sitting at a prefab table that rested on industrial light-brown carpet in the deserted Senate Dirksen cafeteria. On the beige walls behind him hung framed photographs of the Capitol compound, taken nearly a hundred years ago.

The cafeteria had been closed for hours. But he could park himself there, charge his phone and laptop, and work in solitude on his story for the next day. He picked up his ringing cell.

Blocked number. Hmm. Who could that be? "Hello? This is Harris Ward, to whom am I speaking?"

"Don't ask questions. Just listen." The voice on the phone was muffled, as if the caller was using a voice-disguising app. It sounded like a man, but that's all Harris could tell.

"Have it your way. I'm listening."

"You the guy who broke the CNN story on Iran last year?"

"Yes." Harris frowned and shook his head. It was two years ago, but that didn't matter. He didn't want to correct the guy and risk him hanging up.

"You might want to investigate Fort Meade. Looks like they're planning to rig an election in Africa."

"Did you say Africa? Where in Africa? Why would they do that?" Harris pushed his gray-brown hair off his forehead and adjusted his horn-rimmed glasses.

"They want to test their new offensive cyber tool. Rigging elections."

"What country?"

"Don't know. Don't think it matters. It's only a test."

"You're kidding. This is a joke, right?" Harris glanced around the empty cafeteria.

"I'm deadly fucking serious. We're about to pick a president somewhere. You think that's a joke? I ought to hang up right now."

"I'm sorry. Please don't hang up. It's just . . . the irony is astounding. And the hubris. They can't be serious."

"I'm telling you. Within a month or two, the balloon's going up. Some poor schmuck in darkest Africa ain't gonna be president, because of the assholes in the White House and the Senate, mind you. This was their idea in the first place!" His voice grew louder. "Those assholes want to test out a new program to rig elections."

"Unbelievable."

"Well, you better start believing, because it's almost too late to stop it. Look, from what I hear, you're a straight shooter. If that's right, go uncover this shit. Tell the American people. No way they want their government doing this."

"I'm sure you're right about that. Who are you? How do you know about this? How can I be sure what you're saying is true?"

"I've told you all you need to know. Do your job. Ask the congressmen about it."

"I will, but before . . . son of a bitch. He hung up." Unbelievable.

Could this guy be right? Why in the world would the NSA want to rig an African election? A test? He had to be kidding. Would they rig an election to test out a program? *I guess I should ask around, but I can't believe this guy's right.*

And he said the Senate knew. No way.

Chapter Nine

Fred Hendricks threw back the last of his drink and looked Roxy straight in the eye. "I know you didn't start it. But you need to knock that shit off. Look. You don't have to like Roy, but we've all got to work together." He poured himself another shot and leaned back in his desk chair.

"I hear ya, Fred. But something about that guy pisses me off. It's like he thinks, because he's in the National Guard, he's better than the rest of us."

"I get that. But you need to keep it to yourself."

"Hey. It's not just me. Mindy thinks he's a jerk too."

"I don't care!" Fred barked.

"OK, I get it. I'll be good."

Fred took a deep breath and lowered his voice to a rumble. "Listen, Roxy. Jackson's counting on us. His ass is on the line. When Jackson ran for vice president on the Democratic ticket, he burned a lot of bridges. I mean, he's a Republican, after all. Even his staff quit. When Parker won, Jackson came back to the Senate. The majority leader stripped him of the full committee chairmanship to please the hard-liners in the Republican caucus. But he let him keep the defense subcommittee as a consolation prize. I know that's not news to you, but I need you to be smart about it."

Roxy tugged a chair up to the opposite side of Fred's partner desk. She sat down and slipped off her shoes. Then she placed her stockinged feet up on a secretary's note-taking shelf that she'd pulled out from the front of the desk.

"Jackson picked me," Fred continued, "because I've known him for decades. He trusts me. But if I don't do a good job, all the haters will be on Leader Jacobs saying, 'I told you so.' You and I are the outsiders here. Mindy, Stevie, and Dwayne have been on the subcommittee staff for several years. Bernie and Leonard are new. Roy might be kind of new, but they're all a hell of a lot closer to the Republicans than we are." He put his glass down on his desk.

"Jackson doesn't care what party we're in. But his colleagues know that I've been the Democratic clerk on military construction. I've been working for the D's for the last fifteen years. Most senators don't realize I worked for both parties in the old days. There aren't a lot of current Republicans who've been around that long. And as far as anyone knows, I hired you. They'll see you as a Democrat, too." He stared at her.

Roxy nodded. "So, tell me this. I get why Jackson picked you. You know more about appropriations than all the rest of us together. And he knows you don't have an agenda. You'll carry out his policies, not insert your own views. But why would Jacobs let Jackson keep the subcommittee in the first place?"

"Can't say for sure. But a couple things come to mind. Defense was Jackson's subcommittee. The only thing that mattered in the old days was seniority. Nowadays, Republican committee chairmen have to be approved by their members. But there still aren't any rules about subcommittee chairs that I'm aware of. Jackson's senior. But if you ask me, I think it goes a little deeper than that."

Roxy cocked her head and squinted.

"Parker and Jackson always hated each other, right?" Fred shook his head. "That got worse when Parker accused Jackson's good friend, our former Hawaii Democratic senator, Ken Mitsunaga, of having an affair and taking Chinese bribes. Jackson can't forget what Parker did. On the other side, Parker considers Jackson a traitor for running against him on the Democratic ticket."

Fred took a small sip of his drink and spoke again. "And both of them got a short fuse. I know for a fact that they were at each other's throats more than once. Now, it's also pretty obvious that the leader, Jacobs, thinks a hell of a lot more of Jackson than of Parker. And all that shit that came up that Parker might've actually set up Mitsunaga? Well, Parker might've convinced the American public that it was fake news planted by liberal bureaucrats and the media, but I'm pretty sure several of his colleagues don't believe it. I'd bet lots of Republican senators didn't vote for Parker."

He took a deep breath. "You know Jackson never repudiated the Republican Party. He ran on a unity platform. Bipartisanship."

Roxy nodded.

He stared at his empty glass. "But all that's just a guess. My intuition is Jacobs let Jackson keep his subcommittee to show Parker he wasn't going to be bullied. Twist the knife a little in ol' James Fillmore Parker. Remind him the Senate is a separate and equal branch of government in the eyes of those who wrote the Constitution."

"Seriously?"

"Hey. Your guess is as good as mine. That's what I think. But you know what it means, Roxy?"

She shrugged.

"It means we can't let Jackson down. Look it. You're the smartest one around here. But that doesn't mean Roy's a fool. Give him a chance. He might surprise both of us. Now, get out of here. I'm sure you've got better things to do than hang around with this dinosaur. And if you don't, go find something."

Roxy got up and slipped on her black flats. She turned to leave.

"Do me one more favor." Fred's voice stopped her. "Tell Judy she's doing fine. But keep an eye on her. She was throwing that wine down. I don't want to walk in one morning and find her passed out on my couch. Got it?"

"Sure thing, Fred. I'll take care of her. And you take care of yourself. You had me worried this morning."

"Shit, Roxy. Don't worry about me. Just because I didn't turn on my damn phone. I hate being on a leash. Now get outta here." He reached down to grab his bottle of bourbon.

"Right, sir." Roxy took a last sip, gave Fred a knowing look, and walked out.

Chapter Ten

The Burnt Palace

La Paz, Bolivia

Simona Corazon stood up from the intricately carved rosewood table and looked at the men seated in the presidential office. The small gold comb securing her hair in a bun pressed uncomfortably against the back of her scalp, creating the start of an unwanted headache. Despite that, Simona smiled and surveyed the room. She paused and pursed her lips. Her eyes locked on each staff member at the table in turn. "As of today, the Ministry of Interior will be in charge of the lithium fields. Dr. Cordoba, you have six months to increase production."

The gray-haired man with the small goatee to her immediate left raised his head and nodded slowly. Simona smiled and placed her hand on his shoulder.

She looked to the man on Cordoba's left. "Manuel Solo, you'll be in charge of battery production. Under Daedalus, eighty percent of the profits were to go toward cleaning up air pollution. We have no need for profit. Our cleanup efforts will now get ninety percent. The factory workers will share five percent of the profits. I will announce it on my next visit. The remaining five percent will be used to market our products. As soon as the factory is working at capacity, I will dispatch teams from our Commerce Ministry to the capitals of South and Central America to drum up business.

"And you, Miguelito." She turned to the handsome young man seated to her right. "You will be in charge of vehicle production. Your task will be the most difficult, since we must train the workers ourselves. We have the equipment we need and the training manuals the *yanquis* were going to use. But, my brother, yes, it will be difficult. That's why I've chosen you. I know you're up to the task." She leaned over and mussed his dark hair.

He took her hand, squeezed it gently, and smiled at his older sister.

"Questions?" Simona looked at each of them.

A gray-faced older man with plain black glasses and a salt-and-pepper beard cleared his throat with a deep grumble. He looked at President Corazon with a gaze that barely masked his deep concern. "Madame President, Carlos Montoya is going to crucify you. The banks, the tobacco growers, miners, coca growers, they all oppose your decision to nationalize lithium. The editors of the *El Diario* and *Hoy* newspapers have already slammed your proposal. I beg you, Madame President.

"With all due respect, your father—my brother and dearest friend—would never have condoned this. Please, reverse this decision before it's too late. The American president is too mercurial. You cannot be sure what he will do. But, I can assure you, he will not take this lying down. One of his cruise missiles could be headed at us right now!" His deep, lyrical voice exploded into a loud bark as he rose from his chair.

As if shocked by his own boldness, he collapsed back and continued, just above a whisper, "Please, dear Simonetta, my child. I have known you since you were born. I only want what is best . . . what your father would have wanted. I will never desert you. But the election is only weeks out. You cannot throw away your future. Think of your father. Think of your people."

"My people are exactly what I'm thinking about, Uncle Rodrigo. Perhaps you've spent too much time in New York at the UN. Have you become a Yankee fan? The Bronx bombers, they call them. And the mad bomber, that *yanqui* president. Are you a fan of his as well?"

She glared at the old man and continued, "Why would I trust Hans Edison, or any *yanqui*? Edison cheated our Belgian partners out of their company. Now he plans on cheating Bolivia out of its birthright. Don't you see what would have happened if he hadn't been exposed? He would have robbed us blind. Our workers would've been paid slave wages. What would our eighty percent share of the profits matter if he ensured that there were no profits?" She paused. "Oh, he'd make money all right. But it would be through his automobile sales—where we don't share in the profits." She shook her head. "Rodrigo, I'm surprised at you. You seemed so wise when I was a girl. Now I see the real you. You're nothing but a silly old fool."

Rodrigo Corazon shrank in his seat, folded his arms, and released a long sigh. His eyes watered a little.

"And as for Carlos Montoya"—she waved her hands, her voice rising—"let him complain. The people support me. They will never elect a banker president."

Miguel Corazon sat in silence, as did the others. Simona looked at her brother, who seemed to be fighting back tears as he mouthed, *Oh Simona, I hope you're right.*

Chapter Eleven

"Senator Schmidt!" Reporter Harris Ward's voice bounced off the marble walls and floor of the US Capitol corridor, and was drowned out in the cacophony. He waved across the crowded, expansive hallway at the diminutive vice chairman of the Senate Select Committee on Intelligence.

She neither heard nor saw him, but continued her trek from the Senate Chamber doors through the throngs of reporters and tourists. She smiled as she weaved through the crowd.

"Senator Schmidt!" Harris clung to his cell phone and forced his way through the human tide like an Alaskan salmon returning to spawn. The vice chairman twisted her head, searching in vain for who was calling her.

Harris reached her as she waited for the elevator reserved for senators. "Senator! Harris Ward of *Roll Call*. Do you have a minute?"

"Hello, Harris. Isn't it crazy here? School must be out or something. You'd think it was already July with all these people." Schmidt's soft, soothing voice seemed out of place in the chaos, but befit the former first-grade teacher.

"Yes, ma'am. May I ask you a question about your intelligence authorization bill?" He held out his cell to record her comments.

"Oh, Harris. You know I can't talk about intelligence. It's classified."

"Yes, ma'am, but perhaps you can tamp down a lead I'm chasing. Are you aware of a plan to rig an election in Africa?"

"I suppose it's not classified to say I'm not surprised."

"So they *are* planning to rig an election?" Harris tried to keep his voice calm, though he was anything but. *I can't believe this, and I can't believe she confirmed it. This is crazy.*

"What? Who?"

"The NSA."

"The NSA?" Schmidt's tone was incredulous. "Harris, that's crazy. I'm sure the NSA isn't planning to interfere in a foreign election. I thought you were talking about the Russians. I can't comment on actual operations, of course. But, like I said, I wouldn't be surprised if *they* were planning something. The intelligence community has confirmed—this is unclassified, mind you—that they suspect Russian interference in dozens of elections throughout Europe and, of course, here."

She gave him a quizzical look. "You seem like a smart fellow, Harris. What would make you think the NSA was planning to rig an election? And in Africa, of all places."

"Madam Vice Chairman, my source says they're doing it to test a new capability. And he said the Senate is on board with the plan."

"As vice chairman, that I can categorically deny. And as for the administration planning to do such a thing, I can't imagine even President Parker—and you know how I feel about him—I can't imagine even he would approve of such a thing. After what they did to us last time." She paused and looked up at him with a smile. "I think someone's pulling your leg, Harris."

I've been in this business for thirty years. I've got a pretty good idea when someone is BS-ing me. But Harris smiled and nodded. "Thanks for your time, Senator."

The elevator doors opened, and she turned to get on.

He raised his voice. "You don't think Chairman O'Shea would do this without telling you, do you?"

In the mirror at the back of the elevator, he saw the senator's smile fade, her eyes widen, and her eyebrows rise as the door closed.

Chapter Twelve

Rachel Anderson looked up from her desk at the frosted-glass doors that opened into the sterile-looking reception room of the Senate Intelligence Committee.

"Amy, I gotta go," she whispered. "Senator Schmidt just walked in." She hung up the phone and stood. "Good afternoon, Senator Schmidt. Can I help you?"

Senator Schmidt vaguely remembered the curvy young blonde with the big blue eyes. "Hello, my dear. Now, I know he's not expecting me, but is Jim here?"

Schmidt nodded at the police officer who'd stood next to his small desk in the corner.

"I haven't seen Mr. Gates recently, but let me buzz his office and see," Rachel offered. "Of course, you're free to check for yourself. You don't need me to tell you that." She smiled while drumming her fingers on her desk.

"Oh, I don't want to just wander in. Some of the staff might think I'm spying on them." She chuckled. "Please check, if you don't mind. Thank you." She returned the smile and waited.

"Yes, ma'am." Rachel picked her phone back up and hit the intercom. "Mr. Gates, the chairman . . . I mean, the vice chairman is here to see you." She paused for a second. "Yes, sir. I'll let her know." She put down the phone. "He's coming right out. Can I get you anything, ma'am?"

"I hope the call I interrupted wasn't important, dear. It looked like you hung up mid-sentence."

"Oh no, ma'am. Not to worry. It was only my cousin. She just moved to DC from Hawaii. We're thinking of getting an apartment together. But she works way out in Virginia, so I'm not sure it'll work."

"That's nice, dear. It must be good to have family in town. Are you from Hawaii, too?"

"No, ma'am. I'm from Madison. Wisconsin, ma'am. And my cousin Amy isn't actually from Hawaii. She worked there. She's in the air force and was assigned there. She grew up in St. Louis. Now she's working at Fort Belvoir. It's way out in the boonies."

Senator Schmidt suppressed a chuckle, covering her mouth. She waved her other hand. "Oh, it's not that far. Jim and I have visited there a few times. I wonder what's keeping him." She glanced at her watch and muttered, "I haven't got all day."

Rachel's face paled. Her shoulders tensed. "Um, it's nice to—"

"I'm so sorry to keep you waiting, Madam Chairman—or Vice Chairman, ma'am." The Democratic staff director, Jim Gates, popped through the door, his thin blond hair, black glasses, and prominent cheekbones accentuating his frozen smile.

"Jim. There's something I . . . uh . . . need to discuss with you. It'll only take a minute." She glanced at Rachel and the police officer, then back at Gates.

"Got it. Why don't we step into our secure hearing room?" He motioned to the doorway behind Rachel, who reached to open the door.

Senator Schmidt nodded and followed his lead. She smiled at Rachel and proceeded into the next room. The door closed behind them.

"What's up? I mean, it's nice to see you, but I can't remember the last time you stopped in." Gates hesitated. "Is everything OK?"

"That's a good question. I was just cornered by Harris Ward. You know, that *Roll Call* reporter."

"Sure. What's he bothering you with? That guy's always got some angle. Did he want to know what's in the intel bill, like he did when you were chairman?"

"Actually, it's a little more disturbing than that. He told me that the NSA is planning to rig an election in Africa. Isn't that the strangest thing? I told him he was crazy. But then, when he was leaving, he asked if I was sure that O'Shea wasn't up to something and not telling us."

"What? Those basta—excuse me, ma'am." He paused for a second. "You know, I can't imagine they'd do that. Did he have any evidence?"

"He said a source told him what the NSA was planning and that the Senate was well aware of the plan."

"I can assure you, Senator, I'm not aware of any plans to rig an election. And while you and O'Shea have crossed swords in the past, he's never kept things from us." He looked up as if in thought. "O'Shea's pretty old school. I don't think he'd support something as stupid as this. I mean, do we really care which dictator is running which squalid African hellhole?"

"Jim, really. You can't talk like that. Even to me."

"Yes, Senator. Sorry. But why would we bother?"

"Harris said it was some kind of test."

"Test? Hey . . . wait a second."

She tilted her head and nodded for him to continue.

"Two years ago, shortly after you became committee chairman, we told Parker's people we wanted them to explore ways to counter what the Russians had done. I even told them we needed the capability to attack Putin like he attacked us. I guess this could be the result? They could be planning to test an offensive cyber system against a foreign target."

He shook his head. "But that's Russia, not Africa. You know, I still can't see O'Shea supporting it. He's an isolationist, for God's sake. He's one of the new wave of 'bring home the troops' Republicans, like the crazy new guy from Montana. Why would he go along with this?" He tapped his foot a few times and squinted, looking toward the ceiling.

Senator Schmidt checked her watch. "I've got to get going, but I want you to get to the bottom of this. We can't let them do this. I mean, after what happened to us in the last election, who'd believe we'd do the same thing? It just . . . doesn't make sense."

Jim Gates snapped his fingers and pointed in the air. "I've got just the thing to smoke them out. I'll be back with you after I talk to Jean, our NSA analyst, just to be sure. But I know exactly what we need to do."

"Good. Let me know when you've sorted it out." She headed for the door.

Chapter Thirteen

Judy Jameson knocked on the open doorway to Roxy's office. Roxy looked up from her computer screen and saw the young woman blinking back tears.

"Good morning, Judy. I was going to say happy Monday, but what's wrong?"

Judy wiped her eyes with the back of her hand. "Am I in trouble? Is Mr. Hendricks going to send me back to the navy? I thought you said it was OK to drink. What did I do wrong?" Her voice caught on the last word.

"Oh, Judy. Don't worry. You're fine."

"How can you say that? He singled me out, but everyone was drinking—except Roy. Does he hate me or something?"

"Calm down. Fred doesn't hate you. In fact, he told me to tell you you're doing a good job. Everything's OK."

"You're not just saying that, are you? Why'd he pick on me?"

"Look it. Fred's like the *dad*. OK? I mean, he's a gazillion years older than the rest of us. Especially you. So he put on his parental hat and told you to be careful. And to be honest, if he hadn't, I would've told you the same thing after the meeting. It's happy hour in there, but we're not supposed to get too happy. Understand?"

"Yeah, I guess so."

"Maybe Fred came down a little too hard. But you're fine. You're not going to be sent back to the navy, at least not until the bill's done. Like he said, watch what's going on, and you'll learn a ton."

Judy sighed and forced a smile. "So, can you explain what was going on when everybody was talking about both authorization and appropriations? I know we have both Armed Services and Appropriations Committees, not to mention Intelligence. But why do they do the same thing?"

"Good question." Roxy picked at her fingernail. "Think of it like this. It's all part of the separation of powers. You know what we mean by that, of course?"

"Sure, you've got the president, the Congress, and the Supreme Court. They have competing authorities so no one branch of government has total control."

"Yeah, in theory, at least. In Congress, we have our own version of that in our committees. Take us. We're beholden to the Budget Committee, which passes a resolution that tells us how much money we can spend. Right?"

Judy nodded.

"OK. But they don't pass a law. The president doesn't get to say how much the budgeteers want to raise taxes or spend on entitlements. Ya know, like Social Security and Medicare. Or how much we can spend on appropriations to run the government. I mean, he sends up a budget. But Congress doesn't have to pay any attention to it at all. In theory. In practice, it's a lot muddier."

Roxy took a sip from her Big Gulp. "But the Budget Committee can't tell us how much we can spend on the Defense Department versus National Parks or NASA. That's up to our committee. And they certainly can't tell us to buy fighter planes instead of tanks, for example. So here's where the authorizers come in."

She motioned for Judy to take a chair. The navy intern slid into a comfortable red leather armchair.

"So, separation of powers, right?" Roxy said. "Budget says how much in total. We say who gets what."

Judy nodded.

"President can't tell Budget what to do. But he can veto our appropriations bills if he doesn't like how much we spend or how we spend it.

"Now, we also have the authorizing committees. In theory, they're supposed to set policy. Like the idea of a space force. The Armed Services Committee studies whether it makes sense to set up a space force. If the answer is yes, then they write a law establishing the organization.

"When that happens, we come along and say, sure here's your money to set it up. Or—and this is a big *or*—we say, nope. Stupid idea. We ain't gonna give you any money."

"But if we do that, who decides?"

"If we don't give them money, they can't do it, but in practice it's a bit more complicated. Say Senator Brinkman, the chairman of the Senate Armed Services Committee, wants to set up a space force and Jackson says no. You can bet there will be a fight on the Senate floor. So, ultimately, the senators decide."

Roxy released a deep breath and said, "But this is where it gets really muddy. Over the years, instead of just authorizing new agencies or other legislative policy, the Armed Services Committee decided they wanted to authorize what ships we buy or what kind of planes we get or how much we should spend on developing a new bomber." She shook her head. "That's not what the rest of the authorizing committees do. But SASC has established its niche, and the House, the HASC, too. You following me?"

Judy nodded slowly.

"So, who decides? Bottom line, like the space force, Judy, if we don't fund it, it ain't happening. Or like Fred always says, you can't spend an authorization. You need appropriations. But it's not that simple. It's all about power. When there's a disagreement, it comes down to who's got the votes."

"So, if the House says no to cigarettes in commissaries"— Judy's brow ruffled—"and we go along, that would be the rule even if the authorizers wanted to allow sales?"

"OK, we're getting into graduate-seminar stuff here. First, that's policy. It's different than money. The authorizers are supposed to set policy. But in practice, the appropriators try to set policy sometimes. So, yes and no. If Congress says two different things, then the executive branch usually does whatever it wants. In theory, they're supposed to follow the last act. If Congress says no but then passes a subsequent law that says yes, then yes rules. But in these things when Congress is saying conflicting things at more or less the same time, Congress is basically deferring to the White House. It's like saying, 'Mr. President, you can do what you want.'"

"Wow! That's crazy."

"Yeah, don't get me started on the nuances with intelligence programs. I think you've heard enough for this morning. Like I said, you're fine. Just do your job and pay attention to what's going on. OK?"

"Thanks, Roxy. I was so upset I couldn't sleep this weekend. I didn't want to be shipped back to the Pentagon with my tail between my legs. Especially because I didn't think I did anything wrong."

"You didn't. Fred was a little surly all day. He yelled at me that morning. Something's up with him, but you don't need to worry about that. OK?"

"Yeah. And thanks again."

Chapter Fourteen

"Bo-lí-var! Bo-lí-var! Bo-lí-var!"

Standing on the palace's second-floor balcony, facing a crowd of nearly ten thousand, Simona Corazon looked to her side. She covered her mouth and spoke softly to a small man with dark hair standing behind the gold brocade curtains, out of view from the street.

"What are they saying?" she asked.

He whispered, "It's 'Bolívar,' Madame President. They're calling you 'Bolívar.'"

She gave him a puzzled look, tilting her head slightly.

"It's what your supporters call you on the internet. There's a rumor that you're the long lost great-great-great-great-granddaughter of Simón Bolívar, the liberator."

President Corazon squinted at the man behind the curtain. *That's crazy.*

"I know, I know," he whispered. "You can't be his granddaughter. He didn't father any children. But the rumor has spread across social media like wildfire. They've decided your middle initial must stand for Bolívar. I suggest you go along for the ride. Couldn't hurt being linked to Simón Bolívar." He smiled.

She returned the smile, nodded, and faced the crowd, raising her fist to the rhythm of the chant and laughing loudly. After a minute, she put both hands in the air to quiet the assemblage. "Yes, my countrymen and women. Like Bolívar, the father of our country, the liberator that we hold so dear, I, too, am a liberator. He freed us from tyranny. I will free us from *yanqui* imperialism."

The crowd roared its approval.

"I thank you for coming to the square today, and for your support. Together, we will show the bankers in the United States and here in Bolivia. They can't steal us blind. But now, my dear, dear countrymen, I must go back to work. Thank you so much for your support, and don't forget to go to the polls next month."

She grinned, waved, and blew kisses, then backed off the balcony and into her room, closing the French doors and curtains behind her.

"Bolívar, huh." She chuckled, and her advisors joined in. "Luis, make up new posters and billboards in our national colors, saying *Simona B—The New Liberator*. Now, Desdemona, what are the latest polls showing?"

Desdemona cringed a little and looked at her hands. "Well, Madame President, it's not all good."

"What? Why not?" She stared at the skinny twenty-five-year-old in tight blue jeans and a cream-colored silk blouse.

"But it's not all bad, either," Desdemona pleaded.

"Just tell me." Simona trained a steely gaze on her.

"The bad news is that, since your nationalization of lithium, Montoya has doubled in the polls."

"Doubled?" *Oh my God! Could Tío Rodrigo be right?* She glanced over at her uncle and brother, huddled together in one corner. *No. Impossible. Our people will never vote for a banker.* "And me? Where am I?"

"There has been some slippage, but . . ."

Simona's eyes narrowed.

Desdemona's hands shook. The words spilled out. "The good news is, even though you've come down a few points, Montoya is not close. He's at fifteen percent, while you are at thirty-three percent. None of the other eight candidates are above two or three percent."

Simona laughed heartily. "Fifteen percent? Why should I worry?" *I knew that old fool was wrong. A banker? Never.*

"Yes, ma'am. But the only thing is twenty-eight percent of the likely voters are still undecided. And while you're the candidate of choice for millennials, the polls show sixty-nine percent of young people don't plan to vote."

"But they voted for me last time. Surely the polls are wrong."

"Yes, ma'am, they could be. There's a five percent margin of error. And it's possible the polls don't accurately reflect the youth vote. But, Madame President, I have to be honest. The trend doesn't look good. Montoya has coalesced the support of industry and the upper class. Nearly every business owner is tossing his or her support to Montoya. They're pouring money into his campaign. Without the youth vote, it could be close."

"They will vote, Desdemona. You watch. They love me. The people love me. You heard them outside. I am their liberator. We'll ride that love to reelection. I won't let them down.

"Now, get to work on our new posters. I want to plaster the country with Simona B. signs." She chuckled. "Bolívar, huh? I should have thought of that myself. Go now, all of you. Out."

Miguel smiled at his sister as he walked out. He leaned close to Rodrigo. "Uncle, that's the thing. We need capital to start manufacturing electric cars. And you're telling me the banks won't lend it to us?"

Rodrigo shook his head and frowned.

"So, what else can I do? I'll have to talk to the coca growers."

"That, my boy, would be very dangerous. They would just as soon separate you from your head as finance your factory. You would be far better off convincing Simonetta not to nationalize the businesses."

"Yeah, right. She's my sister. I know she loves me. But I wouldn't keep my head if I suggested that. No, *Tío*, we need money. If you can't get the bankers to help, I'm afraid I have no choice."

Chapter Fifteen

"Mr. President?" Steve Simpson poked his head through the Oval Office doorway. "Sir. General McNeal is here to update you on the NSA's project, SWEET REVENGE."

"OK, show him in. Wait a second." He lowered his voice. "Can we talk about that here, Steve?"

"We won't go into operational details. So, yes, sir." The chief of staff motioned for General McNeal to join them and pointed to a seat on a royal-blue couch placed at a ninety-degree angle from a gold armchair.

"How's my favorite general today?" Parker sat in the armchair.

General McNeal stood ramrod straight in front of the couch. Simpson waited in the space next to the couch and armchair, positioned as if ready to defend the president from any outburst or act of treason from the army officer.

"OK, General, have a seat," Parker said. "Cut me off if I say something too revealing, but tell us where we stand."

"Sir, yes, sir." McNeal sat down, keeping his perfect posture. "We have chosen target *M* for the demonstration." He leaned toward the president and handed him a note with the word *Mauritania* written on it.

Parker frowned. "Why there?"

"Three reasons, Mr. President. First, they have an event coming up quite soon. For security reasons, I won't say exactly what that is or when, in this office. But I imagine you know what I mean by *event*."

"Yes, of course."

"Second, they are relatively unsophisticated in their, what shall we call it, um . . . defenses. Understood?"

"Yes, yes." Parker squirmed in his chair.

"Get on with it," Simpson snapped, sensing Parker's impatience. "The president's a busy man."

"Yes, of course. Sorry, sir. And third, it holds no particular strategic importance to us. We checked with the State Department, and they told us—"

"What the fuck?" Parker almost jumped out of his chair. "You told the State Department?" His face reddened as he screamed at the general.

McNeal leaned back against the couch as if to avoid the rush of hot air billowing from the president. He shook his head and gasped out, "No, no, no, sir. We asked for a strategic assessment of several countries in Africa." He continued on hurriedly, as if speaking rapidly would erase that moment. "We didn't say why. And we didn't hint that we were interested in any particular one. But we wanted their expertise to ensure we weren't blundering into more than we bargained for."

"I see. That's all fine." Parker chuckled, his calm demeanor returning. "We can never really trust that striped-pants crew down at Foggy Bottom. That's why I like the military. I know I can trust you." Parker grinned.

"Absolutely, sir."

"Terrific. Now, Steve and I have a different idea for a target."

"What?" General McNeal edged forward on the couch, his knee within inches of the president's. "With all due respect to Mr. Simpson, let me assure you this coun . . . uh . . . target is perfect."

Parker put up his hand. McNeal stopped and eased backward on the couch. "Steve, show him."

Simpson wrote *Bolivia* on the pad of paper he was holding and showed it to the general.

McNeal read it and nearly shouted, "Bo—what? Why?" He paused. "Again, with all due respect, sir, that doesn't make sense."

Parker's eyes narrowed.

"Please, sir, let me explain." McNeal took a deep breath and clasped his hands together as if praying. "Let me remind you this is a test. Our purpose is not to rig an, um, event, but to check to see if we could if we wanted."

"I thought you said you could cause any candidate to . . ."

General McNeal waved his hands. "I'm sorry, sir, but we can't go into those details here."

"Yeah, yeah. OK. But you told us that. Didn't you?"

"We are ninety percent certain that's correct. The purpose of this test is to make sure. The name that Mr. Simpson showed me has a much better defense capability than our choice. Moreover, it is a target with greater strategic importance. If our test is unsuccessful, the ramifications could be much more dire."

"General." Steve Simpson spoke up in a harsh tone. "You don't need to worry about the ramifications. That's not your job." He leaned down, placing one hand on the arm of the couch, and lowered his voice. "The president has made his decision. We just need you to be ready to go when the event occurs. Is that clear? Can the president's favorite general do that or not?" He sneered.

General McNeal looked at Simpson, then over at the president, who grinned. McNeal sighed and sagged a little before sitting up straight. "We can do this. But I have to warn you, something could go wrong."

Simpson glowered. "You need to remember why SWEET REVENGE was authorized. Who the original target was. They attacked us. Now, if you can't take out some tin-horned dictator in a banana republic, what fucking good is it? And, by the way, how would your system do if it's used in the way Congress intended, were that to become necessary?"

General McNeal looked down at his lap. He nodded and glanced back up. "Mr. President, if that's your decision, we'll execute it. But I would be remiss if I didn't provide you my best professional advice. And that is to test it out somewhere else first."

"There's no time." Parker waved his hand at McNeal. "We can't wait for you to do a meaningless test in some shithole. I have full confidence in your ability and that of the fine men and women of the National Security Agency. So, do it. Is that clear?"

"Yes, sir. Absolutely. We'll get right on it. And be assured we'll do our very best not to let you down."

"Very well, General." President Parker stood up and offered McNeal his hand. "Like I said, that fourth star is just around the corner. I'm sure of it."

Chapter Sixteen

The gray helmet-haired frontier woman, first-term senator from South Dakota, sat on the dais, presiding over the Senate. The Vice President of the United States serves as the Senate's presiding officer. But since the early days of the Republic, vice presidents have only presided when a tie vote is anticipated.

Instead, the longest-serving senator in the majority party, normally a septuagenarian or octogenarian, is appointed as a president *pro tempore*. However, it would be cruel and unusual punishment to require the senior legislator to preside over the long-winded speeches and lengthy quorum calls that are common during Senate proceedings. So, first-term senators are dragooned into service as presiding officers, an hour at a time, giving them a chance to learn about Senate rules and procedure.

"Madam President, what is the pending business before the Senate?" Standing at a desk in the first row, near the center of the chamber, Senator Ron O'Shea, the chairman of the Senate Intelligence Committee, smiled, a gleam in his blue eyes.

The presiding officer squawked in a flat, nasally, high-pitched voice, "The Senate is in legislative session."

Senator Ron O'Shea spoke again. "Madam President?"

"The senator from Wyoming is recognized." She nodded for him to proceed.

"Thank you, Madam President." He cleared his throat. "I call up S. 321, the intelligence authorization bill, and ask for its immediate consideration."

"Is there objection to the request?" She paused. "Hearing none, it is so ordered. The clerk will report."

A chubby, middle-aged woman with tortoiseshell glasses and dark hair stood on the lower level of the dais and read, "Senate 321, a bill to authorize appropriations for the intelligence community and for other purposes." She halted and looked toward the Intelligence Committee chairman.

"I ask that further reading of the bill be dispensed with," O'Shea requested.

The presiding officer glanced over toward the other side of the chamber, where the vice chairman of the Intelligence Committee, Kaye Schmidt, was seated. Schmidt nodded, so the presiding officer stated, "Without objection, so ordered."

"Thank you, Madam President." Senator O'Shea looked down to read from a prepared text. "Today, the Senate will consider this vitally important bill, which ensures that our nation is protected from foreign threats—from nation-states that might wish us harm to terrorist cells throughout the world, and sadly, even here at home." He looked up, stared at the television camera focused on him, shook his head, and frowned. "In the interest of time, I ask unanimous consent that my full statement be included in the record as if read."

"Without objection," the presiding officer mumbled.

Sitting down, Senator O'Shea motioned to Senator Schmidt, who sat across the center aisle on the Democratic side of the chamber.

"Madam President." Senator Schmidt stood to speak.

The presiding officer looked over at her. "The senator from New York is recognized."

Senator Schmidt smiled and turned toward her chairman. "Madam President, let me say this at the outset—this is a good bill, and I commend the chairman for all his work on the measure." She spoke softly and with perfect diction, a practice that came naturally to the former teacher.

She gave Senator O'Shea a slight bow. He smiled and waved back, slouching in his chair. Senator Schmidt surveyed the room. The presiding officer, Senator O'Shea, and herself were the only members in the chamber.

Sandy Winthrop, the Intelligence Committee's majority staff director, was seated next to Senator O'Shea. Her light-brown hair was tied back so tight it looked as if each hair was about to be ripped from her scalp. Her taut, gray-tinted skin befitted someone who had been locked in a vault for five months with only minimal exposure to sunshine.

Senator Schmidt glanced at her staff director, Jim Gates. He sat on her immediate left, straight as a rod, the muscles in his neck tense. The top of his balding, bronzed head came nearly up to her shoulder. She counted three more staffers sitting at the back of the chamber behind the low railing that separated the staff seating from the rest of the room.

"But I must inform my colleagues that, most reluctantly, I cannot support it in its current form." She paused.

"What?" Senator O'Shea cried. He sat up straight. He glanced at Sandy, his staff director, who had a panicked look on her face, and then back at Senator Schmidt.

Schmidt cocked her head and grimaced as if to say she was sorry, but she continued, "Mr. President—I'm sorry, Madam President." She gave a sweet smile to the female presiding officer. "Today we learned of a plan by the current administration to interfere in a foreign nation's elections."

Senator O'Shea stood up. "Will the vice chairman yield for a question?"

"I will in a moment, Madam President. But first, if my dear friend would let me explain," Schmidt responded.

He nodded and groaned.

She smiled at him. "Madam President, I said today—and I mean today." She pounded her finger on the wooden desk in front of her. "A few hours ago, my staff confirmed that the National Security Agency is planning to test a new offensive cybersecurity system against a foreign target. They informed my staff, Mr. Jim Gates, and our NSA analyst, Ms. Jean Reed, that indeed the agency is planning what they call a beta test to rig an election."

"What the hell?" Senator O'Shea's voice was clear in the chamber.

The presiding officer raised her eyebrows and pointed her gavel at him. He put up his hands in surrender. She motioned for Senator Schmidt to continue.

"Madam President," Senator Schmidt said, "I have to say I'm shocked, even flabbergasted, that the Republican president would order a cyberattack. How dare he? How dare we, as a nation? Especially after what happened in our last election. And what many intelligence experts say has been happening with regularity in other elections throughout Europe, Asia, and elsewhere.

"When I first heard this rumor in the past few days, I was sure it was erroneous. To learn otherwise has left me horrified and deeply saddened. Therefore, I have no choice but to offer an amendment to prohibit the NSA from going forward with any beta test of any offensive cyber capability designed to interfere in any election." She shook her head and reached for a paper from Gates.

She continued, "Madam President, I send an amendment to the desk and ask for its immediate consideration." She held out the piece of paper.

A young page in a dark-blue suit rushed forward from where he was seated on the floor. He grabbed it and took it to the chubby reading clerk.

The clerk stood to read. "An amendment offered by the senator from New York. On page—"

"Madam President." Senator O'Shea jumped to his feet, waving his right arm. "I suggest the absence of a quorum."

"The absence of a quorum being noted," the presiding officer said, "the clerk will call the roll."

At that moment, the large glass-and-wood double doors at the back of the chamber flew open. The majority leader, Howard "Jake" Jacobs, stormed in and rushed down the center steps toward the chairman. In a stage whisper, he hollered, "What in the Sam Hill you got goin' on here, Ron? You said this was greased. But you wanted to call up the bill so you'd have a chance to talk about it. Now you're accusing Parker of trying to rig an election?"

"Not me, Jake. Kaye." He spoke in a hushed tone. "She jumped us. She's got an amendment to prohibit the NSA from conducting a cyberattack. But, other than for the gotcha effect, I don't know why the flock she's doing it."

The pudgy clerk began reading the names of the senators in alphabetical order to discern whether a quorum was present.

Jake Jacobs, the tall, smooth-talking, flashy-dressing,

Louisiana riverboat gambler of a majority leader spun around. He offered Senator Schmidt a frozen smile and drawled, "Senator Schmidt. You always seemed reasonable. For a liberal, I mean." He continued to grin, cocked his head, and wrinkled his brow. "Why you doing this? You gotta know Parker's not gonna try and steal some election. That's crazy."

"I'm sorry, Senator Jacobs," Schmidt responded. "You're right. It is crazy. I wish it weren't also true. In light of what we learned today, we have no choice. You don't support Parker interfering in elections, do you, Jake? Your president is planning to rig an election in Africa, and soon, from what we hear."

"Now, Kaye, he's the president of all of us."

"Well, I didn't vote for him."

"Who's saying I did?" His brown eyes twinkled.

She shook her head. "Go ahead. Make jokes. But we're going to get a vote on this amendment. And if you try and stop us, you know as well as I that you Republicans will be back in the minority in a year and a half."

Jake turned back to Senator O'Shea, who shrugged his shoulders in apparent agreement. A tall blonde popped through the door from the Republican cloakroom and rushed down the steps. She whispered something in the leader's ear. He nodded.

"I gotta take a call." Jacobs looked at the reading clerk and motioned with his hands for her to slow down reading the names of the senators. Then he walked back up the steps and into the cloakroom.

Chapter Seventeen

"Are you watching the floor, boss?" Roxy burst into Fred's office.

"Yeah, strange shit."

Roy rushed through the doorway, sliding to a stop in front of Roxy. "Sir, I've got that information. Most of it's classified. Should we step into the vault?"

"Tell me what you can here. If I got questions, we can go in the vault."

Roxy sneered at Roy. He smirked in reply.

"All right, you two," said Fred sternly. "Just tell me what you can, Roy."

Roy cleared his throat. "I spoke with the NSA liaison. He um . . . let's say he didn't disabuse the notion of the Democrats' charge."

"Seriously? Holy crap. What a mess."

"Yes, sir. There's more to it than that, but I can't go into any more detail here." He motioned toward Roxy. She threw him a disgusted look. "But there is one more thing."

"Go ahead."

"I spoke to Jonas, that young kid in the Democratic cloak-room. Funny, he thinks I work for the Democrats." He chuckled. "He told me that, yesterday, Jim Gates, the SSCI Democratic staff director, put a hold on the bill but didn't say why. Gates didn't say anything about amendments. So when Schmidt offered an amendment, she surprised the leadership staff. But they were thrilled."

"Why were they thrilled?" Roxy spat, still glaring at him.

"Because they love to see the majority get one-upped, Roxy," Fred growled. He raised his hands, palms upright, as if surprised by the question. "The cloakroom staff and the leadership aides are all about partisan warfare. Any time they can screw around with the plans of the other party, they're giddy.

"Now, look." Fred's gruff tone softened to a paternal rumble. "That doesn't always mean the members feel the same way. But in this case, they might. It's nice to win something, even if it's a pyrrhic victory."

"Sure." Roxy nodded. "But seriously, can we really be planning to interfere in an election?"

Roy shrugged and motioned to Fred. "We can go to the vault, sir. This might go back to that thing a couple years ago when Schmidt was chairman."

Fred sighed and eased out of his chair, masking a grimace probably brought on by his back and stomach pains. He started toward the door. "Sorry, Roxy. Secret crap. You understand."

Roy and Fred left Roxy alone in the boss's office. "Motherfucker. That asshole wants to keep me out of the loop." She stomped her foot once and spun toward the door. "I hate that."

"What's up, Rox? You look like you just ate a shit sandwich." Mindy Abrams was leaning back in her chair, her red running shoes propped up on her desk.

Roxy scanned Mindy's floral-print dress and running shoes and wrinkled her nose.

Mindy glanced down at herself. "I metro'd today. Rockin' the Washington working woman. About to head out . . . if we're free to go."

"Sure. What do we know about intel?" Roxy scoffed. "That motherfucker always insists on saying he has to cut me out. It pisses me off."

"Yeah, I get that. But what choice do they have? Roy's got all that super-secret shit that we can't know anything about."

Roxy let out a deep breath and stared at the ceiling. "I know. I shouldn't get angry. But I always get the feeling he's cutting me out 'cause he knows it jerks me off."

"C'mon, Roxy. You know Fred wouldn't do that."

"Not Fred. The asshole."

"I know what you're saying. But think about it. Fred wouldn't let him get away with that. He wouldn't do that to you, of all people."

"Yeah, I guess. But I get so frustrated." She stalked to her cubicle, crumpled up a piece of paper, and fired it in the trash can.

"Someday you'll probably be in Fred's job," Mindy said. "And Roy, or his replacement"—she snorted—"will have to tell *you* stuff. And *I'll* be out here bitching and moaning that I don't know what the fuck's going on."

Roxy sighed again. "Yeah, maybe so. But it sure as hell won't be Roy briefing me. We should go home. No use sitting around waiting for them to come out of the vault and tell us"—she paused—"nothing." She glanced at the TV and increased the volume. The majority leader was back on the Senate floor.

"This should be good," said Roxy.

The flat, high-pitched voice of the senator from South Dakota rang through the chamber. "The pending business is the amendment offered by the senator from New York, Mrs. Schmidt, number 778."

"Madam President. I know of no further debate on the amendment. I think we can vote on it now," Jacobs mumbled.

The presiding officer nodded. "Is there further debate?" She paused.

Senator Schmidt shook her head.

"All those in favor signify by saying 'Aye.'"

Senators O'Shea, Schmidt, and Jacobs murmured, "Aye."

"All those opposed signify by saying 'Nay.'"

The presiding officer scanned the room. No other senators being present, no one spoke.

"In the opinion of the chair, the ayes have it. The amendment is adopted. The majority leader is recognized."

Senator Jacobs stood in the center aisle, one finger raised. "Thank you, Madam President. For the benefit of all my colleagues, let me say it looks like we're at an impasse on the intelligence bill. The Democrats insisted on offering an amendment seeking to embarrass the president. Now, I want all senators to know we're not going to play that game. I've spoken to President Parker.

"Despite what the senator from New York has accused him of, he has assured me he has no intention of allowing the NSA to interfere in an election in Africa.

"So, Madam President, as I guess we might have expected, our friends on the other side of the aisle are just looking to gum up the works. And it's a shame. You heard the vice chairman say this is a good bill. She commended the chairman for his work. Y'all know this bill is critical to our nation's security. All of us in the Senate, and our fellow Americans, know the many dangers we face. Terrorist cells. Cyber threats. Nation-states that wish us harm. This is vitally important legislation.

"So, why did the senator move to impede progress on the bill? Only she, and perhaps her leadership, know. But I can tell you this—as long as I'm majority leader, we won't stand for shenanigans like this. So, Madam President, I call up S. 1408, and ask for its immediate consideration."

"Holy crap, Mindy!" Roxy shouted over the TV volume. "Jacobs pulled intel. Oh my God, they're dead."

She turned her attention back to the TV in time to hear the clerk read, "A bill to name the post office at Fourteenth and—"

"Mr. President, I ask further reading be dispensed with," Jacobs mumbled.

"Without objection," growled the burly, bald-headed junior senator from Montana as he sat down in the presiding officer's chair. He banged his gavel loudly.

Jacobs smiled and said, "I suggest the absence of a quorum."

"The clerk will call the roll!" shouted the presiding officer. He banged his gavel again.

Roxy hit the mute button and looked over at Mindy.

Mindy rolled her eyes. "That guy needs some anger management classes."

"Which guy?"

"The guy in the chair. Is it Senator Bacon? The new senator from Montana? He sounds like his head's gonna explode." She chuckled a little.

"He's new. Maybe he's never seen the minority get a win. Although, I'm not sure it's really a win. Clearly, Schmidt wanted to force a vote."

"Absolutely!" Mindy chimed in.

"But it's a classic gotcha amendment. If Republicans vote for the amendment, they're all but admitting that their Republican president was planning to fix an election and they stopped him. If they vote no, it's like they're sanctioning an unlawful attack. Lose, lose." She sighed.

"Why did Jacobs call for a vote, then?"

"It's a voice vote. No one's recorded voting for or against it. I guess, from that perspective, Jacobs did the only thing he could. He couldn't have his members support rigging an election. But he didn't want to leave it sitting out there, either. The press will be all over it. And you heard him say the president denied the whole thing. So why not voice vote it? The president's denial probably won't get a lot of TV airtime, except maybe on Fox."

"Then why didn't the Dems force a roll-call vote? You know, really embarrass the Republicans?"

"That's a good question. Maybe Schmidt didn't want to completely blow up the intel bill." Roxy shrugged her shoulders and wrinkled her nose. "But this could fuck us in the end too."

"Why would you say that?"

"'Cause we're bound to face the same thing. And when we do, will Jacobs pull us down?"

"C'mon, Rox. You know it's not that easy. I mean, who really gives a shit if we do intel, other than the intel committee members, right? But you can't run the entire Defense Department *and* the intelligence community if you don't do our bill. We're the fucking Appropriations Committee."

"Yeah, we'll see, Mindy. There's always continuing resolutions."

"Oh yeah? When has Congress ever run DoD on a CR? I mean, for the whole year? You know the answer. Never. And with the R's in charge? They love DoD. No way. Ain't gonna happen."

"Yeah, you might be right, but mark my words: this is gonna fuck us up."

"If you ask me, I think the whole thing sounded like a partisan sneak attack. And when Jacobs denied it, he blew the D's cover on it. I don't think it'll amount to much. Probably blow over by the time we get to the floor." Mindy switched off her computer, stood up, and stretched.

"I'd agree with you, but something Roy almost said makes me think there might be more truth to this than you'd expect."

"Roy?" Mindy scoffed. "Like I'd put a lot of credence in that. We'll see. But I'd bet you a six-pack this is just minority bullshit." She grabbed her backpack. "You ready to head out?"

"Actually, I think I'm going to stick around. With those two secured in the vault without TV or phones, they won't know what happened with the amendment or that Jacobs pulled the bill. Go ahead and take off, though."

"Suit yourself, but you're gonna owe me that six-pack." Mindy stood up, slung her backpack over one shoulder, and headed for the door.

Chapter Eighteen

Steve Simpson stood in the doorway of the Oval Office, a worried look on his face. "Excuse me, Mr. President, I've got some bad news."

Parker looked up at his chief of staff with a wrinkled brow. "Just give it to me."

"Sir, the Senate just approved a Democratic amendment to ban the NSA from beta testing that, uh, cybersecurity thing."

"What the fuck?" Parker slammed his reading glasses down on his desk.

"I just talked to Jacobs fifteen minutes ago."

"Yes, sir, I know."

"I told him we weren't going to rig any elections in Africa. *Africa*, Steve. But how the hell would he know about it, anyway? Some traitor is leaking this crap. I'm calling him back."

"Sir, I'd hold that thought. Don't forget it was Schmidt who raised the issue. She's cleared to know about it. All she had to do was ask the right questions."

"Are you fucking kidding me? Why would McNeal tell the Democrats?"

"First, we don't know it was McNeal," said Simpson, keeping his voice calm and level. "Second, if she asked, he'd have to tell her. The NSA can't keep secrets like this from the intel committees. And remember, in a way, this was her idea."

"You're saying Kaye Schmidt, New York liberal, wants to interfere in foreign elections? Gimme a break." Parker rolled his eyes.

"Not exactly, but it was her idea, when she was the SSCI chairman, for the NSA to figure out how to get back at Russia. This is what the agency came up with. So yes, in a way, sir, she did."

"What do we do now, smart guy?"

"Well, Jacobs pulled the bill after the amendment passed."

"Why didn't you say that in the first place?" Parker snapped.

"Because the intel community knows the Senate voted to ban the test."

"Jacobs pulled the bill. It's dead." Parker waved his arms. "Tell the intel community it's dead and I'm not signing any bill with that amendment."

"Look, Mr. President. We based your campaign on defeating the entrenched deep state, the unelected Washington bureaucracy, and liberal media. I know a lot of that was bullshit rhetoric, but there's some truth to it." He walked closer to the president's desk and lowered his voice. "McNeal wanted to run a meaningless test in Africa. You changed that. It was pretty obvious he wasn't happy. If you go ahead when he knows Congress said no . . ." He hesitated. "To be frank, sir, I'd say we're asking for trouble."

"You think McNeal will blow the whistle?"

"Not necessarily McNeal. He's a good soldier. Bottom line, it'll leak. I'm sorry, sir. You can't do this the way we were planning."

"God damn it, Steve. They really fucked up my plans. What am I supposed to do about Edison now? That little prick threatened me, ya know. He said he'd fuck us in New Mexico if I didn't stop that Bolivian bitch from fucking around in his shit. OK, 'bottom line,'" Parker mimicked his aide. "How much do I have to care about Edison? Can he really deliver on his promise or his threat?"

"Can't say for sure, but it's not something you can dismiss."

"Who is he, anyway? I remember meeting the pipsqueak at that LA fundraiser last August. He looks like one of those grumpy-old-man Muppets with a big head and sloping shoulders. How'd he get rich enough to horn in on the Big Three American car manufacturers?"

Simpson blinked three times. "Despite the gray hair, he's only thirty-five or so. He's a college dropout from Berkeley. The story is he was working with a high school buddy out of a Silicon Valley garage, trying to come up with new software schemes. One night, his pal was looking at a dating website, talking about how so many users lie about their looks or background. Edison realized building an app that validated the accuracy of that information would be huge. So he figured out how to do it by harnessing public records and other info on the internet. Made his first billion before his twenty-first birthday. By twenty-five, he was the fifth-richest man in America."

"Un-fucking-believable." Parker frowned and shook his head. "That's really what this country's come to. Our industrial giants are weak, nerdy software engineers who can't get a date. Where are the Carnegies and Rockefellers? Real men who built real businesses."

"In fairness to Edison, sir, he parlayed his dating-app profits into the electric-vehicle business. So, unlike most new entrepreneurs, at least he's building something and putting Americans to work."

"Yeah, yeah. But what the fuck are we going to do about him now? I'm gonna call Jacobs."

"Sir, you can't talk to Jacobs."

Parker slammed his hand on the desk. "Why the hell not?"

"What would you say? The amendment bans all testing by NSA, not just in Africa. If you call him, he'll ask you, 'What's the problem?' You told him you weren't planning any testing."

"Yeah, fuck. You're right. So, what's the solution to this goat rope?"

"I've got a thought. But I'll need to take a closer look at that amendment and do some research. Give me a day or two. I think we can still skin this cat or rope this goat, sir." Simpson smiled broadly.

Parker glared in return.

Chapter Nineteen

Harris Ward sat at his post in the deserted Senate cafeteria.

He hit "send" and looked up from his keyboard. Early night. Senate was gone. He already had tomorrow's lead story done, and it wasn't even six. He smiled. Getaway Thursdays would do that.

Senators and congressmen were probably causing a traffic jam on Highway 1 at the National Airport exit, rushing to get the hell out of Dodge. He checked his phone and saw that a text had come in. He clicked it.

"Thank You!" it read. The sender was anonymous.

I should be thanking him. Hopefully this put the issue to bed. Harris still couldn't believe they'd actually planned to hijack an election. And what about Parker's denial? Was that a case of "getting religion" after having his cover blown? Or could it be they hadn't really planned on rigging an election? But then why would the guy leak the story? And why would he send a thank-you text?

On second thought, Harris wasn't sure he'd heard the last of this. Maybe he should check in with the Bureau, see if Max Welsh was still at his desk. Normal civil servants would be stuck in traffic at this hour, but Max was no normal civil servant. Harris chuckled. Was anyone at the FBI "normal"?

He scanned his contacts and made the call.

"Max Welsh. FBI. IT Enterprise," answered a fatigued voice.

"Mr. Welsh, it's Harris Ward of *Roll Call*. Do you have a second?"

"Mr. Ward, well if this ain't my unlucky day," he growled.

"Please, call me Harris. I was wondering if you could answer a couple questions for me. On background, of course. Wait . . . did you say unlucky?" Harris squinted at his phone, then put it back to his ear.

"That's right," Max spat. "Last time I talked to you, I nearly got canned. And that conversation was *on background*. Somehow Parker's staff found out it was me who talked to you, and once he got elected, I got demoted. Lucky I still have a job, I guess. Thank God for civil-service rules."

"That's unbelievable. Parker tried to fire you? You told the truth."

"Hey, truth don't count for much these days. Don't you know, I'm part of the deep state. Hell, the whole FBI is. According to Parker, we were all trying to make sure the Democrat got elected. We had the evidence. Parker was lying. Didn't matter. Once Parker got through with us, all the FBI Director could do was apologize for us talking to the press. That'd be you, Ward. Why on earth would I talk to you again? Because I think it'd be fun standing in an unemployment line? I ought to hang up right now."

"Wait. Please don't hang up. Look, I'm awfully sorry about how things worked out. You didn't do anything wrong. All you did was confirm what I suspected. I had a copy of that tape. I saw Parker with Rebecca DeLaurio. He was lying, and he got away with it. But if you hadn't validated it for me, someone else would have."

Max grunted.

"Anyway," Harris continued, "what I'm calling about has nothing to do with the last election." He held the phone a little closer. "I got an anonymous tip that the NSA wants to test out a new offensive cybersecurity system to mess with foreign elections."

"It sure as hell wasn't from me."

"No, I didn't think it was you." Harris rolled his eyes. "But hear me out. I asked the Senate Intelligence Committee's vice chairman about it. She acted like I was nuts. Then two days later, the intel bill's on the floor; she offers an amendment banning NSA from rigging elections."

"Don't know anything about it. Why don't you bother the NSA instead of messing with me?"

"Please, Mr. Welsh, let me finish." He paused for a second and heard a heavy sigh. "So, if my source was wrong, why would Schmidt want to ban it?"

"OK. Let's say, for argument's sake, she was right. Parker's got the NSA planning to rig an election. Big deal."

Harris smiled. *Good. I got him talking.* He didn't say a word.

"I got to think they do that kind of shit all the time. If not them, then the CIA. I'm not in that world. I'm an IT engineer. Don't know nothing about that stuff." His voice raised to a shout. "So again, why are you bothering me, Ward?"

"Because I trust you." *Butter him up. Keep him talking.* "You told me the truth about Parker. I think you're a patriotic civil servant with a job to do. All I'm asking is—could it be true? I mean, could we really rig an election?"

"Hell, Ward, if the Russians can do it, it can't be that hard."

Chapter Twenty

Roxy Fowler stood in the doorway of Fred's office, holding up a small stack of legal-sized papers with scores of numbers on them. "We're balanced. We've spent every dime and not a penny more."

"Thank goodness," Fred muttered. "Jeff Leary and I are supposed to brief the boss tomorrow. Let's get the staff in here for one last session to make sure we've got all our bases covered."

"You want me to call Jeff and Marjory?"

"Nah, we'll do this without the minority."

"What? Fred Hendricks, I don't believe it." She put one hand on her hip. "You've never drafted an appropriations bill without including the other party. After all these years, why are you cutting out Jeff? He's a good guy."

"It's not Jeff. I've shared everything with him. It's Marjory Radcliffe. Unfortunately, we can't trust her. Jeff doesn't trust her."

"I'm not following." Roxy leaned against the doorframe.

"You know that after Patterson died last year, Senator Liz Boyer was appointed to replace him temporarily as chairman of the defense subcommittee."

"Yeah, so?"

"Well, that decision raised a lot of eyebrows among the Democratic members. I mean, she's a first-term senator and she's running defense!" He shook his head.

"So," he continued, "our Democratic full committee chairman, Lackland, explained that she was actually the most senior Democrat who wasn't a subcommittee chairman. You see, she turned down the legislative subcommittee chairmanship at the start of the session. She'd been its ranking member. But she said it was a waste of time."

He gave a look of mild disgust and tapped his fingers against the desk. "Anyway, Lackland told the members it was only temporary. But then the Democrats lost the Senate in the election. And what does he do? He lets her keep defense, albeit obviously as the ranking minority instead of chairman.

"As you might imagine, lots of more senior members looking to move up to more powerful subcommittees were none too pleased."

"Yeah, I heard about that."

"Lackland promised that when the Democrats retake the majority, he'll return to the seniority system. But he basically threw out a hundred and fifty years of Appropriations Committee tradition and precedent. His colleagues were pissed. But no one was going to challenge Harry Lackland of Virginia. I mean, he might be getting old, but he's still tenacious."

Roxy shifted. She loved Fred, but he sure could take his time getting to the point. "All that's awful. But what does it have to do with Jeff?"

"Well, what you probably don't know is Boyer wanted Marjory to be the defense clerk."

At that, she perked up. "No way."

Fred nodded. "'Fraid so."

"That's crazy."

"Anyway, our Democratic staff director, Pat Sistrunk, agreed with you. Marjory was a staffer on the Labor-Education-Health

Committee, after all. She's never worked appropriations. She's never worked defense issues. So Pat got Lackland to appoint Jeff as clerk.

"You know Jeff worked directly for Boyer during her years on the legislative subcommittee. Pat figured Boyer couldn't complain too much. So anyway, the story is Boyer threw a hissy fit. Pat stood his ground. Jeff became clerk, but Marjory was added as his minority staffer. Problem is, now Boyer's always trying to keep Jeff out of the loop. She wants Marjory to represent her."

"But Marjory doesn't know anything," Roxy said. "And if she was on Labor, she's probably not used to doing things in a bipartisan way, like we always do."

"Not the first time a subcommittee ranking member or chairman wanted his or her own guy or gal instead of what the full committee chairman wanted. And not the first time that's caused problems with bipartisanship and a hell of a lot of other things." He sighed. "So, Jeff is telling Marjory what he thinks she needs to know. But he's playing his cards close to the vest."

"That's awful," she said. "At least she won't be there when you brief Jackson and Boyer."

"Well, hopefully not. It's always just the two clerks. Mostly because Jackson likes it that way. But also 'cause sometimes we have to talk about things that nobody else is cleared to hear. But with Boyer and Marjory, I wouldn't be too sure."

"What a mess. So, should I round up the gang so we can put this turkey to bed?"

"Yeah, get 'em in here. Let's make sure there aren't any gremlins out there that'll bite us in the ass."

Chapter Twenty-One

"Desdemona!" Simona Corazon screamed from the desk in her cavernous office.

The skinny young woman popped her head in the door. "Yes, Madame President?"

"Get in here. What's this bullshit?" She held up a three-page pamphlet.

"Ma'am, that's the latest polling data." Desdemona crept a little farther into the room.

"It better be wrong." She threw the paper toward the doorway. "It says Montoya is over twenty percent. Twenty percent! That can't be right."

Desdemona stooped to pick it up. "I'm sorry, but that's what the latest polls show. He's continuing to pick up more support, while the undecided numbers are dropping. The good news is that he's not pulling votes from you. Your numbers haven't changed. You're still way ahead."

"At this rate, he'll catch up before Election Day."

"In theory, but it's not likely. Anecdotal evidence that we're seeing—social media, newspaper editorials, grumbling in the business community—all suggests he's topped out at twenty percent. Like you said, your people won't vote for a banker. You're over thirty, and your support is solid."

"But the undecided vote is still at fifteen percent. They vote for him, he wins."

Desdemona squirmed. "As I said, in theory. In reality, most of the undecideds won't vote. Or they'll split the vote among you, Montoya, and the other eight candidates. No way he'll get all of them."

"OK, Desdemona." Simona smiled a little. "And thank you. I know you're doing your best. Would you please get my brother? I want to talk about his progress in lithium and autos."

Desdemona nodded and walked out. A few moments later, Miguel strolled into the room.

"Madame Bolívar"—Miguel smiled broadly—"how may I serve you today?"

Simona shook her head. "Miguelito, isn't that crazy?"

"Actually, I don't think it's crazy at all. What better way to justify their love for you than to say you're related to the father of our country? It validates their emotional support."

"I'm not complaining." She chuckled. "Why have we not started training new workers for the car factory? I promised the people we'd bring them jobs and cleaner air. Why are you standing still?"

Miguel released a deep sigh. "It's money, Simona. We don't have the capital. Our profits from lithium production are barely enough to pay the workers we need to get battery manufacturing started."

She stared at him for a long heartbeat. "Why haven't you borrowed the money?"

"The bankers won't lend us any."

"What? Why the hell not? Do they want me to nationalize the banks, too?" Simona slammed her hands on the rosewood desk. "If that's what it takes, I'll do it. Miguel, tell them what I said."

"My dear sister, if you nationalize the banks, the people will worry that you'll take their life savings. No, Simona, please. You can't do that. I'll find the money."

"You can't take money from outsiders. I will not be beholden to the *yanquis*."

"Don't worry. Trust me. I'll find the money in Bolivia. I promise." He forced a thin smile.

"OK, Miguelito. I trust you. But hurry. There isn't much time. I want to show the people I meant what I said. We must start training workers before the election."

Chapter Twenty-Two

"OK, Fred, what's gonna get Liz and me in trouble?" Sam Jackson sat at a Formica-topped beige table in the meat-locker-cold vault. The walls were lined with safes filled with thousands of classified national-security documents.

The room had always reminded Jackson of an Airstream trailer.

Jackson's salt-and-pepper crew-cut hair made his large ears stick out. His plain black, Soviet-style, Costco glasses were too big for his small, round face, making the short-in-stature, long-time senator from Washington look even smaller. He stared at his defense clerk across the table, while holding a two-page summary of the staff recommendations for the defense appropriations bill.

Fred nodded. Then he smiled at Liz Boyer. The junior senator from California was known for her great intelligence and sharp tongue. She returned his smile with a sneer.

Seated beside Fred was Jeff Leary, his Democratic counterpart and ten-year veteran of the committee staff. Behind Jeff sat Marjory Stoneman Radcliffe. Boyer had insisted that Marjory attend this sensitive meeting.

Fred looked at Jeff and began, "Well, sir, there are a couple things Jeff and I wanted to mention—"

"What about Parker rigging elections?" Liz Boyer barked at the two staffers.

Behind them, Marjory stifled a laugh.

Unamused, Fred glanced at Marjory. "Senator Boyer, Jeff and I are going to leave that up to you and the chairman."

"Gee, that's bold of you," Liz Boyer retorted, her voice dripping with sarcasm. "Mr. Chairman, we simply must include a ban on election rigging. What Parker wants to do is unconscionable."

"I hear you, Liz," Jackson responded. "But let's think this through. Jacobs pulled the intel bill because of that provision. Is that what we want to happen to us?"

"Sam Jackson, I'm surprised at you," Boyer shot back. "You, of all people, would let Parker rig elections? You lost three years ago because the Russians interfered. Yet, *you* don't have the nerve to take Parker on? Hell. You let him get away with this, Jackson, and he'll be rigging *his* reelection next." She paused for dramatic effect. "I won't support this bill if we don't stop it." She slammed the summary down on the table.

The veins in Jackson's neck pulsated. He took a deep breath and bit his tongue until the pain numbed his other emotions.

"Look, Liz." His tone was sharper than he wanted but more modulated than he was feeling. He tried to take it down a notch. A catfight wasn't going to get him to markup. "I don't like Parker any more than you do. But I want to get this bill done. We can't approve one that Jacobs will throw in the deep freeze. What the hell good is that?" The last sentence came out somewhere between a bear's growl and a bull moose's bellow.

Liz's head jerked back, and her dark eyes turned fiery. She looked like she was ready to blow.

Oh shit. That's not what he'd meant to do. Sam struggled to figure this out before she exploded. They had to move this bill. But Liz was just so damn insufferable. "Now, Senator . . ." This time his voice was barely a whisper.

Fred's eyes popped wide open. He glanced at Jeff Leary, whose face mirrored his. "Mr. Chairman." Fred spoke loudly, but with little emotion.

Both senators turned toward him. "Senators, Jeff and I think we have a solution to this problem. It's not great, but it's probably the best under the circumstances."

"OK, Fred, that's what we pay you for. Right, Liz?" Jackson tried to smile.

Boyer scoffed.

"If we look at this logically, you, Mr. Chairman, can't include that provision in the bill," Fred began.

"Then I sure as hell won't support it. Weren't you listening to anything I said?" Boyer glared across the table.

"Yes, ma'am. I listened carefully to every word. If I may continue."

"Go ahead, Fred." Sam Jackson eyed his staffer curiously. How *would* Fred get them out of this box?

Fred continued, "Jeff and I think you should draft the bill without the election ban, and Senator Boyer can offer an amendment to include the provision." He seemed to rush to get through the second part of the statement before Boyer could blow again.

"That's not bad, guys." Jackson glanced at Senator Boyer. "But I'll need to talk to Jacobs first."

"What?" Liz snapped.

Jackson slowly moved his hands downward, as if to tamp down the rhetoric. "I gotta tell him, Liz. The only reason I'm chairman is because Jacobs wants me in this post. I screw him, and you'll be dealing with someone a lot less charming than me." He grinned at her.

She puffed. "You think you're charming?"

He continued to grin in her direction.

She shook her head. "You old billy goat. You're about as charming as a head-butt." Then a thin smile appeared on her lips.

Fred looked at Jeff and sighed. "OK, then, we'll draft the bill without the provision. Jeff will have the amendment printed for you to offer at the subcommittee mark, Senator Boyer. And, sir, may I suggest the two of you agree, if the amendment passes, we take the bill to full committee and then to the floor. But if it's OK with you, Jeff and I both think if the amendment were to fall, you should tell Chairman Colbert you're sitting on the bill. He'll know he can't report a bill that looks like we approve of rigging elections."

Jackson nodded. "That all sounds good. But if Jacobs says no, I'll have to cancel markup. Sorry guys—I know you've been working like crazy to get this done, but I can't go along without Jacobs. Are we all in agreement?" He turned to Senator Boyer.

She opened her mouth, took a look at the staff, closed her mouth, and nodded.

"Good. OK, Fred." He smiled broadly. "What else is gonna get us in trouble?"

Chapter Twenty-Three

"So, young man, you've come for a loan. Why should I think you'd ever be able to pay me back?" Fernando Roca puffed on his fat cigar and blew smoke at Miguel Corazon. Roca sat with his portly frame stuffed into a chair in the center of the room, framed by two three-foot-tall blue-and-white ginger jars.

Miguel waved cigar smoke out of his face. "We're borrowing the money to invest in Bolivia's automobile manufacturing facility. Once we're up and running, we'll have no problem paying you back." He stiffened his legs to make sure they didn't shake.

"You say 'we,' young man. Perhaps your sister is really the one I should be talking to?" His dark eyes flashed.

"This doesn't involve my sister. I'm the director of automotive activities. It's my decision." Miguel's throat burned as he stared at the older man lounging in an alabaster-white silk-upholstered Louis Seize chair.

Roca lifted the top of the ginger jar to his left and flicked his cigar ash into it. He looked up. "Yet, you said 'we'?"

Miguel steeled himself. Roca had clearly picked this room to meet in because the dark, expensive wood, white marble floors, and vaulted ceiling demonstrated his wealth, while paintings of military generals on horseback in gold-leaf frames boasted of power.

But Miguel wouldn't give the drug kingpin the satisfaction of seeing him squirm. He made sure his harsh eye contact didn't waver. "I was speaking as a representative of the government of Bolivia. We need the money to train workers for good jobs, so they won't need to resort to work as drug mules or slaves." He tried to mask his instinctive look of disgust.

"You want my help. Yet you think it's wise to insult me?" Roca growled. "Why would I lend you money? What makes you think I can afford to underwrite a new factory? Where would I get that kind of cash? And if I had it, what's in it for me?"

"We'll pay you back at the same interest charged by the banks." Miguel trained an icy stare on Roca.

"I can make more money playing blackjack at the Flamingo Casino." He smirked at a tall gentleman dressed in black, standing behind him to his right.

The tall man laughed as if on cue.

"Even cockfighting is a better risk than your fanciful ideas, young man." Roca sat up a little straighter. "If your sister isn't involved, perhaps you should send your uncle to negotiate. At least he's a man of some stature. You're not much more than a snot-nosed school boy." He waved his cigar in Miguel's face.

"Mr. Roca, you're a businessman. Who knows how much longer the government will tolerate coca production in our country? And the Americans' Drug Enforcement Agency's net grows tighter every day. You need ways to invest your money. And I'm sure you're smart enough to recognize a good opportunity. One that could mean the *Cuerpo de Policía Nacional* are not standing on your doorstep every day between now and the election. I mean, the state police have better things to do. Wouldn't you agree?"

"What would the state police want with me? I'm a legitimate businessman."

"Turn me down, and we can both find out." Miguel grinned.

Roca frowned and shook his head. "OK, young man. How much?"

Chapter Twenty-Four

"Larraine, would you tell the folks—staff meeting in five minutes?" Fred Hendricks poked his head through the door of the defense subcommittee's reception area and smiled at the older woman seated at her desk.

She nodded and picked up her phone. "Jeff!" Fred shouted down the Dirksen hallway. "Gonna call a staff meeting. You and Marjory should come. But before that, can I see you for a second?"

Jeff Leary headed back in Fred's direction. Together, they walked into Fred's office, and Hendricks closed all the doors.

"OK, that meeting was a mess," Fred grumbled. "And why was Marjory there?"

"It was close to a disaster. I thought the chairman was going to pull the plug on markup. But probably only after he punched her once or twice. And"—Jeff sighed—"Marjory's there because Boyer insists."

"Yeah, I was thinking the same thing about Jackson. But what the hell would we have done if they started asking specific questions about NSA testing? Marjory's not cleared for that shit."

"I tried to tell Boyer it was a problem. But you got to see her at her best. She's not a woman you want to disagree with. My plan was to interrupt the conversation if we got near that. I figured Jackson would insist she leave. Boyer couldn't argue if the chairman said so."

"I don't envy you, Jeff. She's tough."

"Which one?" Leary smiled.

"Touché." Fred pointed at Jeff. "At least we got the two bosses on the same page. All right, have a seat while I get the troops in here. Let them know where things stand." He reopened the doors.

Roxy was waiting just outside, and the rest of the staff were gathering behind her.

"Everything go OK, boss?" Roxy stopped as soon as she saw Jeff in the room. "Oh, sorry, I didn't know you were in a meeting. You want us to come back?"

"No, get everybody in. I asked the minority to join us in case I forget something."

Jeff looked up from his cell phone. "Marjory's on her way."

"Good," muttered Fred, "let's get started. We don't need to wait. She was in the room."

Roxy's mouth fell open, and she stared at Mindy, who mouthed, "What the fuck?"

Roxy shrugged her shoulders, her eyebrows raised so high they were hidden by her reddish-brown bangs.

"OK, everyone." Fred glanced around the room. "It was a good meeting. The chairman and Senator Boyer approved all your recommendations."

"Even cigarettes?" Mindy blurted out, smiling widely.

"Well, except cigarettes. Both Jackson and Boyer like your recommendation to accept the House ban on cigarette sales on military bases. But neither one of them wants to challenge Colbert. So we'll stay silent on the issue for now."

"And Boyer agreed to that?" Mindy asked incredulously.

Jeff Leary smiled. "I think it's fair to say she doesn't agree with Chairman Colbert. But sometimes, as they say, discretion is the better part of valor. Jackson convinced her she had a better chance of winning this thing in conference by receding to the House than by throwing it in Colbert's face."

Jeff's shoulders sagged as Marjory walked in.

"Thanks for joining us, Marjory." Fred forced a smile.

"Sure, what'd I miss?" Marjory plopped down on the couch when Judy made room for her.

"Cigarettes," Mindy said.

"Oh God. Let me warn you right now, Hendricks. This better work out in her favor. Or you'll see real steam coming outta her ears next time. That little tête-à-tête they had on elections will look like a lovefest compared to this. And on elections, I think you two—"

"Sorry, Marjory," Fred cut her off. "We're not going to talk about that here. OK?"

Marjory scoffed. Roxy raised her eyebrows and cast a sideward glance at Mindy again.

"OK," Fred said. "Jeff, anything else you think I should mention?"

"It was a good meeting." Jeff surveyed the room.

Marjory rolled her eyes.

"Senator Boyer locked arms with the chairman," Jeff continued, "assuming we take care of a couple things which Jackson said he'd do. Specifically, that includes some report language on studying a second manufacturing site for tank production."

"That's right. Is that yours, Stevie Guy?" Fred looked at the Brooks-Brothers-suited staffer.

"Can't say for sure without seeing it." Stevie Guy sat a little straighter in his chair. "Sounds more like procurement than research. It's probably Bernie's."

"Well, the two of you figure it out and work with Jeff, OK?"

Bernie and Stevie Guy nodded at Fred.

"Just so everyone understands," Jeff said, "this language we're working on for Boyer is actually to keep Senator Jefferson at bay. The authorizers included money to start up a second production line in Michigan. We're not pushing to go that far. We think a feasibility study will forestall an amendment on the floor and a food fight with Armed Services."

"That's right," Fred added. "Jackson talked it over with Chairman Brinkman. We give them cover with the study, and SASC won't jump us on the floor. If Jefferson tries anything, Brinkman will let him know he's on his own."

"So he loses." Bernie shrugged. "Surprised you're screwing a fellow Democrat, Jeff."

"Now, Bernie." Fred cast a stern look in his direction. "We're all in this together."

He shifted his gaze to Marjory, who sat stewing on the couch, her arms and legs crossed, one foot bobbing up and down. *Jesus, this shit gets harder every year. That bitch hates me because I work for the Republicans. Some of my more Republican staff wonder why this former Democratic staffer is running the most prestigious appropriations subcommittee for them. I got a chairman who blows gaskets occasionally. And he's being hounded by a new counterpart who's constantly trying to light his short fuse. It's a good thing Jeff's solid. Too bad Boyer doesn't get that.*

"OK, everybody, markup's on for Tuesday at ten. Larraine, please send out the notices to the members' offices. Let's keep our eyes and ears open for anything new cropping up. You've done a great job. Now we have to show everyone. Thanks. And, ah, Roy."

Roy perked up.

"I need to talk to you briefly in the vault before you head out today."

"Yes, sir." Roy smiled as if glad to be singled out. "I'm ready when you are."

"All right. Check your messages before you go home. Bernie and Stevie Guy, hang around until you figure out who's got Jeff's language on tanks. Anything else?"

Mindy raised her hand. "Sir, you tell the full committee about cigs?"

Fred smiled. "We're gonna wait on that a while, Mindy. I want to keep them worrying. Don't want them to have time to think up some harebrained idea. OK. Thanks again, everybody. C'mon, Roy. Let's get this over with." He stood up slowly, bracing with his arms to minimize the pain in his back.

Chapter Twenty-Five

"Jake, it's Sam."

"Mr. Chairman, you got that bill ready to go? I'm counting on taking it up next week. Getting it done before recess. That still work for you?" Majority Leader Jacobs was standing in his Capitol office, staring out the window down a long expanse of green grass. The Washington Monument loomed in the distance.

"We're on track for markup tomorrow in subcommittee, Jake. Colbert's gonna take it up Thursday in committee. But I need to talk to you about one thing."

"Don't like the tone of your voice, Sam. You're not gonna say something to ruin my day now. Are you?" Jacob's smile started to fade.

"It's the election mess. Parker's plan to screw around some-where."

"Oh, I talked to him. He's not doing it. That's all a ruse by the Democrats to mess with us. You don't need to worry about that."

"That's the thing, Jake," Jackson said slowly. "I can come up and talk to you about this, but my staff has looked into it. Not sure it's quite what our dear president might've implied. Can't say much more on the phone. Should I stop by?"

"Hell, Sam. Just tell me what you can on the phone."

"OK. My minority partner, the Lizbitch, won't let us mark up without offering the same amendment."

"Can you beat her?"

"And let them crow that we're for rigging elections? C'mon, Jake, you know better than that. Hell, you accepted the amendment on the floor. How the hell can we vote it down now?" Jackson's voice rose a little.

"Now, Sam, don't get your undies in a bunch. But if you accept that amendment, how am I supposed to call up your bill? They've got us boxed in."

"Jake, think about it. Are we for rigging elections? Hell no." Jackson paused and took in a deep breath. "If Parker's planning to rig an election, we'd have to condemn it. Wouldn't we? The Russians interfered with our election, Jake. Hell, I might be vice president now were it not for that. I know you supported Parker. But, Jesus Christ. Look what he did to Mitsunaga."

"C'mon, Sam. What choice did I have? Our party is your party, too, ya know. Isn't it, my friend? We nominated the bastard. Mitsunaga's a good guy. You and he are my friends. But, as leader of the Republicans, I had to support our nominee."

"I hear ya, Jake. All that's ancient history now. I'm back. You made me chairman, and I'm grateful. But no way we can vote this down."

"That's your choice, I guess, Mr. Chairman. But I'm not sure that bill will ever see the light of day. We got a judge or two we can vote on next week."

"Wait a second, Jake. We're talking the defense bill. This ain't intel authorization, transportation, or the Coast Guard, or something. When has a Republican majority not done defense approps? Never. You know that. We have to do it. If we gotta take a Democratic amendment that tells us we shouldn't be rigging elections, I'm not sure what's really wrong with that. Fuck Parker if he's telling you to kill the amendment. We need to move this bill." Jackson sounded ready to blow.

"Alright, Sam. I'll check with Parker. I haven't talked to him since he swore he wasn't interfering in elections. His staff bitched a little, but I didn't get a blast from the Oval. If he green-lights it, you're good to go."

"Jake, why the hell do we care what Par—"

"Sam!" Leader Jacobs snarled, losing his Southern gentility. "I just told you, I'll talk to him. Now, go home and have a couple drinks. Calm down. If you don't hear back from me tonight, you're good to go. Christ on a crutch, Jackson. Don't go having a heart attack on me. I need a couple of smart senators like you on our side. God knows we don't have any to waste."

"OK, Leader. Sorry. Reminds me of the old adage: Silence is golden. I'll try practicing it for a change, and I hope you do as well, in this case." Jackson hung up the phone.

Chapter Twenty-Six

Steve Simpson stood in the Oval Office, nodding at the president.

President Parker spoke into the phone. "That's right, Leader. You heard me. Go ahead. Sam Jackson's an asshole. I don't forgive you for giving that traitor the defense subcommittee. But he's your problem. If that motherfucker wants to accept the amendment, I won't oppose it. I already told you the NSA isn't going to fuck around in any African election." He paused and listened.

"OK. I'll be even clearer. The NSA won't be rigging any elections. Period! You got my word on that. Probably won't be good enough for Jackson, but it sure as hell better be good enough for you." He waited for a response.

"Good. Now get me my damn judges. I've got more than"—Parker glanced over at Simpson, who raised three fingers on one hand and five on the other—"thirty-five noms pending. Do your job."

Parker slammed down the phone and squinted toward his chief of staff. "You're sure about this, right?"

"Yes, sir. If they take the same amendment, it bans the NSA from interfering in any election. Under our new plan, that's no longer a problem. I talked to the NSA deputy, General McNeal. To be frank, I can't say he's thrilled with the idea. But he's got two jobs. One is as the head of the Army Intelligence Command. They work with the NSA folks up at Fort Meade, but they also have a unit at Fort Belvoir, near Alexandria, Virginia. That outfit is separate from the NSA, but they have access to some of the same technology. McNeal agreed he'd direct his NSA staff to hand over the tools for rigging elections to the army. Nothing in the amendment says the army can't attack a foreign country's election."

Parker crossed his arms and leaned back in his chair. "You're telling me the army can rig elections? That's hard to believe."

"It's a little complicated. Please, hear me out. Last week, in the presidential finding you signed, we suggested that the Bolivian government may be producing and distributing cocaine. The Drug Enforcement Agency and the intelligence community think there could be a connection between the Bolivian president—well, the Corazon family—and drugs. Under this finding, you tasked the intelligence community *and* the Defense Department to take out drug lords. So, White House legal counsel says you can task the army to take out President Corazon by rigging her election."

"Heh-heh. Good work. Serves the Bolivian bitch right. Teach her to fuck around with American businesses, and ol' President Parker. She doesn't know what she's up against, does she, Steve?"

"Got that right, sir. If this goes as planned—and McNeal's certain it will—come August, she better hope her family made a lot of money running drugs, because she'll be out of a job."

Chapter Twenty-Seven

Roll Call reporter Harris Ward leaned against the back wall in the packed hearing room of the Dirksen Senate Office Building. A number of conversations throughout the room blended together in a raucous din.

Seventy-five folding chairs had been set up for the audience. The first row was reserved for the staff of the defense subcommittee members, two per senator.

A handful of young staffers had arrived early and grabbed all the seats in the second row. The men wore navy-blue sports coats, striped ties, white shirts, and khakis. The women had on summer dresses. Interns.

Older men in suits and women in Washington-chic business attire filled the remaining seats. Lobbyists.

The door was still open, and a long line of people waited to get in.

A brawny, middle-aged, African-American man with graying temples and a thick mustache stood blocking the doorway. He stepped aside as senators arrived with their staff members. Another black gentleman, smaller and a little younger, motioned to Harris and others, many carrying small tape recorders and reporters' notebooks, to squeeze in a little farther to make room for a few more people before the doors were closed. Two more made it in before the larger black man shut the door and stood blocking the entrance.

Harris scanned the room. At the front, several committee staffers sat behind the raised wooden dais in the overstuffed armchairs usually reserved for senators. More staff sat against the wall behind them on wooden chairs with upholstered backs and seats.

Directly in front of the dais were four rows of matching chairs. Harris recognized many of the staff sitting there. Most were defense staffers for the senior members of the committee. A few were full committee professional staff.

The defense subcommittee's professional staff sat near the center of the first few rows. Harris spotted Fred Hendricks there. His Democratic colleague, Jeff Leary, sat across a small aisle on Fred's right. To Fred's left, a few of the other majority subcommittee staff were seated. The chair on Jeff's right was empty. Must be for Boyer's new gal, Margie or something. Next was Pat Sistrunk, the short and rotund Democratic staff director for the committee. A couple others, whom Harris had seen before in the Democrats' committee office, sat to Pat's right.

Harris looked around for Marty. He spotted the bushy black beard, curly hair, round face, and pudgy frame of the majority staff director near the door, behind the dais.

Long, forest-green-cloth-covered tables butted up against one another in the shape of a large, hollow box. It dominated the center of the room. Nineteen copies of the draft bill and expository report had been placed on the table next to senators' wooden name plates and microphones. In one corner inside the box, a heavyset, gray-haired gentleman sat holding a mini-typewriter to record the subcommittee's actions.

Harris counted ten senators around the table. Subcommittee Chairman Jackson sat front and center. Full Committee Chairman Colbert sat on Jackson's left. The two seats to Jackson's immediate right for Boyer and Lackland were empty.

Where was Boyer? Harris jotted down a note. He looked up. Could there be a problem? He didn't recall a defense subcommittee markup where the subcommittee's ranking minority member was absent. Harris checked his watch—10:10 a.m.

Hmmm. And Lackland not here, either? That was really curious.

Jackson looked around and motioned Fred Hendricks forward. Harris couldn't hear the chairman but read Fred's lips: *Where the hell is she?* Fred looked over at Jeff, who shrugged, palms up. Fred raised his eyebrows, shook his head, and gave a little shrug. Jackson scowled.

Youch. Not a good start for the new staff.

Jackson glanced at the clock hanging on the back wall. He picked up his gavel. *Holy crap, is he gonna start without his ranking member?* The chairman grabbed the gavel by its head and tapped the handle gently a few times on the wooden sound block.

The audience mostly stopped speaking or lowered their voices. A few of the members ceased their conversations and turned toward the chairman. Jackson tapped a little harder. More members fell silent. He stared at those who didn't until the room was quiet. *He's actually gonna do it.* Harris started to write himself another note.

"Colleagues, ladies, and gentlemen in the audience," Jackson began. "I'm sorry we're running a little behind schedule, but our ranking minority member has been detained." He glanced over his shoulder at Jeff Leary, who was looking a tad pale.

Jeff nodded.

"We're confident she'll be here, along with Senator Lackland, in just a minute. As many of you know, the subcommittee won't proceed until a quorum, a majority of our subcommittee members, is present. We have that, but I ask you to be patient for a few minutes. We should get underway shortly."

That was damn reserved for Sam Jackson. Harris scratched out a second note. Checked his watch again—10:15. If Jackson spoke again, odds were it'd be a nuclear blast.

The back door behind the dais opened. Liz Boyer, trailing Marjory Radcliffe, plowed her way through the staff and marched toward her seat at the table box. Senator Lackland, cane in hand, ambled behind. The staff quickly cleared a path for the elderly former chairman.

As Lackland approached the table, he waved to his colleagues and shook the hands of both Chairman Colbert and Senator Jackson. He bent down to whisper something in Jackson's ear. The subcommittee chairman nodded, a thin smile on his lips. He patted the older man's forearm and motioned to gray-haired Pat Sistrunk to pull out the former chairman's chair.

Harris smiled and scribbled a quick note: *Old-school senatorial courtesy, not sure Boyer saw the memo on that.*

Bang! The gavel came down sharply—extra sharply, perhaps. "The subcommittee will come to order," Chairman Jackson called. *Bang!* The gavel sounded again, just as loudly. Jackson scanned the room as if trying to stare down each and every person.

He took a deep breath, cleared his throat with a grumble, and looked at the printed text before him. "Today, the subcommittee is meeting to consider the defense appropriations bill for the coming year. Senator Boyer and I are presenting our recommendations jointly, as has long been the tradition of this committee and *especially* this subcommittee." His voice roared throughout the room.

Well, he can't yell at her directly, so I guess he'll bellow at us. Harris suppressed a chuckle.

Jackson continued, "In this bill, we're providing nearly seven hundred and twenty-five billion dollars for activities of the Department of Defense, the intelligence community, and other purposes."

The last clause came out as a mumble. "This amount is nearly five percent more than was provided by this subcommittee last year. It fully funds the brave men and women who serve all of us. All of us," he repeated and looked up from his text. "And let me remind my colleagues, and everyone here, that very few choose to wear the uniform of our country. Less than one percent of Americans put their lives in harm's way to protect the rest of us."

He stopped and surveyed the room. "Fully funding the Defense Department, giving our soldiers, sailors, airmen, and marines the weapons they need, the food and fuel they require to carry out their missions, and the assurance that we will take care of their families, is something we should all support." He looked back down at his text, mumbling, "This bill does all those things."

A few of Jackson's colleagues looked at their watches. He glanced up at the clock. "In the interest of time, I'm going to stop here and recognize the senator from California, my ranking member, Senator Liz Boyer."

Senator Boyer looked up and offered a saccharine smile. "Thank you, Mr. Chairman. Let me begin by telling my Democratic colleagues that you and I have worked closely together on this bill. I can't say I like everything in it. But I credit the chairman and his staff for formulating a bill that, with a change or two, all members should support."

She paused for a second and sat up straighter in her chair. "One thing I cannot support, though, is the lack of language banning the president from rigging elections. Did the chairman forget that the Senate voted just a few short weeks ago to do that? Why in God's name would the senator from Washington not include that language in this bill?" She slowly scanned the Republican side of the table. "What are you all afraid of? Your president? I, for one, am not. What I fear is the White House going out to rig a foreign election. After what happened to us . . . to you, Mr. Chairman. Have you forgotten about the last election already? Did Leader Jacobs brainwash you before restoring your chairmanship?"

Senator Lackland placed his hand on her right forearm. She looked over at him. He leaned toward her and whispered something. She frowned, but nodded.

Jackson sat bristling. "Does the senator have an amendment she wants to offer? If so, I'd hope she'd get on with it. This markup is dragging a little long."

"I certainly do, Mr. Chairman."

Fred Hendricks jumped out of his seat and whispered in the chairman's ear.

Jackson nodded. "If the senator would suspend," he said, "I'm reminded by the clerk that we need to vote to report the bill, subject to amendment, of course. We need a majority of subcommittee members here to make that motion. If the senator would please offer that motion first, we can get on with the committee's business. Then those members with other commitments can leave."

Jeff Leary tried to hand Boyer a piece of paper.

She glared at him. "Mr. Chairman, I'd prefer we take up my amendment first."

Jackson covered his microphone and leaned toward her. "Now listen, Liz." He spoke softly, but his strong baritone carried throughout the room. "You can make the motion first, or I'll get Colbert to do it. It's a courtesy, and a sign of bipartisanship. I'm affording you that opportunity. Is that clear?"

She sneered at him. Senator Lackland touched her arm again, and she sat back. "Yes, sir, Mr. Chairman."

She snatched the piece of paper from Leary. "I move the subcommittee be discharged from further consideration of the bill S. 2119, that the bill, subject to amendment, be reported to the full committee, provided that the bill conforms to its subcommittee allocation for budget authority and outlays, and provided further, that the staff is authorized to make technical and conforming changes to reflect the subcommittee action."

"Is there objection to the motion or further debate?" Jackson growled. "Hearing none, the clerk will call the roll."

Fred Hendricks stood up. He read the names of the Republican members by seniority, except the chairman. The six Republicans present all voted aye. Fred then read the Democratic names, starting with Senator Boyer.

She grimaced and looked at Senator Lackland, who nodded in her direction. "Aye," she sighed.

All the other Democrats voted aye. Fred came to the end and said, "Mr. Chairman?"

Jackson barked, "Aye."

Fred handed the chairman a marked-up sheet of the subcommittee members' names. Jackson stared at it. "The ayes are twelve, the noes are zero. A majority of the members having voted in the affirmative, the bill will be reported to the committee."

Harris Ward jerked his head up. What was Jackson doing? He'd failed to specify that the bill would be reported *subject to amendment*, despite Boyer's motion. This could be interesting.

"Mr. Chairman!" Boyer screamed.

Jackson raised his hand but didn't look in her direction. "The clerk will now read the names of the absent senators." The chairman voted aye by proxy for each missing Republican. Liz Boyer, still stewing, did the same for the four missing Democrats. Fred handed the chairman a second roll-call list.

"The ayes are nineteen, the noes are zero. The bill will be reported subject to any amendment." A smile crept onto his lips as he leaned closer to his microphone. "Does anyone have an amendment?"

The room broke out in spontaneous laughter.

Harris relaxed. So the chairman wasn't trying any funny business after all. Just making a dig at Senator Boyer.

Chairman Jackson lifted his head, grinning.

"Mr. Chairman." Liz Boyer smirked as if to say, *I hope you enjoyed your little joke.*

"The senator from California, my partner and neighbor to the south, is recognized."

"Mr. Chairman, I have an amendment that the staff is distributing." She looked around. Marjory and a younger woman handed a copy of the amendment to each senator. Staff of absent members reached out to snag copies.

"My amendment is exactly the same as the amendment which the Senate unanimously approved on the intelligence bill. I want to explain to all my colleagues why I think this amendment is so—"

"Would the senator yield?" Without waiting for a response, the chairman continued, "We're prepared to accept the amendment."

"That's fine, but I have a statement."

"In the interest of time," Jackson rattled off, "I ask unanimous consent that your full statement appear in the transcript of these proceedings as if read. All in favor of the amendment signify by saying aye."

The Democrats and most Republican members voted aye.

"All those opposed?"

No one spoke.

"In the opinion of the chair, the amendment is adopted. Now."

"Mr. Chairman!" Senator Boyer screeched. "I want a roll-call vote."

"Senator, no one voted no. Is a roll call really necessary? Is there any other business to come before the subcommittee?"

"Mr. Chairman, I know my rights. I demand a roll call on my amendment."

Jackson looked around, frowning. He growled, "Is there a sufficient second?"

All the Democrats, including Lackland, raised their hands.

Jackson shook his head. "Apparently, there is. All in favor of the amendment from the senator from California should vote aye, those opposed no. The clerk will call the roll."

Fred Hendricks stood and began to read the Republican names. Only four Republican senators were still present. Colbert had left after the bill was reported favorably.

When they reached Senator Mannington of Idaho, instead of voting, he spoke, his voice rising with each word. "Mr. Chairman,

I have to tell you I'm outraged by these outbursts from our minority colleague. Outraged. Who are we to tell the president what he can and can't do in the interest of national security? Why are we so eager to tie his hands? Mind you, President Parker has already informed the majority leader he's not planning to interfere in a foreign election. Isn't that good enough?" He looked at his colleagues on the other side of the box. "Do you think this is some kind of game? And what if it becomes in our national-security interests to do so? This is a slippery slope, Mr. Chairman."

"Mr. Chairman!" Boyer shouted.

Jackson banged his gavel so powerfully he cracked the sound block, and a woodchip flew into the middle of the room. He jerked back a little, but hollered, "The senators will cease. This is not a debate. It's a vote. Senator Mannington, how do you vote?"

"*No!*" shouted Mannington. He slammed both hands on the table and stood up, knocking over his chair onto the staffer seated behind him. He stormed out of the room.

Jackson glowered at him and then looked stone-faced at Boyer. "The clerk will continue reading the names."

The other Republican members and all the Democrats voted aye.

Fred called out, "Mr. Chairman?"

Jackson let out a large sigh, tilted his head in Fred's direction, and grumbled, "Aye."

Fred called the names of the absent members. Their proxies were voted. He handed the chairman a roll-call tally sheet. Without looking at it, the chairman said, "The ayes are eighteen, the noes are one. The amendment is adopted."

Roxy handed the chairman a piece of paper while Jeff Leary did the same for Boyer.

The chairman mumbled, "We have a package of twenty-one amendments that have been cleared by both sides. You'll find a copy of it beneath your draft bill."

As several senators scrambled to find the two-page list, Jackson continued, "Without objection, the amendments will be adopted *en bloc*."

The chairman picked up his gavel. "Is there anything else to come before the subcommittee?" He paused for less than half a second. "If not, the bill as amended will be reported to the full committee." He banged the gavel. "The full committee intends to take up this bill on Thursday."

The murmuring in the room gave way to a thundering cacophony. The chairman shouted over the noise, "I thank all members for their cooperation. The subcommittee is adjourned, subject to the call of the chair." He banged the gavel a little more gently and leaned back in his seat.

Senator Boyer pushed back her chair and departed without looking at him.

Fred knelt on one knee beside Jackson. Harris Ward shuffled through the departing crowd, hoping to get a chance to ask Jackson a few questions and hear the queries of his colleagues. He tried to read Fred's lips and caught part of the conversation. Fred was apologizing for the way it went but said at least it was approved. He added something about the full committee.

Chairman Jackson sighed, shook his head, and then nodded in Fred's direction.

Probably Fred was telling him Boyer was Colbert's problem now. He'd have to deal with her at the full committee markup.

Harris got within earshot to hear the chairman responding to a question on tank production. Fred added on to the chairman's answer. The subcommittee had included report language on the subject in response to a request from Senators Jefferson and Boyer.

"Mr. Chairman," Harris shouted. "Seems like you're doing a lot for your minority."

The AP reporter chimed in, "Was that *for* or *to*, Harris?"

Chairman Jackson smiled. "This committee has a long bipartisan tradition. You all know that. But we still have some rollicking debates. You heard Senator Boyer say she supports the bill. That's all I can ask."

"What about cigarettes?" shouted a woman from *Politico* sporting bright-blue glasses.

"What about 'em?" The chairman held his smile. "They're bad for you."

"Did you ban their sale on military bases?"

Jackson looked at Fred, who barely shook his head. Jackson returned his attention to the twenty-something reporter and frowned. "Nope."

"But Mr. Chairman, the House did," said the *Politico* reporter. "You acknowledge they're bad for you."

"Do you really think we should tell our brave men and women in uniform they can't smoke? After all they do for us?"

Harris noticed that Fred had a pained look on his face. Chairman Jackson had spoken out against smoking for twenty years. By the look on Fred's face, Harris guessed Fred had already told the House—or maybe just his minority counterparts—that Jackson would recede to the House ban in conference.

This could get interesting. He jotted down a quick note.

"Mr. Chairman." Harris caught Jackson's eye. "Why did the minority insist on offering the ban on election interference? The

Senate already voted on it. Is there more to this story than you're letting on?"

"If you want to know why Boyer insisted, I suggest you ask her," he responded without skipping a beat. "The president's already said he's not doing it."

"So, are you confirming that the White House isn't planning on interfering?"

"Didn't you hear me?" He shot a frosty look at Harris.

"Chairman Jackson, are you expecting more fireworks in full committee?" Harris didn't recognize the young Asian reporter who asked the question. Perhaps a blogger or something.

"You'd have to ask Chairman Colbert. Subcommittee approved the bill unanimously. All the Democrats voted in favor. I'm sure Chairman Colbert will get the same support in committee." Jackson smiled widely.

Harris chuckled. Yeah, probably so. But if the Democrats had brought this issue up again, who knew what lay ahead? This could rival some of the historical fights in the Senate.

He tapped his notebook. *Senator Jackson's an old pro,* he mused. If he was willing to accept the amendment, it was likely he had the go-ahead from Leader Jacobs. That would mean the White House had signed off too.

He thought back to the cryptic phone call and the follow-up text from his mysterious source. There was more to this story than met the eye. He was sure of it.

And after today's fireworks, Jackson better watch his back if he sees Boyer come in with a cane.

Chapter Twenty-Eight

"What the hell happened, Fred?" Roxy followed Fred into his office across the hall from the Dirksen hearing room.

He slammed his brown accordion folder onto his desk.

Roxy ground to a halt. "Boyer acted like she didn't know we were going to accept her amendment. I thought you said the chairman told her he'd take it."

"As you said, 'acted.' It was all a show, Roxy. Makes me think the Democrats are gaming us. Gaming Jackson. It's bullshit."

"I dunno, Fred. I think it's just Boyer being Boyer. She's been a loose cannon as long as I can remember. Like a couple years ago when she offered that amendment to freeze members' pay and jumped the full committee chairman. I swear you could see a little steam coming out his ears. But he quickly accepted it. So, this time, she asked for a roll call." Roxy paused for a second. "I guess she's learned something since she got here. Force a vote. Try to really screw the other side."

"You're probably right, Roxy. Well, go round up the troops. We got to make sure we get all the changes put in the draft bill. Jeff and our dear friend Marjory are probably waiting in the reception area. We need to get started. The editors have to make the corrections and turn around the bill and report tonight so we can send copies to the full committee members tomorrow morning."

Chapter Twenty-Nine

"Senate Intelligence Committee, Rachel speaking."

"Rachel, it's Amy. Can you talk?" Sergeant Amy Anderson spoke into her phone, her voice just above a whisper. Her stomach jumped as she waited for the intel committee's receptionist to respond.

"Hey there, cuz. Sure, I can talk. All quiet here since the leader pulled our bill. Half the staff is AWOL, and I haven't seen any senators for weeks. The mood's pretty tense, but yeah. What's up with you? Find a place yet?"

"I'm renting a small condo right now, month to month, but it's pricey. I need to find something more permanent. I mean, I'm gonna be in town for at least a couple years. I told you how this stuff works. Wouldn't be surprised if my next gig is in the Pentagon or up at the fort. Meade, that is. I could be stuck in DC for years. Boy, I miss Hawaii. I'm gonna forget everything I learned about surfing, pupu platters, and local boys. But listen. I got something serious to ask you. 'Kay?"

"Sure."

"Remember you told me the Senate passed an amendment banning election, umm, stuff?" She paused for a second and twirled a finger in her fiery curls. "Hey, can you go secure?"

"What? Me? No, Amy, I don't have a secure phone." She snickered. "I'm the receptionist."

"OK, I'll keep this unclass. Remember that amendment?"

"Of course I do. That's what's caused us so much trouble. My two staff director bosses aren't even talking to each other. I thought Sandy was going to kill Gates."

"So, what if I told you we're doing that stuff now?"

"What stuff?"

"You know. Like those other guys were gonna do."

"What? That's impossible. The Senate said no."

"Well, we are. It's giving me the heebie-jeebies." Amy swallowed.

"You should tell someone." Rachel's voice had taken on a concerned tone.

"That's why I called you."

"What can I do?"

"Can you tell your boss?"

"No way. I mean, if I tell Gates, my old boss, he'd blow a gasket and might blame me. That's just the kinda guy he is. If I tell Sandy, I mean, she's as twitchy as a mouse in a snake pit. I think she might accuse me of being a commie, or something. Besides, you're military. From what I understand, we don't really control you. That's the Armed Services Committee. Oh yeah, and the appropriators. They do everything. That's who you should talk to. You need to talk to the appropriators."

Amy's pulse hammered in her ears. "C'mon, Rachel. How would I do that?"

"Beats me. But it's really not ours. And as for me, there's nothing I could do, anyway. I don't want to get in trouble. I need this job. I'm not as smart as you. I didn't join the air force and get my college degree paid for. I've still got tons of student loans to pay off. I have to take care of this on my lonesome. No way I'm asking my dad. He still hasn't forgiven me for leaving Madison." She paused. "Maybe somebody you work with knows one of the appropriations staff. That's the only thing I can think of."

"OK, Rachel. Thanks anyway. Hey. Want to get together this weekend? There's a pool here. We could wear bikinis, make a couple drinks with those little umbrellas, and pretend we're on Hawaii's North Shore dreaming of ten-foot waves and beach boys. I could make poke or a pupu platter."

"Poo-poo? Amy. Ewww. What?"

"Pupu, silly. That's what they call appetizers in Hawaii. Oh, Rachel, I miss Hawaii. DC's got stuff to do, museums and all, but Hawaii was wonderful. I should've quit the air force and stayed there." She lowered her voice again. "And then I wouldn't be worried about this stuff. It's terrible. I don't know what to do."

"Talk to someone you work with," Rachel whispered. "But be careful. OK?"

"Yeah, OK. Love ya, cuz."

"Love you back. I'll call Friday and let you know about Hawaii." Rachel giggled and clicked off.

Chapter Thirty

The defense subcommittee staff was seated in the back of the Senate Chamber, each with an accordion file containing a copy of the newly printed defense bill and its accompanying report, as well as background information they might need as the Senate began consideration of their bill.

"Mr. President, I send an amendment to the desk and ask for its immediate consideration," Jackson mumbled into the microphone.

"Roxy! What's the amendment?" Judy Jameson gripped a large three-ring binder that contained a copy of all the amendments that had been filed on their bill. "How can I track them if I don't know what we're doing?"

"Relax, Judy. It's a placeholder. Fred always gets the chairman to offer a noncontroversial amendment first."

"Why?"

"'Cause under the rules, it's the pending business, and no other amendment can be considered until it's disposed of."

"I'm sorry, Roxy, but—"

Roxy held a finger up to her lips as a member of the Sergeant at Arms staff, a doorkeeper charged with monitoring entry onto the floor and keeping order, scowled at the staff bench.

Judy Jameson lowered her voice to a whisper. "But I still don't understand."

"So, we have a list of, what? A hundred fifty amendments that have been filed, right?" Roxy said.

Judy nodded and pointed at her notebook. "Yes, 157 at last count."

"Right. But that doesn't preclude any senator, like George of Tennessee, for example, coming to the Senate floor and offering an amendment that's not on the list and jumping the chairman. But if there's already an amendment pending, the chairman can object to Senator George or anybody else offering anything. We control the floor."

"Oh, I see."

Roxy's nose twitched. "And we know George is gonna do something stupid. He does on every appropriations bill. The press calls him a maverick because he's always messing with us. We know he's a gadfly."

Judy looked perplexed.

Roxy took a deep breath. "He knows his amendments aren't going to pass. He's lucky to get ten senators to vote with him most of the time, but this way he gets on TV. He gets to decry the process and complain how Washington is so messed up. And how we're spending all this money. And nobody knows what it's for."

Roxy paused, glanced at the doorkeeper, and lowered her voice.

"If he were serious, he'd pick out a few programs or things and try to cut them. But he knows we and the chairman can defend what we're spending and Jackson would probably embarrass him. So, he offers an amendment to cut funds in appropriations bills by some arbitrary amount. That way he doesn't need to know anything about any of the bills and what they're funding."

"But if—"

"I'll explain more later," Roxy whispered, nudging Judy and nodding toward the stony-faced doorkeeper.

Judy nodded. "Thanks. You sure know a lot about this stuff."

"Hey, I learned from Fred. He's the best. OK, now take your list of amendments, show Jeff the ones our staff thinks we should agree to, and see if Jeff can clear them for the minority."

"But he's sitting down where the senators sit." Judy glanced nervously at the doorkeeper again. "Can I go down there?"

"Yeah, you can, but three things. First, don't sit in the big chairs. Those are only for senators. Sit in the empty, small chair right next to Jeff. Second, if Boyer comes in, walk up the aisle back here immediately. And don't walk in front of her. Go up the other aisle." Roxy's voice had a bit more urgency to it. "And under no circumstances go in front of the desks and into the well area. We aren't allowed down there. Not even Fred or Jeff. OK? After you talk to Jeff, come back up the aisle and around the back of the room to our bench. Got that?"

Judy's hands started to shake, and she clutched her binder. She looked a little bobble-headed. "OK." She took a deep breath and stood up.

"You'll be fine, Jameson." Mindy had been watching the scene unfold from her seat on the other side of Roxy. "Just don't vote."

Roxy elbowed her. "Hey, I resemble that remark." They both suppressed giggles as the floor monitor scowled at the staff again. Judy looked a little confused but started toward the Democratic side of the chamber.

Chapter Thirty-One

"Mr. President? It's Hans Edison again. If you're making progress on getting my factory back, I sure as hell don't see it." The billionaire entrepreneur sounded agitated on the speakerphone. "My vice president of South American operations was denied access to my factory in La Paz today!"

President Parker picked up the receiver. He frowned at his chief of staff, who was hovering over him. "Listen, Hans. I told you I'd take care of it," Parker growled into the phone, then paused, listening. "Good. I'm a busy man. I don't have time for this." He slammed down the phone. "That motherfucker."

"Sir, don't worry about him," Steve Simpson said. "In a month, Montoya will be president. Hans will get his shitty factory back, and you'll have New Mexico locked up." He paused for a second. "Mr. President, General McNeal is outside. He's ready to brief you on our plan."

"OK. Show him in."

Simpson cracked open the door and waved the general inside.

McNeal marched into the office. "Mr. President, thank you for seeing me."

"Of course—anything for my favorite general." Parker snickered and put out his hand, welcoming McNeal to a seat on the couch. "Where are we?"

"All good, sir. We've migrated the software to Belvoir, and we're ready for beta."

"General." Steve interjected with a smile. "Try that again. In English, this time."

"Oh, yes, of course. Excuse me, sir. Mr. President, we're all set to go. My analysts are trained and ready. They have what they need to execute SWEET REVENGE against target *B*, and we'll launch that operation as planned at zero eight hundred on the target date."

"That's 8:00 a.m., right?" Simpson looked like he was ready to throttle the general as he translated army speak. "Give us the details."

McNeal sat at attention. "I can't go into more specific details here, but I can promise you, by the end of the day, you'll have your man, and Cor . . . the incumbent will be done."

"That's good enough for me, General. Can't thank you enough." Parker looked at his watch and stood up to end the meeting. "Keep Steve in the loop as you get closer. We can't have any screwups on this. Right, General?"

"Absolutely, sir."

"Good. And you might want to order a shiny new star for that uniform. The three you got are looking a little lonely. Heh-heh."

Parker watched as Simpson ushered McNeal out the door and closed it. "Jesus Christ, Steve. No more fucking meetings. What time am I teeing off?"

"Three, sir. At Burning Tree."

"Burning Tree, great. No bitches slowing down play. Get the car."

Chapter Thirty-Two

"OK, gang, we got the UC. Six more votes, and then final passage tomorrow. Judy, give us an update on amendments." Fred looked over at Judy Jameson. She was squeezed between Roy and Bernie on the couch in Fred's office, cradling her three-ring binder.

"Yes, sir." Judy sat up straight. "There were a total of 184 amendments filed. We cleared sixty-three. Jeff or Marjory cleared fifty of those. By my count, ten senators offered amendments that were agreed to by voice vote. Roxy and Bernie did three packages that made up the rest of the amendments cleared by both sides. They were agreed to . . ." She tilted her head. "Is it *en bloc?*"

"That's right." Fred nodded at her, smiling.

"Then we had six . . . seven . . . eight"—she counted from her two-page list in the front of her notebook—"nine roll-call votes. Three passed, and the others were defeated." She looked up. "But what I don't understand, Mr. Hendricks—"

"Fred."

"Yes, sir." She cleared her throat. "Fred." She gave a shy smile. "What I don't understand is what happens to all the rest of these. We still have more than a hundred amendments filed. But you said the unanimous consent agreement—the, uh, UC—only allows votes on six."

"Well, in short, they die." Fred grinned, and the staff began to laugh, applaud, and high-five each other.

Judy shook her head, her dark curls bouncing.

Fred quieted the staff. "OK. Fair question, Judy. Under the UC, we'll have votes, and I quote, 'on or in relation to' six amendments.' One is Senator George's. What's that again. Roxy?"

"It's a one-percent cut to the entire bill. So, roughly $7.25 billion. It's a general reduction. He's not saying what should be cut, but that the total in the bill is reduced. Leaves the cuts up to us, I guess."

"What an asshole," Mindy muttered.

"Alright, Mindy." Fred looked at her in mock anger. "Senator Pierce is adding another hundred million for health research, right?"

"Yes, sir." Leonard nodded and shook his head in disgust.

"We've got Jackson's placeholder in case we need to do something. That most likely will go away. Boyer's got a placeholder, too. Hopefully that also goes away."

"You sure, boss?" Roxy had a thin smile.

"Good point, Roxy. What's Jeff saying?"

"Nothing." Roxy shook her head. "Said Boyer insisted on having a placeholder if the chairman did. But knowing Boyer . . ."

"Yeah, right. Who the hell knows what she'll do. What else?"

"Andrews has the amendment to pull the troops out of Afghanistan," Roxy added.

"Like that'll ever pass," Bernie scoffed.

"And Lee?" Fred scanned the room.

"He wants a milcon project," Mindy piped up and rolled her eyes. "Never gonna happen."

"Yeah, my old colleagues on the military construction sub-committee don't see the humor in the defense subcommittee sticking our nose in their business." Roxy smiled.

"Well, he's the whip. He's getting a vote," Fred declared. "How the hell does Jackson tell him he can't offer his amendment?"

Judy looked at Roxy and mouthed, *Whip?*

"Assistant majority leader, Jameson. Number-two Republican," said Roxy.

Fred looked around. "OK, great work, everybody. We're in the home stretch. Judy, just to clarify about all those missing amendments. The way the Senate works, members file a lot of amendments. Most of the time, senators have no intention of coming to the Senate floor and offering them. But filing lets their constituents know they're working. And, who knows, we might just accept them." He paused for a breath. "Bottom line, we know members are serious when they come to the floor and actually offer their amendments. You said we cleared fifty-plus amendments. I wasn't keeping exact track, but I'd bet most of those were never debated."

Judy nodded. "I think only thirty-two amendments were actually offered. We acted on, I think, sixty-three total."

"Exactly," Fred said. "So, amendments are filed, but no one offers them. Most die. Now, everyone, tomorrow's Thursday. Recess starts as soon as we're done. You all need to make some time for your loved ones. And on that note, Sunday afternoon you're welcome to come by the cabin with the family. I'll cook up some burgers and dogs. And I'll get plenty of beer and some sodas for the kiddies." He glanced at Roy and winked. "And anyone else. Now, listen. This ain't no command performance. You got something better to do, do it.

"But, for any of you who don't know, my cabin's got a dock on the Patuxent River. You can swim, go tubing, relax. Sailboat's not gonna be available. It's down for some maintenance. But it's a great place to unwind. God knows we all need to do that. I'll fire up the barbecue at four and put some food out around five. Then we all start preconference with the House staff on Monday. So, go home now. Kiss your wives, significant others, or pets. Tell them it's almost over. But be on the floor tomorrow morning at nine-thirty sharp."

Fred waved them out of his office.

Chapter Thirty-Three

Roy let go of the doorknob when the phone on his desk rang. *Crap. Who could that be?* He looked at his watch; it was already 9:20 a.m. He sighed and answered, "Appropriations, Roy speaking."

"Hello, is this Mr. Peterson?" Roy could barely hear the soft voice. Sounded like a thirteen-year-old girl braving her first call to the pimply fourteen-year-old boy she had a crush on.

"Yes, this is Roy Peterson. Who's calling please?"

"Are you the army guard captain, Roy Peterson?"

"Yes, ma'am. Who are you, and what's this about?" Roy's voice hardened a little.

"Yes, sir. This is Sergeant Amy Anderson, sir. I'm currently detailed to Fort Belvoir for INSCOM. I have some information that I think someone in Congress ought to know."

"Listen, Sergeant." His voice filled with sarcasm. "If you have *information*, why don't you talk to your CO about it? We're kinda busy here, trying to get a bill done. I don't have time for some silly schoolgirl game. Did Mindy put you up to this? Is she trying to make me late? Get me into trouble?"

"Who, sir? Sir, I got your name from Master Sergeant Baker. He works for the NSA. He told me you worked for the Senate Appropriations Committee, sir. He said you do your reserve duty at NSA sometimes, and you handle the NSA's budget. He said he's met you a couple times." Her words spilled out, one on top of the other.

Sergeant Baker? Could this be legitimate, or are they screwing with me? Roy glanced down at his watch. *Shit. Now I'm late. Fred's gonna kill me.*

"Listen, Sergeant, or whoever you are. I've got to run. Call me back next week, if you really have something to tell me." He hung up the phone, grabbed his accordion folder, and ran out the door.

Fred Hendricks stood facing the staff bench in the Senate Chamber. "Where the hell is Roy?" He turned toward Roxy.

She shrugged and glanced at the door, which was just opening. "He's walking in right now."

"OK, good. Who's up first, Jameson?"

Judy looked at her list and glanced at Roxy with terror in her eyes.

"Fred, the UC doesn't say who goes first," Roxy responded for Judy. "But Andrews just walked out of the cloakroom. I'm thinking he probably wants to be first up."

Fred nodded. "This one's yours, Mindy, let's go. We'll sit down there and listen to the rant. Jackson's supposed to be on his way."

Roy walked up.

"Where the hell've you been?" Fred demanded. "I said nine thirty."

"Sorry, sir. I got a weird phone call as I was headed out the door."

"Sit your ass down on the bench."

Roxy guffawed.

Roy glared at her.

"C'mon, Abrams." Fred and Mindy headed down the aisle toward the Senate well and sat in the two staff seats wedged between the senators' chairs in the first row. "Poke me if Andrews says something important. I'm gonna see if I can sleep with my eyes open."

Mindy chuckled. "Yes, sir."

"And nudge me if the chairman arrives." He winked at her.

Near the back of the chamber, Andrews began to speak, and Fred groaned. Mindy suppressed a giggle.

 Fred yawned, listening to Andrews drone on.

Finally, Jackson approached. "How long's he been speaking?"

"Eighteen of his thirty minutes, sir," Fred replied.

"I'll only need two. I'll say the president will withdraw the troops when the Joint Chiefs say it's time and that we just voted on this in the defense authorization bill three weeks ago. Anything else?"

"That'll probably do the trick, sir. We've got some talking points that Mindy drew up." Fred nodded toward her, and she smiled. "Not sure you need all this, but there's some good arguments here." He handed the chairman a four-page, typewritten list of bullet points.

Jackson plopped down next to Fred and began to read. He nodded as he flipped the first page. Yawned after the second. Then he perked up, focusing on Andrews, who had started talking about the illegality of keeping troops overseas unless there's a declared war.

Jackson rolled his eyes and leaned over to whisper to Fred, "Ya know, he's right about this, but it doesn't matter. The White House has the War on Terror authorization from right after 9/11. They use it as blanket authority to wage war wherever and on whomever they want. Not just this president, but all of them since 2001."

"Yes, sir," said Fred. "But it seems to me this goes back to Korea. Congress hasn't declared war since 1941, but we've been in a near-constant state of combat ever since. First Korea, then Vietnam, hell, the Falklands, Lebanon, the War on Drugs, Al-Qaeda, Iraq, Afghanistan, ISIS, Syria, and on and on and on."

"Careful. Your liberal roots are showing. You're with me now."

Fred sat up a little straighter and opened his mouth.

But Jackson held up his hand and smiled. "You're fine. As soon as the peacenik shuts up, I'll speak. If he hasn't used up all his time, I'll see that the clock continues to run against both of us. Should take ten minutes, then I'll move to table the bastard." He grinned widely, and Fred chuckled.

Then Jackson looked over at Mindy and waved the sheaf of paper. "Talking points are really good."

Mindy beamed.

"But I don't think we need to get into all this. I'm sure you understand." He handed the notes back to Fred.

Mindy's shoulders slumped.

Jackson looked across the room, where Andrews was wrapping up. "Here we go." He rose from his seat. "Mr. President?"

The presiding officer, the junior senator from Florida, nodded at Chairman Jackson.

"Mr. President, the senator from Massachusetts is a fine speaker. A gifted orator. Why, I could sit here and listen to him all day." He nodded in Andrews' direction. "So, I say to my friend—and he is my friend, Mr. President—I might not be as eloquent as you, Senator."

"The senator will speak through the chair." The presiding officer raised his eyebrows and looked pointedly at Jackson.

"Excuse me, Mr. President. Of course, I won't address the good senator directly. The rules don't allow that. He is most eloquent, but that doesn't mean he's making sense."

The presiding officer raised his gavel.

Jackson smiled at the first-term senator presiding over the Senate and raised both his hands. "Mr. President, the Senate voted on this amendment a few weeks ago. I'm not sure why we have to do it again. Now, that is the senator's right, but if the senator has new information that could sway members, I didn't hear it in the beautiful speech he just offered."

Jackson took two steps into the center aisle, pulling his microphone cord with him. He retraced his steps while continuing to speak. "Moreover, Mr. President, while the senator's remarks were mighty fine, he failed to point out that the Chairman of the Joint Chiefs and the Secretary of Defense have testified to Congress repeatedly that it would be 'dangerous and ill-advised' to pull our troops out at this juncture. 'Dangerous and ill-advised.' Those are the Secretary's words, not mine. But I agree with them.

"Mr. President, senators have heard this debate before. We're here today to pass the defense appropriations bill. The time to debate this policy was on the defense authorization bill." He paused for a moment. "And we did! The Senate already told my friend, *no!*" Jackson's voice boomed throughout the chamber. He looked around as Andrews shuffled off the Senate floor, shaking his head. "I suggest the absence of a quorum and ask the chair how much time is remaining on the amendment?"

The presiding officer leaned toward the assistant parliamentarian, who pressed a white button to turn off his microphone.

She whispered instructions and released the button as he said, "The time in favor of the amendment is two minutes. The time opposed is twenty-six minutes. Under the unanimous consent agreement, time will be charged equally against both sides during the quorum call. The clerk will call the roll."

Jackson sat down. "So, in four minutes, all his time will be gone. I'll yield back my time and move to table it. Now, we wait."

Chapter Thirty-Four

At the back of the Senate Chamber, Fred leaned over the short railing and huddled with his staff. Some were seated on the bench, and a few stood next to it.

"All right, everyone," Fred said. "All we've got left is the two placeholders. Once Jackson comes back, he can vitiate the quorum call and withdraw his amendment."

"What about Boyer?" Roxy's voice was a little too loud and caught the attention of a newly hired so-called doorkeeper.

The young man strutted over to Fred's group. His dark hair was cut so short that, from a distance, he looked bald. Fred stared at him, taking in the ill-fitting suit—the jacket sleeves barely reached his skinny wrists—short-sleeved, white dress shirt, and clip-on tie. Scuffed shoes completed the outfit. He looked more like a nerdy intern than a doorkeeper.

"This is your last warning," the doorkeeper said. "I want everyone sitting down, and if you need to talk, you gotta leave the floor. This is the United States Senate, not happy hour." He sneered and pointed at the bench.

Fred rolled his eyes and motioned for everyone to sit down. "I'll check with Jeff. I can't imagine it's more than Boyer said. Just a placeholder because the chairman had one. Looks like we're done."

He glanced at his watch.

"Rox?" Mindy spoke in a stage whisper loud enough for all her colleagues on the bench to hear. "Who's the new floor Nazi?" The staff guffawed loudly. The doorkeeper pointed a warning finger at them from his post next to the door.

"Shh-shh," Roxy admonished while suppressing a laugh.

"Whoever he is, he's stylin'," Mindy whispered again.

Roxy elbowed her, trying to hide a smile.

Fred shook his head and walked down the aisle, back to the staff seat in the first row.

The majority leader entered the chamber through the center doors at the back of the room and strolled down the aisle. At his side strode Senator Margaret Johnson from Maine. The staff had started calling her *sea turtle*. Short in stature, a little slow moving, with an oval-shaped head and pointy nose, she fit the profile well.

But the real reason for the moniker was her front-runner position on *Roll Call*'s top-ten endangered senators list. The popular Democratic governor of Maine, who was being compared to Jack Kennedy, had announced his candidacy for her Senate seat. Early polling showed he had a sixty-five percent approval rating to her thirty-five. Seventy percent of the poll respondents favored him in a head-to-head election. Like the sea turtle, Senator Johnson didn't look long for this world.

"Fred?" The leader smiled and addressed Fred at the front of the room. "Senator Johnson has a question."

Fred stood up, a bit surprised. He hadn't realized the majority leader even knew his name. "Yes, sir! Ma'am?"

Roxy rushed toward them, taking each of the wide chamber steps in a single stride.

"Fred," Senator Johnson started. "Fred, I was told that you were including a provision that kept the air force KC-135 aerial refueling tanker aircraft at Bangor. But my staff says they can't find the provision in the bill. I'm sure you know how important this National Guard unit is to national security. I'm a member of the Armed Services Committee. We included this provision in our bill. Didn't you do the same?"

Fred hid a smile. *Should I remind the senator and inform the majority leader that the air force chief of staff testified that, due to budget cuts, he and the Secretary were consolidating squadrons onto fewer bases? And that, in light of the soon-to-be-retiring older KC-135's stationed at Bangor, shutting them down made good sense? No, probably not.* "I'm sorry, ma'am, that provision didn't make it into the bill."

"It didn't!" the senator snapped and turned toward the leader. "Jake. You promised me you'd take care of this. I need this for my campaign. Why isn't the provision in the bill?"

Jacobs looked sternly at the defense clerk. "Fred, I can't believe you didn't include the senator's provision. How did this happen?"

Oh shit. News to me. I mean, Christ, the Armed Services Committee included it in the authorization bill. There isn't any need to put it in the appropriations bill, too. Unless you thought the DoD authorization bill wasn't going to get enacted. I can't tell 'em that. "I'm sorry, the provision isn't in the bill."

The leader frowned at Fred, then turned toward Senator Johnson. "I'm sorry, Margaret. There's nothing we can do now. The bill's done except final passage. Tell you what. I'll talk to Chairman Jackson. Maybe something can be done about it in conference."

"This is terrible, Jake. Fred, how could you leave this out? It's vital to national security." She glared at both of them. "You better be able to fix this in conference, Jake. I need this."

"Oh, absolutely, Margaret. Like I said, I'll talk to Sam. I'm sure he and Fred can fix it. Isn't that right, Fred?"

Fred blanched and opened his mouth, but no words came out.

"Now, don't worry, Margaret. Fred knows what to do. Don't cha, Fred?"

Senator Johnson threw her hands in the air and shuffled off.

Jacobs gave Fred a knowing smile. "Sorry about that. I'm sure you understand. Just do the best you can." He clapped Fred on the shoulder before turning back up the aisle.

As Fred sat down, Roxy slid into the seat next to him.

"What the hell was that?" she asked.

"Oh, Roxy, you know—shoot the staff."

She wrinkled her nose and shook her head. "Jeez Louise, I thought the turtle might peck at you with her beak."

Fred raised his eyebrows. "That's enough. Back to the bench. Jackson just walked in. Let's wrap this up."

"Where are we, Fred?" Jackson smiled as he reached the first row of Senate seats.

"Mr. Chairman, all we've got left are the two placeholders for you and Senator Boyer."

"OK. Let's get them withdrawn and go home."

"Yes, sir. But we still don't know what Boyer's gonna do."

"Oh, hell. She can't be planning to offer an amendment, can she?"

"Don't know, sir. I probably shouldn't say this, but after her subcommittee shenanigans, who the heck knows?"

"Guess so. What's her staff saying?"

"Jeff's clueless, sir. And we haven't seen Marjory, Boyer's gal. So I hate to say it, but anything is possible."

Mary Beth Anderson, Jacobs's head staffer on the Senate floor, poked her head out of the cloakroom door and approached Jackson. "Supposedly, Boyer's on her way. But they didn't say whether she was planning to withdraw her placeholder."

"Oh, Christ. Thanks, Mary Beth. What's Jake saying about getting outta here?"

"You're the last vote, sir," she replied. "Once the two place-holders are withdrawn, we'll go to third reading, final passage, and then go home."

Liz Boyer blasted through the side door next to the Democratic staff bench, Marjory in tow. As she reached the minority floor manager's seat across the aisle from Jackson, he stepped over to her.

"Liz, what say we withdraw our amendments and go home?"

"You can withdraw yours, but I'm not," she said in a sharp tone, then raised her hand. "Mr. President."

The presiding officer acknowledged her.

She vitiated the quorum call and continued, "I send an amendment to the desk and ask that further reading be dispensed with."

The junior senator from South Carolina, as presiding officer, leaned in to receive instructions from the assistant parliamentarian. Then he nodded and said, "The clerk will report the amendment."

Senator Boyer explained her amendment was the same as language in the House-passed defense bill banning the sale of cigarettes on military bases. She spoke for five minutes on the dangers of cigarettes, and then concluded with a harangue against the Republicans—particularly Sam Jackson—for not including the House language.

When she finished, Jackson stood, threw up his hands, and noted the absence of a quorum. By that time, the committee staff director, Marty Barons, had arrived on the floor. He summoned Fred Hendricks to the staff bench.

"What the hell are you doing, Hendricks?" Marty's high-pitched voice squealed. The doorkeeper motioned for him to lower his voice.

"Nothing I can do, Marty. Can't stop a senator from offering an amendment, can I? Remember, when the elephants stampede, the pygmies get crushed."

"Let me tell you something, Hendricks. You better hope this thing—"

Pat Sistrunk, the Democratic staff director, blew through the large glass-and-wood doors of the chamber and stomped down the aisle to where Senator Boyer was sitting. He directed Jeff and Marjory to leave and sat down next to the senator. His eyes narrowed, and the veins in his neck pulsed visibly.

Boyer glared at him, and they proceeded to have a heated yet stifled conversation until Boyer stood up, wagged her finger at him, and stormed out.

"What could that be about?" Marty whispered.

Fred grinned. "I think the Lizbitch forgot her ranking member's from Virginia. Tobacco isn't king in the commonwealth like it once was, but it's still got deep roots in the state. Shit, Philip Morris's headquarters is in Richmond. Lackland isn't immune to that. My guess? Pat spelled out the facts of life for our West Coast friend."

Marty's mouth fell open.

"Funny how these things sometimes work themselves out. You better scurry back and tell the chairman how you solved this one, buddy."

As if on cue, the committee's senior Democrat, Senator Lackland, slowly pushed open the heavy doors. With a hickory-wood cane in his right hand, he stepped onto the floor.

Pat Sistrunk sprang to his feet and rushed over to him. They spoke for a moment. The senator nodded and shuffled to the well next to the dais. He walked up to Sam Jackson, who stood up.

Lackland smiled and offered Jackson his left hand for a shake. Then he spoke softly.

Jackson nodded and patted the hunched, older gentleman on the back. Pat Sistrunk directed Jeff Leary to show Boyer's amendment to Lackland. The old man stared at it and shook his head. He turned toward the dais, mumbled something, and was recognized by the presiding officer. Then Lackland spoke quietly without a microphone. Fred couldn't make out what he was saying, and he knew hardly anyone else could, either: not the staff in the back of the room, the folks in the gallery, or those watching on TV.

Meanwhile, Jackson watched from his seat. He crossed his legs and held his hands in a loose prayer grasp. A thin smile appeared on his face.

The presiding officer nodded. "Without objection, the pending amendment is withdrawn. The question is now on the amendment from the senator from Washington, Mr. Jackson."

Jackson stood, reached out to shake Lackland's hand again, and said, "I withdraw my amendment."

"The amendment is withdrawn." The senator from South Carolina looked down at the parliamentarian, listened, and nodded. He drawled, "The bill will be read for a third time."

"I ask for the yeas and nays on final passage," Jackson said.

"Is there a sufficient second?" asked the presiding officer.

Lackland raised his hand.

The presiding officer nodded. "The clerk will call the roll."

"Ho-ly shit," whispered Mindy on the staff bench. "Never seen that before. You, Roxy?"

Roxy shook her head. "But methinks Jackson ain't gonna be receding to the House on cigarettes now. Like Fred always says, Mindy, some members are hard to help."

Chapter Thirty-Five

"Is this Carlos Montoya?" The woman's voice on the phone was firm but friendly.

"Yes, it is." Carlos leaned over his huge oak desk in his spacious office at *Banco Nacional* and held his cell phone up to his ear. Sunlight streamed through the large windows, adding to the luster of the room decorated in earth tones. *How did she get my private number?*

"Please hold for the president."

The president? Which president? She didn't sound like one of Corazon's people. Montoya switched hands with the phone and flipped the page of a thick financial document he was reviewing.

"Mr. President? Heh-heh."

"I'm sorry. This is Carlos Montoya, not the president."

"Well, you'll be president soon, Mr. Montoya. May I call you Carlos?"

"I'm sorry, but who is this?" he asked sharply.

"What? You're asking *me* who *I* am?" the voice growled. "It's Jim Parker, Carlos. Parker. As in *President* Parker."

"Oh my goodness!" Carlos sat straight up. "Mr. President. What an honor. Thank you for calling." He pushed back from his chair and stood without thinking. "What can I do for you?"

"For one, you can give me back my factory, Carlos." There seemed to be a smile in the American president's voice.

"Your factory? I'm sorry, Mr. President. I don't understand."

"The car factory, Carlos. The one you guys nationalized."

"Oh. But I thought that belonged to Hans Edison. And I—"

"It's American, God damn it. That means it's mine." Parker's tone hardened.

"Oh, I see. But, Mr. President, why are you calling me? Simona Corazon is President of Bolivia. I'm just a candidate trying to replace her. I can't give you back your factory."

"As I said, you'll be president soon enough. And I expect you to sign an order first thing returning my factory."

"Sir, if I were president, I can assure you I'd do just that. Simona Corazon's actions, nationalizing lithium and the auto factory, are terrible for business, and for banks. Foreign investment in Bolivia has dropped to zero since that stupid stunt. It's killing us. But there's nothing I can do."

"I'm counting on you as a man of your word to fix this when you win."

Carlos began pacing the room. "Mr. President, excuse me, but I don't know where you're getting your information. I'm running to protest Corazon's ill-advised nationalization plans. But, to be frank, I cannot win. The people support Simona."

"That's not what I hear."

"Mr. President, it's true. The *inteligentsia* and industry objected when she nationalized the plants, and I surged in the polls. But the latest polls show that I'm still fifteen or twenty points behind."

"I wouldn't pay too much attention to the polls. Those amateurs said I wouldn't win either, and look what happened. Mr. President, you're going to win. Trust me."

"I wish you were right. But, with all due respect, your information is wrong. I—"

"God damn it, Carlos. I just told you, you're going to win. Don't pay attention to the polls. They're always wrong. My intelligence agen—" He cut himself off. "My experts are saying the polls are wrong. We're watching Bolivia very, very closely, Montoya, and you're gonna win. You're gonna be president. And when you are, I want my fucking factory back."

Carlos pulled the phone away from his ear, wincing at the loud voice on the other end. *He's a madman. What can his experts be thinking? She's going to win. How can I argue with crazy?* "OK, Mr. President, that's wonderful news. I can't thank you enough. And once again, I assure you, I'll return your factory. Thank you so much for calling." Montoya returned to his desk and pressed a button underneath it, signaling an aide. He nodded as the president thanked him again and hung up.

Jonas Mendoza, a twenty-five-year-old, short, fat, and already balding, Harvard-educated wunderkind, stood in the doorway. "Sir, you wanted me?"

"Damnedest thing, Jonas. I just spoke with the American president. He said I'm going to win the election. Does that make any sense?"

Jonas shook his head rapidly. "No sir, no sir, no sir. It's impossible. You can't get more than twenty-five percent of the vote. Corazon won't get less than thirty. She'll probably top forty. Game, set, and match."

"President Parker was adamant. I have to say, he sounded strange, unstable."

"Yes, sir, many in the American press contend the president's unstable. The White House calls it fake news. But it's been known for a long time that he has a sharp temper. Perhaps he's just angry."

Montoya chuckled. "He *was* angry; that's for sure. But he was also sure I'd win."

Jonas shook his head again. "Sorry, sir. Won't happen."

Montoya put up his hand. "I hear what you're saying, but the Americans have many resources. He mentioned his intelligence agency experts told him this."

"Sir, they're wrong. The only way you could win is . . ." Jonas paused. "If they rigged the election."

"What? Impossible. Bolivia's a free country with a strong democracy. There's no way they could rig our elections." He spoke in a quizzical tone. "Could they?"

"It would be difficult." Jonas clasped his hands in front of him. "We still use paper ballots. The technology the Russians use corrupts computerized data. But, if the Russians can do it, you can be sure the CIA can. Sir, if you like, we can increase our election monitors to keep an eye on it. Frankly, we probably should. You need to know what's going on."

Montoya nodded and dismissed his aide. He stared absently as the young man departed. *They wouldn't do that. I know we've had our problems with the Americans in the past, but we're a sovereign nation. America has always respected democracy. No. Jonas must be wrong.*

Chapter Thirty-Six

"Cannonball!" Lester Peterson screamed and jumped off the rickety dock. His curly black hair flattened out, and his water wings slipped from his biceps to his wrists as he hit the water. Roy grabbed the four-year-old and readjusted the safety floats. Lester dog-paddled back to the ladder and climbed up, ready to go again. His mom, Julie, sat on a blue towel on the dock, wearing a modest black one-piece and sporting hot-pink nail polish on her fingers and toes. Her feet made gentle ripples in the water below.

"Chow's ready," Fred hollered, standing at the screen door off the cabin's kitchen in his plaid shirt and tan shorts. He placed a plate of burgers and hot dogs next to a disposable container of potato salad on the picnic table's red-white-and-blue plastic tablecloth.

Stacks of paper plates and napkins sat on the table, along with jugs of ketchup and mustard, some plastic spoons and forks, a crumpled Safeway bag, and two open bags of potato chips. A large ice chest rested on one of the benches.

Mindy pulled out a Budweiser and wiped the water off on her oversized Bethany Beach T-shirt. She dried her hands on her khaki shorts and flinched as a wayward ice cube from her beer landed on her bare toes.

"No more cannonballs, Lester. Time for a hot dog." Roy climbed out of the water and grabbed a T-shirt. Julie picked up her towel and wrapped it around her waist.

"But I wanna do more cannonballs, Dad." Lester stood on the dock and crossed his arms.

"After we eat, buddy. The river will still be here. Eat a hot dog, and we'll let you swim some more. Deal?"

Lester frowned. Didn't budge.

"I think Mr. Hendricks has ice cream bars. You eat a hot dog, and Mom will let you have ice cream." He offered his hand to shake on the deal.

"Chocolate?"

"Oh, I'm sure. What other kind of ice cream would Mr. Hendricks have?" Roy smiled.

"OK, deal." Father and son shook on the agreement. Lester took off, running toward the picnic table.

Roxy sat in the shade on one of four redwood Adirondack chairs positioned halfway between the dock and the cabin. She balanced a plate with potato salad and a burger on her lap, holding a beer in her other hand.

"Oh, that looks good." Julie smiled at Roxy as they passed by. "I could use a beer."

"They're in the ice chest on the picnic bench. Help yourself. And there's Coke in there, too, Roy." Roxy snickered.

Julie glanced at Roy, who was frowning. "C'mon, Roy. I'm famished." She grabbed his hand and dragged him toward the food.

"See what I mean?" Roy barked. "She's a bitch."

"Oh, Roy. She's just teasing. I'm sure it seems a little odd to them that you don't drink. But that's your choice. Now, relax. We're here to have fun. Look at Lester. He loves it here."

"Yeah." He paused for a second. "I should have a beer just to show her."

"No, you shouldn't. You won't be having any beer," Julie snapped and squeezed his hand a little.

"I know. I know." He sighed. "But she ticks me off."

"The burgers smell great, Fred," Julie called out to their host, waving.

"Thanks. C'mon and get some food before it gets cold."

Mindy perched on the wide arm of Roxy's chair, holding a beer in one hand and a hot dog in the other. "Nice day, huh?"

"It's beautiful. Not too humid. Somebody must've imported the weather from New England. Doesn't feel like July in Maryland," Roxy replied.

"So, Rox? Did Fred ever explain what happened to Boyer?" Mindy looked around, making sure Boyer's staffer, Marjory, wasn't at the barbecue. She smirked when her eyes landed on Jeff and his frumpy wife, Sarah, standing with Fred near the picnic table. Jeff wore a green polo shirt, khaki slacks, and loafers. Sarah was sipping wine and wearing a pale blue-and-white-flowered muumuu, big straw hat, and white sandals. Her mousy-brown hair covered half of her freckled face, and large sunglasses hid most of the rest. Jeff held a beer in one hand, and Sarah's hand in the other.

"Nuh-uh. Hey, Fred!" Roxy waved at the boss to join them.

Fred, Jeff, and Sarah headed their direction.

"Crap, Roxy. Jeff's coming too. How can we ask about Boyer?" Mindy whispered.

"Jeff's cool, Mindy. But we'll bore Sarah to tears if we rehash all that happened on the floor."

"Yeah, Roxy," Fred said. "What's up? You remember Sarah, right?"

"Sure, hi." Roxy smiled at Sarah and introduced Mindy. "She does O and M."

"So, Fred." Roxy tilted her head to the side, shielding her eyes from the filtered sunlight peeking through the trees. "What really happened to Boyer?"

Jeff laughed and looked at Fred. "Yeah, Fred. Tell us."

Fred smiled. "I think you should be asking Jeff that question."

"OK, so let's keep this in the family. Right?" Jeff leaned in a little.

Mindy and Roxy nodded.

"So, we're on the floor and Boyer is nowhere to be found." Jeff looked around, as if checking who was within earshot. "I found Marjory and started to ream her out about Boyer's absence as we were trying to finish the bill. She snapped at me, saying Boyer was thinking about offering the cigarette amendment. I reminded her about Jackson's willingness to agree to it in conference. She said Boyer wanted to get it on the record. Said she didn't trust Jackson, or any 'effing Republican.' I told her she'd be wise to take her chances with Jackson. She said, and I quote, 'Liz doesn't take chances.'" Jeff laughed.

The others joined in.

"But what about Lackland?" Mindy asked, running her finger around the rim of her beer.

"Well, the way I see it, I work for Lackland, since Boyer didn't want me as her clerk. So, I made sure Pat Sistrunk knew what Boyer was thinking. Pat's in his office watching the Senate floor on TV. As soon as she offered the amendment, he let Lackland know, and you saw the rest. Pat came to the chamber and told Senator Boyer she could withdraw the amendment or Lackland would get consent to do it for her. If she resisted, Pat told her"— he leaned a little closer and lowered his voice—"Lackland would call a meeting of the committee Democrats immediately and strip her of her acting defense subcommittee ranking-member status."

"*Holy shit!*" screamed Mindy. Roy and Julie looked up from where they were sitting with Bernie and his wife, Jane. Roy shook his head and motioned toward his preschooler. "Oops." Mindy slouched. "Sorry."

Jeff continued, "Since most of our members didn't think she should be heading up defense anyway, the handwriting was on the wall. You all saw her storm out. Lackland came in and killed the cigarette amendment."

"Jeez Louise. Did you know this was coming, Fred?" Roxy asked.

"Yes and no. I know Lackland well enough to know he wasn't going to allow the Senate to vote on an amendment banning cigarettes on his watch. When I saw Pat come on the floor, I kinda figured he was sent to break the news to dear Senator Boyer."

"*Wow!*" Mindy roared.

"Calm down, Mindy." Roxy elbowed her in the ribs. "So one more thing." She looked at Sarah. "I promise, Sarah, this is the last inside baseball question. Fred, what was going on with you, Jacobs, and Senator Johnson? You said 'shoot the staff.' What did you mean?"

"Oh, you know, Roxy. Jacobs came up to me and acted like we were supposed to have put Johnson's stupid amendment in our bill for him. Of course, he never asked us to put it in. Not the kind of thing I'm gonna forget. And not the kind of thing Jackson's gonna fail to mention."

"But why 'shoot the staff'?"

"C'mon, Roxy. Think about it. Jacobs couldn't let Johnson know that he didn't tell us to put it in. She's up and she's the sea turtle, right?"

Roxy shrugged.

Fred sighed and continued, "He's protecting his relationship with her. He's written her off. But he doesn't want her to know. In case he needs her on a vote before the election. Instead, he blames the snafu on the staff. She walks away pissed at me, but not at the leader . . . ergo, shoot the staff."

"That's terrific," Mindy said, laughing. "I got to remember that."

Chapter Thirty-Seven

"Tell you what. I got a lot going on right now. But if this is as important as you say, I can get away for lunch tomorrow. OK? Let's meet at Epic Smokehouse. It's near the Pentagon City Mall."

That was how Roy Peterson found himself agreeing to meet with Sergeant Amy Anderson at the barbecue joint. She said she'd be in her air force uniform and he could recognize her by the red curly hair. He told her he'd wave when she walked in.

And there she was. He got up from his seat at a corner table in a secluded area of the long, narrow restaurant, next to the wall of windows, and waved in her direction.

She walked over. The name tag *Anderson* on her uniform left no doubt he'd met his "date." She wore a concerned look as she strode toward him. Her green eyes darted around the restaurant, focusing on a half dozen people in various military uniforms.

"Hello, are you Mr. Peterson?" She gave a half smile as he offered a hand to shake.

He nodded and motioned for her to sit down. Roy noted the cyberwarfare badge on her uniform, but wasn't familiar enough with air force ribbons to recognize all the others.

So, she was in cyber. Explained the NSA connection. Man, she looked so young to be a technical sergeant. Must have been promoted early. *She's cute enough, her looks alone might have done the job. I like the freckles and little nose. And she's got a nice, trim figure. Maybe she's an athlete.*

"Jeepers, Captain Peterson, I had no idea there'd be so many soldiers and sailors here. I hope no one recognizes me." She continued to scan the patrons in the restaurant.

"Actually, I chose this place mostly for that reason, figuring you'd blend in. If we met on the Hill, you'd stick out like a sore thumb, and I might see someone I know." He paused. "Besides, the food's not bad. So, tell me what's so important. And, please, call me Roy."

"If someone recognizes me, how will I explain meeting you here?"

"First, it's highly unlikely you'll see someone you know. But so what if you do?" He glanced at her hands—no wedding ring. "Just tell them it's a blind date. You know, like that 'it's just lunch' app. I got the bigger problem. I'm married. A little harder to explain if we see someone *I* know." He tried to smile. *Not often I get to have lunch with a cute redhead. Might as well enjoy it.*

Amy took the seat across from Roy. "I guess we should eat something. I've never been here before. What's good?"

"Burger's good. Barbecue ain't bad. My wife likes the salad with pulled pork. I guess it depends what you like." He squirmed a little in his seat. *Probably good mentioning my wife again. I can't have her getting the wrong idea.*

"I like burgers." Amy giggled. Her voice sounded more relaxed. "So, what's it like working on the Hill? Do you see the congressmen all the time? Do you get to talk to the president? My cousin works on the intel committee. She's a receptionist. But she sees senators a lot."

Roy cocked his head. "Wait a second. I thought you had vital information you needed to tell me. Is this some game? I'm a busy man." He signaled for a waiter to take their orders.

After the waiter left, Amy turned her attention back to Roy. "I'm sorry, sir. Just trying to be friendly. Yes, I have something terrible to share. But you can't tell anyone I told you, OK?"

"Sure. But what's the super-duper secret?" He frowned, regretting his decision to meet.

"So, I work at INSCOM."

He looked at her air force uniform, and his skepticism grew.

She leaned forward in her chair and lowered her voice. "So, what if I were to tell you we're getting ready to interfere in an election?"

"Bullshit. The Senate's already voted to deny NSA the authority to do that."

"But we're not the NSA. We're the army. This isn't an intel action. You know, what we call Title 50. It's Title 10, the military."

"OK, slow down. First, you're air force, not army. Second, what do you know about Title 10 and 50? What's your game here?"

Amy sat straighter in her chair. "Sir, I'm detailed to the Army Intelligence Command at Fort Belvoir. I've been in the air force for more than ten years. Most of that time, I've been working for the NSA. That's the reason I know the difference between military ops and intel ops."

She paused as the waiter brought over their burgers. "Yum, this looks good." She smiled at the waiter and waited for him to leave, then her face grew serious again. "Anyway, INSCOM needed someone with my skill set—software and cyber. I guess they're a little short, because the new cyber command is scooping up all the talent."

She took a big bite of her burger and wiped off the juice dripping down her chin before she continued, "A couple weeks ago, we got a whole new batch of stuff from Fort Meade. Anyway, it's stuff you'd need to rig computers that count ballots. I'd heard about the flap in the Senate with my old agency, the NSA, and the election rigging. So, when I saw this, I knew right away what was going on. I thought I should tell someone. And my friend at the NSA, Sandy—Master Sergeant Baker—suggested you."

"But once again"—Roy bent forward—"the intelligence community wouldn't be fixing an election after we told them not to."

"But that's just it, sir. It's not intel. We're doing it under counter-drug authorities in Title 10. I don't know all the details. But I know there's lots of stuff we're authorized to do. I mean DoD, not intel, under counter-drug ops."

"OK. Let's say I believe you. What's fixing an election in Africa got to do with counter-drugs?"

"Beats me. But who said anything about Africa?"

Roy leaned in a little closer and scanned from side to side. "That's where the NSA was going to fix an election." He sighed. "But they cancelled it," he whispered and pounded his index finger on the table. He looked in her eyes. "And in case you don't know, that's all classified. You can't repeat it." He pointed at her cyber badge and air force ribbons. "With your background, I'm sure you're cleared for this stuff." He leaned back in his chair.

"Yes, sir, I am. But it's not Africa. It's Bolivia."

"Bolivia!" Roy nearly shouted. A couple of guys seated two tables away looked in their direction.

Roy leaned in again and lowered his voice. "Why would we rig an election in Bolivia? This is supposed to be a beta test. That's why they chose a corrupt African dictatorship to mess around in. Bolivia's a democracy. This doesn't sound like a beta test."

"No, sir. From what I can tell, this is the real deal." She leaned in so close he could smell her floral perfume, almost close enough to kiss. "They intend to make some guy named Montoya the winner." She lowered her voice a notch. "Technically speaking, it's really neat what we can do. How we can manipulate votes. We've been messing with their computers for a couple weeks now. We're all set to go. Election's the Sunday after next."

"You're serious?"

She nodded, leaned back, and raised her eyebrows. A sheepish smile crossed her face.

"Who else knows about this?"

"Sir, the commander, General McNeal, knows. He's the one who signed the order."

"McNeal. He's the deputy at NSA." He leaned back in his chair, nodding slowly. "OK, it's starting to make a little more sense."

"Yes, sir. With the emphasis on cyber, the NSA is having even closer working relations with the military services. So he's dual-hatted."

"Yeah, that's right." Roy crossed his arms. "Who else?"

"Can't say for sure. We've got a real small team. I report to Major Whitehall. Everything's compartmented pretty tight. I know two spec-4's—the army calls them specialists these days. They deal with some of the technical details. I don't know if anyone else has put two and two together and understands what we're about to do." She slouched a little in her chair. "So, what do we do now?"

"I think you go back to work and forget we met. I've got to tell my boss. My instinct? He'll want to make sure what you're saying is legit. I'm mean, it's awfully hard to believe. Bolivia? Why?" He raised his hands in question. "But if it's true, the Capitol dome's gonna explode. No way Congress is going to approve an attack on Bolivia's elections."

◆ ◆ ◆

From a white sedan, illegally double-parked outside Epic Smokehouse on the corner of Fourteenth and South Fern streets, two people watched the restaurant's interior through the glass back doors. The dark-suited passenger snapped photos of a couple in the restaurant. In the bottom corner of his window, a laser microphone was aimed at the glass ashtray sitting on the table between the two diners. The mic picked up sound vibrations from their voices as they bounced off the ashtray. Those sound waves would be analyzed by a computer and transcribed. As the couple got up to leave, the sedan pulled out into traffic. The photographer looked at the driver. "Any idea why we're watching these two, Burt?"

"HQ suspects she's leaking classified information. Computers picked her up talking on a nonsecure line and red-flagged a few keywords. Told us to track her movements for thirty days. Routine shit. Nothing much usually comes from these things, but we got to collect the data. Not a bad chick to follow. I hope her blonde friend comes back this weekend for another pool party. Nice rack. Just wish the bikinis were a little skimpier."

"Yeah. I got some great shots, especially when chickie number two bent over. Bazoomba."

Chapter Thirty-Eight

Drug kingpin Fernando Roca stood on the veranda of his five thousand square foot, French-provincial style beach cottage on the shores of Lake Titicaca. Winter temperatures were mild here during daylight hours, but chilly at night. He looked out at the cloudless, sapphire sky reflected on the surface of the water. Small waves lapped the shoreline below his manor house.

"Mr. Roca. As your financial advisor, I must warn you the move is very risky."

"Risk? What risk? I loan the boy fifty million *bolivianos*. He trains his workers and pays me back . . . with interest, Ricardo. You should like that. It's a legitimate business opportunity. The kind you're always encouraging. You won't have to worry about the Drug Enforcement Agency.

"Plus, it's safe. Surely, the government has seven million US to secure the loan."

"But Bolivia is not securing the loan. Your agreement is with Miguel Corazon."

"What's that, Ricardo? Who did you say?" Roca placed a hand behind his ear as if he hadn't heard correctly.

"Miguel Corazon, sir," Ricardo muttered as if irritated by his patron's attempt at humor.

"Corazon. Yes, that was it. Why would that name be familiar?" Ricardo sighed.

"That's right. Gee, this loan is sounding better every day. I loan the president's brother fifty million and he . . . what do we say . . . he owes me. Not just the money, Ricardo. He *owes* me. The press would be shocked to learn that the Corazon family was taking drug money, wouldn't they?"

"Yes, sir."

"And if the national police tried to raid my factories, do you know what it would take to have them turn around with their tails between their legs and apologize? One phone call. That's it. I'd say, 'Young man, I want those uniformed functionaries out of my factories, immediately.' Doesn't that sound good? And all that for only fifty million. Ricardo, you're the money man. How many months does it take me to earn that sum?"

Ricardo shrugged. "Maybe six."

"And if we aren't worried about the police, I'd say less. So, my friend, it seems a small price for, what do the *gringos* say, for a get-out-of-jail-free card."

"But what if he can't pay you back?"

"If Miguel Corazon fails to pay me back, the president will no longer have a brother. But the Corazon family is well positioned to pay me back."

"But there's an election coming soon. What if she loses? Who'll pay you back then?"

"Corazon lose? Simona *Bolívar* lose? That's crazy talk. To whom? Montoya? That fraud. He'll be lucky if his own mother votes for him. And the others, the seven dwarfs? Not one of them will get three percent. Admit it, Ricardo. This is a sound business decision, even if it's not one you thought of. Relax, my friend. Enjoy the view." His stomach growled, and he smiled. "Come. I'm hungry. Let's get lunch."

Chapter Thirty-Nine

"OK, guys," said Fred Hendricks, smiling and nodding at Mindy, Roy, and Stevie Guy in turn. "I called you three into the vault to talk counter-drugs. I'm still getting up to speed on this. We didn't have counter-drug ops in milcon. So, Mindy, give me a little refresher on DoD's counter-drug program."

"Yes, sir. I did a little more research after we talked this morning. DoD's involvement with counter-drugs goes back to 1986 when President Reagan signed the executive order that started the War on Drugs. In 1991, Congress finally changed Title 10 US Code to formalize DoD's role.

"So, here are three relevant sections that I pulled out of a Joint Chiefs of Staff memo on the subject. First, the general policy statement." She looked down at her notes to read out loud. "The DoD counter-drug mission is:

"'Conducting strategic, operational, and tactical intelligence collection (consistent with the law) against illegal drug trafficking originating in or transiting through their respective areas of responsibility (AORs) to support cueing of foreign and domestic LEAs.'

"LEAs are law enforcement agencies," she added.

"Huh," Fred interjected. "'Consistent with the law.' You'd

think that'd go without saying. Wonder why they added that? What else, Mindy?"

"Yes, sir. This might be interesting. DoD's role is also:

"'Coordinating with other USG agencies to suppress illegal drug activities in production, processing, and transshipment countries.'"

Suppress illegal drug activities. Could that be a rationale to rig an election? Pretty thin reed, if you ask me. Fred's expression was quizzical, but he just nodded at Mindy.

"Yes, sir. And I thought this was interesting, too, as a blanket policy statement from the same document." She cleared her throat and read from her notes again.

"'Those who contribute to the production, transport, sale, and use of illegal drugs and laundering of drug money present a threat to the national security of the US.'"

"So, if a country is contributing to the illegal drug trade, we've labeled them a threat to national security. Interesting. Anything else, Mindy?"

Mindy shook her head, took a deep breath, and glanced at Roy and Stevie Guy, who appeared to be monitoring every word. "Sir, just wondering. Does that help? If I knew what you were looking for, I might be able to find something of more use."

"Sorry, Mindy. This gets into some classified stuff that you're not involved in. I'm sure you understand."

Mindy nodded, with a look of mild disgust.

Fred smiled. "I appreciate the background. Now, if you'll excuse us, I need to talk to Roy and Stevie a little. But before you go, when are you starting your discussions with the House staff on conference?"

"Started this morning, sir." She beamed. "Made great progress. We'll be ready to go whenever the formal meeting with the members is set up."

"That's terrific. Good work. Oh, and one more thing. Let's not tell the House about this just yet."

Mindy nodded again and left the secure room.

After she closed the heavy steel door, Stevie spoke. "Sir, two things. First, the intelligence community has become quite involved in the War on Drugs. It's written a lot of findings on counter-drug ops."

Stevie opened a red manila folder. "I have one here that came in a couple weeks ago. For your eyes only." He shot a look at Roy. "Pretty routine. Didn't see much new in it. I was gonna show you after we finished the bill. Let you decide if you thought the chairman needed to see it." He handed it to Fred.

Fred scanned the document. It was an updated list of drug kingpins and countries suspected of sponsoring drug trafficking. His eyes spotted Bolivia, which was highlighted as a new entry. Bolivia, huh? Could this be the authority they were using to rig its election? Pretty convenient. Bringing down the President of Bolivia could weaken the government's role in drug trafficking, in theory. Assuming their president was personally involved. He tut-tutted under his breath and glanced at Stevie, then at Roy.

What do I do with this?

Roy wasn't cleared to read the finding. And Fred couldn't tell Stevie about the NSA rigging the election.

I guess it's my problem. But one thing's for sure—I got to tell the chairman ASAP. Just wish I felt certain of Roy's info.

"Holy mother of God," Fred muttered quietly. "OK, Stevie. Lock this up, but keep it close. I'll need to show it to the chairman soon. Let me talk to Roy for a second."

Roy perked up, wearing a big grin.

Stevie walked out and Fred began, "So, Roy. Not much I can tell you."

Roy's smile evaporated.

"I need to talk to the chairman. But before I do, I'd really like to meet your source. Why don't you try and arrange a meet for after work near the Capitol. Think you can get her to do that? I don't want to waltz in and brief the boss with these crazy claims. Oh yeah, and tell her not to wear her uniform. Don't want her to stick out like a sore thumb."

Chapter Forty

"Desdemona!" Simona Corazon screeched from her office. The sound reverberated throughout the second floor of the palace.

In the anteroom, Desdemona's eyes widened, and her mouth fell open as she leaped from her chair. Miguel Corazon stood next to her, glancing at a paper.

He motioned for her to stay calm. "Relax. It's just the stress of the campaign. We're less than two weeks out. She always gets like this when we get close to Election Day." Miguel offered a calming smile. He cocked his head to the side, indicating that Desdemona should go into the presidential office.

Desdemona smiled at him. She took a deep breath and knocked on the open door. "Yes, Madame President?"

Miguel drew a few steps closer to the doorway, listening.

"Where am I supposed to be going for the last five days of the campaign?"

"I have your schedule here. Next Wednesday, you will travel to the lithium fields. It'll take all day, but the reporters will see you with the workers. You should get great press on the progress being made."

"Good."

"On Thursday, we'll travel to Santa Cruz. A rally has been organized for that evening."

"Why am I going to Santa Cruz? Those businessmen hate me."

"Madame President, it's the largest city in the country. You can't ignore them. Plus, the rally is a chance for your supporters to remind undecided voters how popular you are. Forget the businessmen. This is about the workers."

"OK. What about Sucre?"

"Yes, ma'am. We plan for you to hold a parade and election eve rally in Sucre. We want Simona Bolívar to parade through the streets as Simón Bolívar did nearly two hundred years ago. We think it's an excellent way to cap off your campaign."

"And here in La Paz?"

"On Friday, and of course you'll be here on Election Day."

"Is that when I visit the auto factory?"

Miguel poked his head in. "We're not sure that's a good idea."

"Why not? The workers love me. Remember the outpouring of support I got when I nationalized it? I must go."

"Simona, there isn't much to see. We don't think the time is right."

"Not much to see?" Simona screamed. "Why not? What's wrong? Have you failed me, Miguelito?"

"No, sister. But progress has been slow. I explained it to you. The banks were unwilling to lend us money."

"Then we'll nationalize them too. Get Rodrigo in here. He's the Finance Minister. This is his fault."

"Simona, it's not Tío's fault. He's done everything he can. But it's taken me time to raise the funds."

She trained an icy scowl on him.

"Don't worry." He held up his hands. "I have the money now to train the workers. We'll start soon. However, today, the factory is still idle. It wouldn't be wise to tour a factory filled with machines but no workers. Trust me, my sister. This will all work out. Once you've won, I think the bankers might even change their minds. But for now, we can begin to train workers, maybe as early as the Monday after election."

"Where did you get the money, Miguel? You didn't ask the *yanquis*, did you?"

"No, it was from local agricultural businessmen who support you. It's homegrown." He stifled a chuckle but kept a serious look on his face.

"Very well. You're my brother. I trust you. Now, both of you, get out. I need to think about my speeches for this week." She waved them away.

Chapter Forty-One

Judy Jameson's curly black hair preceded her, peeking into H-140, a white-walled, medium-sized hearing room in the Capitol. Her curls were followed by large, black-rimmed glasses, which obscured her brown eyes. She clutched an accordion folder stuffed with papers that looked as if they'd spill onto the floor with the slightest bump.

The first thing she noticed was the table and chairs in the shape of a large box, like the committee used for markup. The center of the box, covering nearly half of the entire room, was empty. On the left side, an older man in a brown suit and matching tie sat at the far corner of the table. She'd never seen him before.

He was flipping through a thick stack of papers that looked like the printed notes for conference that she had in her accordion file. A lot of younger men and women holding similar accordion files sat against the wall behind him. She didn't recognize them, either.

She spotted Roxy and Mindy on the other side of the room against the wall, and her shoulders relaxed. Turning that way, she stumbled over the first of three rows of folding chairs to her immediate right. They were separated by a narrow aisle from the chairs at the table. Roxy beckoned her to join them.

"Hey, Jameson, what's with the specs?" Mindy called out over the chatter.

Judy adjusted her glasses self-consciously. As she approached the two women, she whispered, "I can't wear my contacts. I think I got an eye infection. Maybe it's all the long hours, or the lack of sleep."

"Yeah, that kind of stuff happens every year." Roxy shook her head. "Me, I always seem to power through but get sick as soon as we get done. This stuff takes a toll on you. Not sure how Fred's been doing it for forty years."

"Mr. Hendricks has been here forty years?" Judy's eyes widened.

"That's what he told me a few weeks ago. He seems fine, though. A lot of that time was on milcon, and, frankly, that's nowhere near the stress of trying to manage a defense bill.

"Hey! Fred's here with the chairman. OK, everybody, we're getting close."

Chairman Jackson walked around the table and sat down. Fred sank into the chair next to Roxy's, directly behind the chairman. Jeff Leary took the other seat beside Fred.

Jackson waved at the white-haired congressman across the room and scooted his chair back. He whispered, "What's that fella's name again?"

Fred leaned forward and murmured in the chairman's ear, "That's Thaddeus Harlow, Republican from Kentucky. From what I understand, the only thing he ever asks about is military recruiting."

Jackson nodded.

"The tall, skinny staffer standing behind him is Al Kittenger," Fred continued. "He's Chairman Jones's clerk."

"Oh yeah, I recognize him. Seems like he's been doing this awhile."

"Yes, sir, twenty-five years. Been defense clerk for fifteen."

"So he's a pro." Jackson turned toward Jeff. "Where's Liz?" His words came out in a soft growl.

"I'm sorry, sir," Jeff replied. "We're told she's on her way."

Jackson looked up. Chairman Jones, the aging Democratic congressman from Louisiana, walked in, leaning on his cane. Jackson gave him a wave and a smile. "Mr. Chairman," he called out. "It's good to see you."

"And you, Senator," Jones responded. He waved the hand holding the cane and nearly whacked a female staffer.

Following right behind Jones was the ranking Republican, Larry Chalmers, a balding, short, round man.

Larry smiled and waved at Sam Jackson. "Mr. Chairman, heh-heh. Bet it feels good to be called *chairman* again. Huh, Sam?" His head bobbed as he spoke. "You're looking good, my friend."

Quickly, congressmen filed into the room and grabbed the seats on three sides of the table. Jackson sat alone on the Senate side. After a few minutes, the newest member of the Senate subcommittee, Jason Coleman, joined him, a befuddled look on his face.

"Mr. Chairman," Jones called out in a Southern drawl, "y'all ready to proceed? We got a series of votes this morning, so we best get started. That alright with you, Senator?"

"Senator Coleman and I are ready, Mr. Chairman, but my ranking Democrat is still on her way. I suggest we give her another minute."

Jones spun around in his chair and sneered at Al Kittenger, who stood up and whispered something in the chairman's ear. Jones nodded. "OK, Mr. Chairman, but I got *all* my members here." He grinned. "The House is ready to proceed."

Jackson grinned back at him and faced Jeff. "You need to get Liz here now, or I'm going to start without her."

"Yes, sir." Jeff stood up to leave, but just then, Boyer waltzed into the room.

Boyer glanced to her right, spotted Jackson frowning at her, and glared back. She looked to her left and smiled as Chairman Jones stood up, bracing himself on the table.

"Chairman Jones, if you aren't a sight for sore eyes." She weaved through the narrow passageway between the seated members and House staff, making her way over to the chairman.

She squeezed his hand and pecked him on the cheek. "You're looking younger than ever, Mr. Chairman," she leaned in and whispered in his ear. He threw back his head and laughed. She patted his hand and nodded to Congressman Chalmers, then made her way to her seat next to Jackson. Her assistant, Marjory, sat down next to Jeff Leary.

Chairman Jones banged his gavel. "This meeting of the conferees appointed by their respective houses on the bill H.R. 1253, making appropriations for the Department of Defense and for other purposes, will come to order." He read from an oversized three-ring binder. "I move that the conference be closed in order that members may discuss classified information. For the information of senators present, please note this vote is only for the House conferees. All those in favor?" He banged the gavel. "Opposed?"

No one in the room spoke.

"The motion is approved. The clerk will clear the room as appropriate. Senator Jackson, you are charged with making sure all remaining Senate staff are cleared to discuss top-secret information."

The House staff escorted the half dozen reporters huddled near the door out of the room. A few House staffers were also instructed to leave. Jackson gave Chairman Jones a thumbs-up.

Once the doors were closed, Chairman Jones spoke. "If it's OK with you, Senators, I'll call out the page numbers as we flip through the items in conference. As you can tell from the more than two hundred pages in front of us, we have thousands of items to adjudicate.

"For the benefit of all members, the staff is proposing resolution on certain items. Their shorthand recommendations—HR, SR, or HWA—are printed in the right-hand margin. If the margin next to an entry is blank, that item remains open. We'll debate the open items one by one after we go through this entire document." He looked up. "I want to thank the staff on both sides for their hard work. But, if there are any staff proposals on which members have questions, I suggest they reserve those items for later discussion. In this way, we can proceed expeditiously to agree to these other proposals."

"We're all set, Mr. Chairman." Jackson scooted his chair up close to the table and opened his binder.

When Jones reached page twenty, Congressman Harlow called out, "Mr. Chairman, what is the disposition of item number five on this page?"

Al Kittenger whispered something in Chairman Jones's ear. The chairman nodded, then said, "As it says here, Congressman, HR. The House will recede to the Senate."

"But Mr. Chairman, why would we give in to the Senate? The House cut fifteen million from the joint recruiting and advertising budget. You said at our markup, Mr. Chairman, this makes a lot of sense."

"I know what I said, Thaddeus, but the Senate's arguments were persuasive. And we've all heard from the Secretary of Defense about this proposal. Would the gentleman like to reserve on this?"

"Mr. Chairman, you know as well as I do that the joint advertising program is a waste of taxpayer dollars." He started to read from a piece of paper a staffer had handed to him. "Over the past ten years—"

"Would the gentleman like to reserve?" The chairman's tone was a little louder.

"But, we've already spent over four hundred—"

"Would the gentleman like to reserve?" the chairman barked and banged his gavel.

Thaddeus Harlow looked up. Everyone in the room was staring at him. Congressman Chalmers was signaling him to shush.

He nodded. "Ah, yes, Mr. Chairman, I would, but first, I want to—"

Bang! The gavel sounded again.

"The gentleman reserves." Chairman Jones flipped the page. "Page twenty-one."

Chapter Forty-Two

"Mr. President." Chief of Staff Steve Simpson put his cell phone down. He turned around in the front passenger seat to view the president in the back of the limousine.

Parker looked up. "Yeah, what is it? And no bad news, Steve. Especially nothing that's gonna fuck up my time at Camp David. Got it?"

"Sorry, sir. The good news is this won't affect your trip." He took a deep breath. "But army counterintelligence is reporting there might be a leak about our upcoming election plans. If you get my drift."

"What the fuck? Who's talking?"

"Sir, the army picked up some key phrases on an open phone line a couple weeks ago. So they started following an enlisted woman who works at Fort Belvoir. Last week, they saw her meet with a staffer, a National Guard captain, by the way." Simpson grimaced. "I hate to say it, sir, but he works for Senator Jackson on the defense subcommittee."

"Oh fuck." Parker slammed his hand down on the leather seat. "Not Jackson. Not the fucking appropriators. Those motherfuckers will fuck me any way they can. Jesus Christ, Steve.

What's wrong with these people? Don't they know it's treason to leak secrets? I want that bitch locked up. Now!"

"Yes, sir. I hear ya." Steve chose each word carefully. "But we can't just lock her up, sir. The army can't say for sure that she's done anything illegal. And if she's talking to a cleared Hill staffer, she's protected under whistleblower laws. If we tried to lock her up, we'd have to tell a hell of a lot more people about this."

"God damn it, Steve. I want her stopped. We can't let her fuck this up. I need New Mexico. Corazon has to go down. I won't have American factories nationalized. Not on my watch, Steve. Stop her. I don't care how you do it."

"God damn it. The election is right around the corner, and he hasn't done a thing!" Hans Edison screamed at his assistant from a plush chair on his private jet. "What are the polls saying? Parker insisted she was going to lose."

"I'm sorry, sir," the assistant replied. "She's up by at least twenty points. There's simply no way she loses."

Edison frowned. "How much am I going to lose if she gets away with this?"

"In terms of investment, less than fifty million. In terms of potential, billions."

"Jesus Christ. We've got to do something. Parker's fucked this up. I want her gone. And if Parker can't fix it, I'm going to work my ass off to make sure he loses."

"Sir, I've got an idea. I'll be honest. It's a long shot. But I think I've found a way to embarrass her and show that nationalization is hurting Bolivia. It could hurt her on Sunday."

Edison scowled. "Then what are you waiting for? We've only got a few days."

"Yes, sir."

Chapter Forty-Three

"So, what else, gang?" Fred glanced around his office at the staff.

Judy raised her hand. "Can I ask a question, sir?"

"Sure." Fred smiled at the intern.

"It looked like all the House members were there today. But only Jackson and Boyer, plus Coleman, were there for the Senate. Where were all the other senators?"

"Well, senators are so busy they're always supposed to be in three places at once. Our full committee chairman, Colbert, was chairing an agriculture subcommittee hearing. Senator Mannington chairs the Energy Committee. He's holding hearings on climate change this week. House members generally only belong to one or maybe two committees at most. It's a lot easier for them to show up at these things.

"Roxy, how many items were reserved?"

"I think about twenty. All from the House members, except the one Coleman did." Roxy glanced at Bernie.

"Yeah, Bernie. That was yours. Wasn't it?" Fred asked.

"Yes, sir. I talked to Coleman's staffer about it. He wasn't sure why his boss did it. I'm betting it's 'cause he sat there like a bump on a log for two hours, probably not really having a clue what was going on. Anyway, he reserved it. That means we haven't resolved if we're going to spend fifteen million or fourteen million eight hundred thousand on designing a new engine for the army's medium-truck program. In a seven hundred billion dollar bill, the only thing he wants to fight about is 200K for a truck." He shook his head.

The staff guffawed.

"OK, settle down, everybody," said Fred. "That was great work today. I think we've whittled the open items down from 250 pages to about twenty. I want you to get back on the phone with your counterparts now and see if we can close more items before tomorrow's session. The chairman won't be happy if he walks in and sees a ton of open items. Al promised me no more games. That goes for you too. Let's get this done."

"Does that include the items the House reserved?" Roxy asked.

"If their guy insisted on reopening the item, they probably ain't gonna take no for an answer. So, try to get it closed, unless it's really smelly."

"Like the Carolina shipyard bailout, right?" she said.

"Yeah." Fred nodded. "Like that. The big four are gonna have to solve that one."

"One more thing, if I can." Roxy raised her hand.

Fred nodded.

"What's up with Boyer? She hardly spoke. The only thing she did was kiss Jones."

The staff howled.

"Beats me, Roxy. Maybe she learned her place after Lackland took her to the woodshed, but that'd be pretty out of character. My guess is she's biding her time, waiting for the right spot to throw a monkey wrench in."

"But kissing Jones?" Roxy groaned. "He's ancient."

"Hey, she served in the House. She was on appropriations for a couple years. Maybe she likes him. Old guys certainly like her—Lackland gave her defense, after all. Enough questions. Phone the House, then review the new conference notes, and go home. Let's get 'er done. Thank you all."

Chapter Forty-Four

"Listen, Sara," Harris grumbled. "There's no news. Jones closed the conference, and all the journalists were thrown out. How can I write a story if, as far as I know, nothing happened?" He paused, holding his cell away from his ear as his editor shouted through the line.

"I know we've got to remember our readers," Harris said, fighting to keep his tone level. "But, from what the staff said after the session broke up, all they did was approve the easy stuff. There was nothing on cigarettes, no news on ships, tanks, or airplanes. And from what I hear, nobody said boo about election rigging. So, I'm all ears if you got an idea for a story. Christ, Sara. The biggest news was probably that Boyer pecked Jones on the cheek, and the old guy didn't have a heart attack." He smiled at the familiar cackle on the other end.

He continued to listen, then said, "Yeah, I got it. I'll think of something." He put down his phone and opened his laptop. He stared at the blank screen for several minutes. Finally, shaking his head, he wrote:

Five minutes after opening the conference meeting where senators and congressmen divvy up more than seven hundred and twenty-five billion dollars for the Depart-

ment of Defense and the intelligence community, Chairman Woodrow "Woody" Jones, a Democrat from Louisiana, moved to restrict attendance to those with top-secret security clearances. His motion forced reporters and a half dozen House staffers to be ushered from the meeting.

Everyone understands the legitimate need to restrict access when the nation's secrets are being discussed. All too often, though, the people's right to know is thwarted "in the interests of national security" as public meetings are closed. Access is limited to "members and cleared staff."

There is nothing classified about the continued sale of cigarettes at military facilities or a proposed bailout of the South Carolina-based Charleston Marine shipyard. But the people will be left in the dark about these until it's too late to affect the outcome.

And what of the issue of tampering in foreign elections? Yes, that subject is classified. But the issue has already been debated twice in open forum in the Senate. Why should it be resolved behind closed doors, away from the press and public?

With Chairman Jones's action today, the people will only learn the resolution of thousands of differences between the proposals approved by the House and those of the Senate after the conference has been completed and the final bill is posted online.

Is this reporter's contention that all these will be determined in private an unlikely hypothetical? To the contrary.

If history repeats itself, as it almost always does in dealing with appropriations bills, the conferees, having "met in free and open conference" as they did for five minutes earlier today, will not meet again. Instead, the issues will be resolved, as this reporter has proffered, with only a few senators, representatives, and staff present. And then the completed thousand-page document, with enormous implications for all Americans, will be sent to each respective House for a single vote on whether to approve the seven hundred and twenty-five billion dollar spending bill.

And they call this democracy.

Harris stopped writing and read the copy. *This is garbage. How am I going to write a story worth reading?*

Chapter Forty-Five

"What do you mean we're cancelling the trip to the lithium fields? What the hell is going on? Desdemona!" Simona Corazon shouted toward the hall.

Desdemona peeked in the doorway. "Yes, Madame President?"

"Why are we not going to the lithium fields today?" she demanded, drumming her fingernails on the stack of paper in front of her. "You said it would get great press. So why not go?"

Desdemona shrank. "The Interior Minister says it's a bad time."

"Bad time? But we're four days out from the election. It can't be a bad time. What the hell is going on?"

Miguel strolled past Desdemona into the office. "It seems the workers are about to go on strike."

"What?" Simona drew back as if she'd been slapped. "Why? The workers love me. Why would they strike?"

"Minister Cordoba believes it's outside agitators."

"This must be Montoya. He knows he's losing. He's desperate. We must stop this now."

"We all agree with you, Simona. But Cordoba says it's not Montoya. He believes these men were hired by Hans Edison. Your minister thinks he can stop the strike. Convince the workers that you will take better care of them than Hans Edison. But right now, the situation does not make for a good story."

"Jesus Christ. The God-damned *yanquis*. This proves they'll stop at nothing to defeat me. They want to turn Bolivia into an American colony. I'll show them, Miguel. I'll win. Isn't that right, Desdemona?"

"Yes, ma'am. The polls show you climbing above forty percent. Montoya has fallen below fifteen, and none of the other candidates matter. The election is a lock for you, Madame President. Unless you make a huge mistake. Going to the lithium fields at Salar de Uyuni would be a mistake. I don't think it'd cost you the election, but you shouldn't take the chance. Let Minister Cordoba talk to the workers. After the election, you can visit and reassure them of your continued support. Winning will mean a great deal more to them than a campaign spectacle with the press pushing them out of the way to get better pictures."

Simona pursed her lips and nodded slowly.

"Today you should stay in La Paz," Desdemona said. "Tomorrow, you'll rally the workers in Santa Cruz and show your overwhelming support in Montoya's stronghold. On Sunday, you'll prove you can even win there."

Chapter Forty-Six

Jones, chairman of the Subcommittee on Defense of the House Committee on Appropriations, banged the gavel as he scanned the hearing room.

Ten House subcommittee members were present, including his ranking member, Larry Chalmers. Across the room sat Jackson and Boyer, flanked by two dozen staffers seated against the wall.

"Mr. Chairman," called Jones, "the staff has put together a third proposal for us. We're down to eight pages. Senator, what's your pleasure?"

"If I may, Chairman Jones," Liz Boyer said. "I think we should talk about the Senate's proposal banning this administration from interfering in foreign elections."

"I think that's a mighty fine idea, Senator, but the House would like to defer on that subject just now. I'm sure you understand. It's classified."

"Actually, Mr. Chairman, I don't. I can't see why the House Democrats—"

"C'mon, Liz," Jones drawled, a twinkle in his eye. "There ain't no cameras here. I assure y'all we'll get to it in due time. But today we'd like to close out the remaining items with the other members present. If you catch my drift." He offered a conciliatory smile. "Charlie wants to talk about the Charleston Marine shipyard. Go on, Charlie. Tell the senators about the terrible things the navy's been doin' to the good folks of South Carolina."

Republican Congressman Charlie Harkins raised his thin six-foot-six frame from his seat. "Why, thank you, Mr. Chairman." His deep baritone boomed across the room. "My shipyard's being robbed blind by the navy." He stared across the table at the Senate side.

Chairman Jackson scooted his chair back and discreetly turned his palms upward while keeping his eyes on the South Carolina congressman.

Roxy placed a paper on the table in front of the chairman and whispered in his ear, "The House is proposing bill language to pay the Charleston Marine shipyard in South Carolina seventy-five million dollars to cover its cost overrun to complete a navy merchant marine ship designed to carry ammunition and fuel.

"The navy contends the shipyard is responsible for the losses that the yard incurred following a tropical storm that hit the coast of Carolina five years ago. FEMA has already awarded the shipyard thirty-five million, which it says is the right amount for the damage caused by the storm. But the shipyard says its costs were much higher."

She paused for a second as the chairman nodded. She looked back at Fred, who motioned for her to continue.

"The Secretary of the Navy says the additional shipyard losses are the result of mismanagement. That they just want the navy to pay them to modernize their yard. If the Senate agrees to this, it'll establish a precedent, which, the navy says, could ultimately cost the government hundreds of millions. Defense contractors will use this bailout as justification for charging DoD for problems of their own creation."

Jackson held up his hand. "Congressman, staff tells me your shipyard is responsible for these losses. Isn't it correct that FEMA has already paid your shipyard . . ." He paused and tilted his head toward Roxy.

She whispered in his ear.

"Thirty-five million dollars for damages caused by the storm?"

"Yes, Mr. Chairman, but that's a pittance compared to the costs we've been hit with. This storm was historic."

"But staff tells me the Secretary of the Navy says the shipyard's management caused the overruns."

"No, Mr. Chairman. It was the storm."

"Staff says it was your company's leadership that caused the problems."

Charlie Harkins slammed his fist on the table. "The navy's lying. You want to know what's causing the real problem? I'll tell you what the real problem is, Senator. The real problem is the Senate staff!"

Roxy jerked her head away from the chairman. Fred grabbed her jacket and pulled her back, motioning for her to take her seat.

Jackson stared at the congressman, then looked over toward the House chairman. "Mr. Chairman, I think a recess is in order. I, for one, need a break."

"All right." Congressman Jones smiled. "The conference will stand in recess, subject to the call of the chair." He banged his gavel and looked at Sam Jackson, a sly grin frozen on his face.

With his eyes locked on the House chairman, Jackson frowned and shook his head slowly.

◆ ◆ ◆

"What did I do wrong, Fred?" Roxy whimpered.

Fred rested his feet on his desk. "Nothing. Harkins just didn't like you contradicting him. Facts can be nasty things."

"But what happens now? Are we gonna bail out Charleston Marine? That would be terrible."

"Well, Chairman Jones recessed subject to the call of the chair without saying when that would be, so I'm betting these formal meetings are over. The next member meeting will probably be only with the big four. I figure there's almost nothing left on the list that the four clerks can't resolve when we meet later to-day—except for cigarettes, your shipyard bailout, and election rigging." He released a heavy sigh. "If I had to guess how that's gonna go, Jackson will give in on the bailout. He'll stand firm on keeping out cigarette language after Boyer tried to screw him in the Senate. As for elections, well, I still got to talk to someone about that. That's about all I can tell you. But the good news is we should be done by tomorrow night. The members will want to go home for the weekend."

Chapter Forty-Seven

Sergeant Amy Anderson sat at the Thunder Grill bar inside Union Station, nursing a Negroni. The building itself was incredible. She'd heard it was at least a hundred years old or something, but that didn't detract from its beauty. The cavernous open space, the rounded, gold-trimmed ceilings, the statues near the roofline. Gorgeous. She could hardly believe it was a train station. All these shops, restaurants, and bars with hundreds of people coming and going. Truly amazing. Good place for a meetup too.

Amy hoped she looked OK. She checked her outfit in the mirror behind the bar. Hair was getting a little long—she was starting to look like Little Orphan Annie again. This Fred Hendricks guy was supposed to be important. Staff director for the defense subcommittee. Major Whitehall would probably keel over if he knew she was meeting him. And her cousin Rachel had said she had to dress up a little.

At least she still had her Hawaii tan. And her green blouse, with one button unbuttoned, was pretty, not slutty. She was ready.

Mr. Peterson had said Mr. Hendricks had short gray hair. She wondered fleetingly how old he was. Hopefully he'd recognize her. It would've been a lot easier if she'd come in uniform, but Mr. Peterson had told her not to.

A gray-haired man wearing a dark-blue suit, pale-blue shirt, striped tie, and brown loafers walked in with a slight limp. He looked over at the bar. Could that be Mr. Hendricks?

My gosh! He was so *old*. Like her granddad. He looked right at her and started her way. This was it. OK. She took a deep breath and told herself to smile.

"Hello, are you Sergeant Anderson?" He smiled as he approached. The wrinkles in his face grew even deeper.

"Yes, I am. Mr. Hendricks? Please, call me Amy."

He signaled to the bartender and growled, "Johnny, gimme the usual." He motioned to the barstool next to her. "Mind if I sit?"

She smiled and nodded.

He sat with a heavy sigh. "Thanks for agreeing to come, Amy. It's got to seem a little weird meeting some strange man in a bar. I hope you came by Metro and didn't have to pay to park. It can get a little steep."

"The Franconia-Springfield station's right near my apartment. So it was perfect."

"OK, I promise not to keep you too long."

"Oh, don't worry about me. I'm nobody. You're the important one. At least that's what my cousin Rachel says. She works on the intel committee."

"Intel? Really?" He paused, a curious look on his face.

"You're probably wondering why I didn't go to her? I did. But she said her bosses wouldn't want to hear about this. They're still upset about not finishing their bill. And this was the major reason."

He chuckled a little and took a big swig of his drink.

"Anyway, she was afraid they'd get mad at her. And fire her or something. So she told me to talk to the Appropriations Committee, and my friend at NSA knows Mr. Peterson, so I called him. And here we are." She managed a smile.

He held up his glass, and she clinked hers against it.

"Cheers," he said and took another big swig.

Amy took a sip of hers.

"What's that you're drinking?" he asked.

"It's called a Negroni."

"Good?"

"It's not bad. They're better in Hawaii. But everything's better in Hawaii." She giggled.

"You're from Hawaii?"

"No, but I was assigned there, at the RSOC—ya know, regional signals ops center—at Lualualei. Do you know Hawaii?"

"Not really. Been there a couple times. We used to have a senator from Hawaii on the committee. Traveled there with him a few years ago. You've probably heard of him. Ken Mitsunaga."

"Oh, I know all about him." She leaned closer to Fred and whispered, "I'm the one who found that Chinese spy in Los Angeles that caused him so much trouble."

"What?" His face looked incredulous.

"No, really. I was working at the RSOC, and we got this encrypted message from LA. I was curious. So my friend Sandy, the guy who knows Mr. Peterson, told me what it said. Then he told his bosses about it. They told the White House, and then President Parker, well, he was a senator then—"

"Yeah, I know the rest of the story. And now you're telling me you also know about this election thing?" He squinted at her.

"Weird, isn't it? I keep getting caught up in this stuff. I guess I'm just lucky or something."

"So, what exactly do you know about this *stuff?*"

"OK." She took a deep breath. "A few weeks back, I was given a new assignment with, like, four other guys. Major Whitehall—

he's my boss—gave us all this new software from the NSA and told us to get ready to do a beta test on it. But in this case, instead of, like, running a simulated test on the program, we're supposed to actually"—she leaned over to whisper in his ear—"attack Bolivia." She sat back and stared into his gray eyes, which snapped up to meet hers.

Was he looking down my blouse? Nah. Probably just concentrating. He was actually kind of handsome for an old guy. Pretty eyes, kind smile, and sexy voice. *Gosh, I hope he believes me.*

◆ ◆ ◆

Fred almost couldn't believe his ears. Almost. But as distracting as the view down her shirt had been when she'd leaned over, he knew he'd heard her correctly.

"Unbelievable," he finally muttered. "OK, Sergeant, I'm not a technical guy. I mean, I'm kind of a dinosaur, or Neanderthal, I guess, when it comes to new gadgets and software and stuff. Maybe you can explain how it works. So I can tell my boss, Senator Jackson."

"Jackson?" she said in that cute, high-pitched voice. "Didn't he run for vice president? I voted for him. I didn't trust Parker. I mean, when the truth came out about Mitsunaga, I was sure he was gonna win. All my coworkers and my neighbors in Hawaii said they were gonna vote for him. But he lost. I couldn't believe it."

"Yeah. It's a shame." His tone grew a little sharper. "But tell me how this computer stuff works."

"Oh yeah. There are several ways to manipulate the data. First, and this is really classified."

He nodded as she leaned over to whisper again. This time, the brown edge of her areola was barely exposed as he looked down her blouse. He forced himself to listen.

"So, first thing is we've tapped into the Bolivian election operations. Now, in Bolivia they still use paper ballots. But all the data gets inputted into the election monitoring computers."

Each time she spoke, she gestured with her hands and a little more of her breast crept free of her bra. The saliva in Fred's mouth thickened, and he knocked back another gulp of his drink.

"We'll get the data the same time the Bolivians do." She leaned back and took another deep breath, then leaned over again. "So, as the votes come in and are counted by the computer, we can alter the totals by either increasing the total vote or adjusting the results to favor a candidate."

She sat back again and spoke a little louder. "I'm guessing this is probably like what the Russians do in Europe, and maybe here too." She took a big sip, finishing her drink. She leaned even closer to him, and her bra visibly shifted. Her nipple popped all the way out. She flinched and put her hand to her chest, readjusting. "Oh goodness!"

He smiled and finished his drink. "Care for another?"

She regained her composure. "Sure. I got nothing else to do. My cousin's at the beach this week. I don't know anybody else in DC . . . but there's one more thing I need to tell you that's classified."

He nodded and signaled the bartender for two more drinks. "OK." His gaze slipped down again.

She leaned over, but this time she pressed her right hand against her blouse, keeping that free-spirited breast from jumping out again. "The election is next Sunday. We've been told to adjust the votes to make sure that a guy named Montoya beats the current president. Her name is Cortisone, or something like that."

Amy's eyes scanned the bar as she spoke. She jumped in her seat. "Oh my God!" she continued to whisper, putting her hand up to her mouth to hide what she was saying. "There's two guys over there, sitting in the corner. Fortyish. Wearing dark suits that don't quite fit them. I think I've seen them before. What would they be doing here? You think they're following me?"

"Nah, I imagine it's a coincidence. Ain't no law against coming to a bar after work."

"No, Mr. Hendricks, I don't think it's a coincidence. We're miles and miles away from Fort Belvoir. And since Belvoir isn't close to a Metro station, it's a pain to get here from there. I took a bus home and changed clothes before I came. Jeepers. You think I'm in trouble?" She reached for her fresh Negroni. Her hand was shaking so much she spilled a little on the bar. She set the drink back down.

"Hey, relax. First, you're not doing anything wrong. There's nothing you could tell me that I don't have a security clearance for. Second, all we're doing is having a drink. Like I said, I'm sure it's just a coincidence." He looked in the mirror behind the bar. "Yeah, I see 'em. They do look like military cops. Maybe you're right. Like I said, don't worry. You're fine. Tell you what. Let's leave together. I'll spring for your cab. Always tons of cabs outside 'cause of the trains coming in."

He placed two twenties on the bar. "Hey, Johnny." He signaled the bartender to come over. "See those two guys in the corner, look like ex-jarheads?"

Johnny nodded.

"I think they might be following my friend here. What say you talk to 'em a little if they try and leave when we do?"

Johnny looked at the young woman and back at Fred. A smile crept onto his face. "Sure thing, Fred."

"You don't need to pay for my drink, Mr. Hendricks," Amy offered.

He waved her off. "Don't worry about it. I can afford it. And call me Fred." He winked at her, stood up, and gulped his bourbon. Using two hands, she picked up her nearly full Negroni and chugged it. She exhaled, jumped off the stool, and grabbed her black leather clutch. He placed his hand on the small of her back and led her out of the bar.

"C'mon." He pushed her out the door into the main hall and hurried them through the big glass doors at the front of Union Station. Glancing over his shoulder, he spotted one of the guys rushing out of Thunder Grill, looking around. "Taxi!" Fred hollered so that half the people in the cavernous Union Station could hear.

Outside, he grabbed Amy's hand and pulled her to the right, away from the street. "Change of plans." They quickly walked past several stone archways along the front of Union Station and around the corner of the building. "OK, Amy, we're gonna run now. People will think we're late for our train."

They ran back into the building through a side entrance separate from the main hall, and past a couple restaurants. He guided them to the right again, near the rear of Union Station, and they headed in a full sprint toward the doors to the trains.

Fred stopped suddenly, causing Amy to slip on the floor. He reached out and grabbed her free arm, helping her regain balance. "Quick," he said. "In here."

He pulled her into a small gift shop and pushed her behind a circular rack of greeting cards. He squeezed in next to her, breathing heavily.

"Are you OK, Mr., um, Fred?"

"Yeah, I'm just a little too old to be running from cops. Let's wait a couple more seconds." His breathing slowed. "Make sure they're not still following us. Pretend you're looking at cards."

She nodded. After a minute, he walked over to the doorway and looked in both directions through the glass storefront.

He waved her over. "I think we lost them. Now, you're gonna walk out this door and to the right. Don't hurry this time. Don't want to catch anyone's eye. Head straight toward that McDonald's over there. Then walk past it. There's a door to the outside. I'll be right behind you."

"OK, but I really got to pee."

"Yeah, OK. If you can hold it for five more minutes, I got a plan."

Chapter Forty-Eight

Fred sat on the sagging brown couch in his English-basement apartment on F Street Northeast, a block and a half from Union Station. His tie was loose, and his suit coat hung on the back of a wooden chair.

What was he doing? Why had he brought her here? Yeah, she was a cute little thing, but he was old enough to be her grandfather. Besides, did he really want to get involved in this mess?

Amy came out of the bathroom with a big smile. "Whew, I feel better now. I'm glad your place was so close. I couldn't hold it much longer." She stood in the living room/kitchen and surveyed the spartan décor of the small apartment. "How long have you lived here?"

"My wife and I bought this town house a long time ago, when this area was real run-down. I wanted a place near the Capitol so I wouldn't have to drive all the way to Reston every night. I figured we could rent out the upstairs, and I could crash here when I didn't feel like driving."

"So, you're married." Amy's voice seemed tinged with concern.

"Divorced. My wife and I split up, geez, about thirty years ago, after eight long years of unhappy marriage."

"Oh, sorry." She tilted her head and offered a thin smile.

"Nah, probably for the best. I wasn't a great husband. Spent too much time at the office, and there were . . . assorted other bad habits. Anyway, she got the big house in Virginia, and she gets the rents from upstairs." He pointed up with his thumb. "I live here for free."

"Jeepers, this place is pretty small to call home, isn't it?

"Oh, I just crash here. I got a cabin on the Patuxent River in southern Maryland. That's my home. But it ain't fancy, either. I don't really care too much about houses and things. Why don't you sit down? I'll call you a cab. No way those guys know where we are. You're safe now."

"But they know where I live," Amy whimpered. "I'm pretty sure I also saw them in a car at my apartment complex. I'm afraid to go home. What am I gonna do, Mr. Hendricks?"

"It's Fred, OK? You'll be fine. If they were going to arrest you, they would've already done so. Like I said before, you haven't done anything wrong."

"Then why are they following me, Fred?"

"Good question." Could these guys be from the White House? This involved Parker, after all. Who knew what shit he'd order. If these were black-ops guys, yeah, she could be in trouble. But if they were pros, it wouldn't take them long to find her here, either.

"Listen. Don't take this the wrong way, but you can stay here if you like. You can have the bedroom. I'll sleep here on the couch."

"Oh, gee. I don't know."

"Hey, like I said, I'll call you a cab. You got some place you can go? You mentioned a cousin."

"She's out of town. Are you sure it'd be all right? I mean, you shouldn't have to sleep on the couch."

In another life, that's an opening I'd be rushing through. He smiled. "I'll be fine. I usually fall asleep on the couch anyway.

But you should do what makes you feel most comfortable. Going home might be the best thing."

"No! I can't go tonight. I'm afraid they'd snatch me in the dark. I'll go home tomorrow in the daytime."

"OK. Well, it's still early. Are you hungry? There's not much to eat here. Not sure I want to call for takeout and have to answer the door in the dark. I mean, just in case." He paused for a second. "I can microwave some popcorn."

"I love popcorn. And I'm pretty hungry."

"All right, popcorn it is. You want something to drink?" He chuckled. "Don't think I can rustle up a Negroni, but I got cold beer and some Maker's Mark bourbon. That's about it. Oh, and tap water, of course."

"Maybe a beer. I'm still a little shaky. It might help calm me down."

"If you're looking to relax, I'd say have a boilermaker."

"What's that?"

"A beer with a shot of whiskey. Hell, I might even join you. My nerves ain't what they used to be." *Damn, like I said, another lifetime.* He stood up, bracing one arm on the couch to reduce his back pain. He walked into the kitchen area.

She followed him. "I'll try a boilermaker."

Fred poured two shot glasses full of whiskey and opened a couple bottles of Flying Dog Pale Ale. "OK, Amy, you chug the shot and then follow that real quick with a swig of beer. You'll be relaxed in no time flat." *Especially after two Negronis the way Johnny mixed them.*

She nodded, picked up the shot, and clinked his glass. She threw it back and gasped. Her eyes looked as if they'd pop out of her head.

"Beer, Amy. Drink the beer." She grabbed the bottle and drank about half in a few quick gulps. He chuckled and drained his shot.

"My gosh! You drink that stuff all the time, Fred? Straight?"

"Yeah. It's an acquired taste." He picked up his beer and took a long pull, then opened the cabinet and threw a pack of popcorn into the microwave.

"This beer's pretty good," she said.

"Yeah, not bad. They're brewing it locally these days."

Amy started to sway a little. "I think I need to sit down."

"Good idea. I'll bring the popcorn out in a minute. Make yourself comfortable. The couch ain't bad."

She plopped down right in the middle of the couch and set her beer bottle on the glass coffee table.

Fred came over and put a bowl of popcorn on the table. He sat on the arm of the couch. "What time you got to be at work in the morning?"

"Oh, I'm off till Sunday at O-seven-hundred. Then we're on duty till we're done, which probably means sometime Monday." Her arms flapped around as she spoke.

"Lucky you, I guess. I got to brief the chairman on this stuff tomorrow morning, and then we'll meet with the House leaders. Hopefully for the last time. Think we're going to finish the bill tomorrow. Then it's just getting the staff to finalize the paperwork and giving the House subcommittee members time for a quick review. Then we'll post the final bill online. But it'll make for a very long day tomorrow."

He glanced over at Amy. She was starting to list left. *Oh shit.* Maybe that boilermaker wasn't such a good idea. "Hey, you feeling OK?"

Amy tried to sit up straight. "I think I need to lie down."

"I'll give you a hand." Fred stood up. Amy tried to stand and fell backward onto the couch.

"Whoops." She giggled. "OK. Here we go." She made another attempt and swayed a little.

Fred grabbed her by the arms. "I got you. Just put one foot in front of the other."

He led her into the bedroom and pushed the covers off one side of the bed.

"OK, turn around, Mister Fred, I got to get ready for bed." She giggled again.

He turned to the side, facing the full-length mirror on his bathroom door. *I know I shouldn't watch, but what if she loses her balance? She could hit her head on the nightstand. Then what would I do?*

Amy struggled to undo the buttons on her blouse and open the clasp in the front of her bra. She managed to wiggle out of half her clothes, dropping them to the floor. Her alabaster breasts were framed by her bronze skin, the pink nipples a shock of color.

She wobbled around to face the bed. Fred stared at her silhouette. She reached behind but couldn't quite maneuver the button at the top of her skirt.

"Can you help me? I can't get the button."

Fred undid the button and lowered the zipper on the back of her skirt. Turning around again, he watched in the mirror as she dropped her skirt on the floor. She was wearing cream-colored thong panties. Her bottom was round and shapely and as white as her breasts, a stark contrast to her tan legs. Fred took a deep breath.

She put one knee onto the bed and started to fall. Fred spun around and caught her, grabbing her rib cage right below her breasts. He helped her get her other knee on the bed and guided her toward the center.

She looked up at him and smiled. "Thanks. You're a good person, Mister Fred."

He smiled. Amy collapsed. Fred stood staring at the nearly naked girl in his bed. *My God, she's beautiful. Shit, oh dear. In another life.*

He leaned over and reached out to pull the sheet over her. She was already snoring softly. He folded her clothes and placed them neatly on a chair, then went back into the living room and ate all the popcorn.

When he finished his beer, he checked his watch. Only nine, but he had to get an early start in the morning. Might as well hit the sack. He walked into the bedroom, carrying his suit coat. Light coming from the living room spilled in.

Amy had rolled over onto her back. Her panties had gotten twisted, and Fred could see curly, reddish-brown hair peeking out. He couldn't help but stare for a moment. *Oh, Lordy.*

He opened the closet door, took off his tie, belt, and pants, and hung them up. He tossed his shirt and socks into the clothes basket on the closet floor. Then he grabbed clean clothes for the morning and carried them into the bathroom. He brushed his teeth and threw some water on his face. Stared into the mirror at the old guy looking back at him. *I know what you're thinking, grampa. Just grab the bedspread and a pillow and hit the couch.*

He walked back into the bedroom. Amy was lying on her side now, snoring a little louder.

With a sigh, he cracked open the bathroom door and switched on a light so she'd be able to find her way if she woke up.

Fred pulled the sheet over her again and grabbed the bedspread and extra pillow. He walked out and tossed them on the couch, then stopped, staring. He turned around and went into the kitchen, poured a large glass of water, grabbed a couple aspirin from the cabinet, and carried them into the bedroom.

Chapter Forty-Nine

"Mr. President? Before you leave for Camp David, I thought you should know that the air force enlisted woman was followed to a bar near the Capitol this evening." Simpson walked quickly across the White House lawn, following after the president.

Parker was ignoring him. The president quickened his pace toward the Marine One helicopter.

Simpson continued, "Army Counterintelligence says she met with Fred Hendricks. Do you remember him?"

Parker shrugged and shook his head but didn't turn around.

"I knew him a little when you were on the Hill. He's the staff director on Jackson's defense subcommittee."

"What the fuck? That bitch can't shut up."

Simpson chewed his bottom lip. "It might actually be a little worse. Hendricks has been working on appropriations for a long time. But get this, sir. He worked for the Democrats."

"You said Jackson. Did you mean Liz Boyer?"

"No, sir, that's just it. Jackson hired him to run the subcommittee staff this year."

Parker stopped, twirled around, and screamed, "We've got a Democratic staffer running the Republican defense subcommittee? Why would Jacobs go along with that? This proves what I've said all along. Jackson's a fucking traitor. Not just to me, but to the entire Republican Party. Jacobs needs to get a new chairman."

"Yes, sir." Simpson caught up to the president. "Not much we can do about that. But I think we've got a real problem here. First, the gal meets with the staffer who handles intel. Now she's meeting with that guy's boss. That's all probably being done so they can brief the chairman. Jackson's bill is in conference right now. Sir, my bet is he's gonna fuck you."

"How can he, Steve? The election's in three days. Montoya will be elected before he gets his bill done. And I'd veto that bill anyway."

"Practically speaking, if the Democratic-controlled House and the Republican-controlled Senate approve it, you can't veto it."

"I'm the fucking president, I sure as shit can." Parker continued toward the helo again, with Simpson trailing him.

"Not a bipartisan defense appropriations bill. What would you say? They wanted to stop you from interfering in foreign elections. You'd cripple your reelection chances. No, sir, if we can't stop Jackson from putting a ban in, your hands are tied."

"But the election will be over already. She'll be toast. Burnt to a crisp. We win. Besides, if this gets out, my base will still support me. She nationalized a fucking American company. She deserves to go down."

"Well, your base, maybe," Simpson said firmly, "but that's not enough for you to win next year."

"OK, where's the talkative bitch? Tell McNeal to pick her up and scare some sense into her. Make her take it back. She needs to tell the staffer she made the whole thing up."

"Problem, sir. The army lost her. She left a bar with Hendricks, and they lost her."

Parker stopped just outside the helo. He bellowed, "Jesus Christ, Steve! Isn't there anyone in this fucking government that can do something right? This is McNeal's fault. Tell him to fix it tonight! God damn it. I'm fucking going to Camp David, and I'll expect a report in the morning that you've fixed this shit."

"Yes, sir. I'll do my best."

"Not your best, Simpson." He climbed aboard Marine One. "Fix it."

Chapter Fifty

Amy opened and closed one eye. Her mind picked out a strange dresser and chair in the semi-dark room. *What? Where am I? Oh, my head.* She opened both eyes.

Light streamed in from the bathroom. The door to the bedroom was closed. *Oh, yeah. Fred's place.* They'd had boilermakers.

She spotted her clothes folded on the chair. *Oh shit. What happened?* She jerked herself up on one elbow. The pain in her head exploded.

A piece of paper, folded in half, was sitting on the nightstand, next to a large glass of water and two little white pills. She grabbed the paper. The pounding in her head made it tough to focus, but she forced herself to read:

> *Amy, I had to go to work. I'm guessing the best thing for you now is my antidote for a hangover: take the aspirins, drink the water, and try to go back to sleep. In a half hour, you'll start to feel a little better.*
>
> *If you're worried about your clothes, don't. Nothing happened. You got undressed and into bed on your own. Like I told you last night, the couch was fine for me.*

There's not much to eat and no coffee. Sorry. But you're free to stay as long as you need. Just pull the front door shut when you leave. It locks.

And I don't think you need to worry too much about the guys following you. If they wanted to arrest you, they probably would have already.

But if something comes up and you need to reach me, my email address is on the bottom of this note. I've got a real busy day, so I probably won't get time to check it until late tonight.

You're a sweet kid, Amy. And brave. Thanks for letting us know about the election rigging. Don't worry. We'll stop it.

Fred

Amy put the note back on the nightstand. *That's so nice of him.* She groaned. *But my head's killing me. Guess I should take his advice. With that stuff he drinks, he's probably got a lot of experience with hangovers.*

She tossed the pills in her mouth and took a big sip of water. *Oh, that tastes good.* She lifted the glass and drained it, then lay down and drifted back to sleep.

Chapter Fifty-One

"Mr. Chairman," Fred said with a smile, "thanks for coming over to our vault this morning. We got you coffee. Hopefully, that'll make this a little less painful."

Jackson harrumphed, took a seat at the table, and had a large sip. "Alright, Fred. What's so important you needed to see me at eight thirty?" He looked at the other staffer in the vault as if trying to remember who he was.

"Sir, it's the only time Betsy said I could get on your calendar before the big four's meeting at two this afternoon. Let me reintroduce you to Roy Peterson—he covers the NSA for you. We've had a very disturbing development in the election-rigging controversy. I want Roy to explain it to you." Fred sat next to Roy, across from Chairman Jackson, and motioned for Roy to begin.

"Yes, sir." Roy bobbed his head. "Good morning, Mr. Chairman. At Fred's request, following the flap on the intel bill, I visited Fort Meade and confirmed that the NSA had been planning to test a new offensive cyber weapon to influence elections. The test included a real-world intrusion into the election in Mauritania."

"Why the hell are they doing that?" Jackson grumbled.

"NSA leadership, specifically the deputy, Army General

McNeal, felt that the only way they would know for sure if this new tool worked was to actually use it. They chose Mauritania because of its limited ability to detect an intrusion into their elections and because it—"

"But why are we interfering at all?" Jackson barked.

"Sir, after the last election, Intelligence Committee Chairman Schmidt demanded that the administration develop the means to attack Russia's elections, as it's believed Russia attempted to do to us."

"They did attack us. I think that's why we lost," Jackson snapped.

"Yes, sir. But—"

"Roy"—Fred placed his hand on Roy's forearm—"let's skip to where we are now. The chairman doesn't have a lot of time."

"Yes, sir. With the provision in the intel bill, like in our bill— your bill, sir"—Roy corrected himself—"the NSA cancelled its planned attack on Mauritania."

"So we should drop the provision. That's gonna piss Liz off. Jesus, what a mess," Jackson grumbled.

"Sir, it's worse," Fred said. "What Roy found out is that Parker plans to test out the capability against Bolivia instead."

"What?" Jackson scowled at Roy. "He can't do that. We passed a law."

"It's not a law yet," Fred said slowly. "But more importantly, the bill's language only precludes NSA from carrying out the attack. They're gonna have the army do it."

"The army? They're not allowed to do that stuff. Are they?" The chairman raised his eyebrows.

Fred nodded. "Roy has a source inside the Army Intelligence Command, INSCOM. They've been directed to hack Bolivia's presidential election on Sunday."

Roy's lips tightened. "I was approached by an air force technical sergeant two weeks ago. She gave me the whole story. At Fred's suggestion, I went back and verified that she's legitimate—not some crazy conspiracy theorist. She's been working for NSA for more than a decade and is now assigned to Fort Belvoir in an offensive cyberwarfare cell. They're the ones who'd do this, if the army was tasked."

"So Parker wants to mess with Bolivia. Why Bolivia? And why the army?" Jackson sneered.

Fred turned to Roy. "Thanks, Roy. I need to speak to the chairman alone now." After Roy stood up and left, Fred continued, "Sir, the army's being tasked under a new counter-narcotics finding from the Director of National Intelligence to go after Bolivia's president, Simona Corazon, for narco-trafficking. That would, in theory, give them the legal authority to interfere in the upcoming election."

"There are lots of countries where corrupt government officials are probably involved in drug dealing." Jackson leaned forward. "Why target her?"

"I can't say, sir. But she recently nationalized the holdings of Edison Electric in Bolivia. And you know, sir, Hans Edison did support Parker in the last election."

"So that's it. Shit, Fred. We can't let him do this."

"Yes, sir. I completely agree."

"How do we stop it?"

"I suggest, when you meet with your colleagues this afternoon, you tell them all about it. Convince them to put language in the conference report that bans anyone in the US government from interfering in a foreign election. Not just the NSA."

"Whoa. Are you sure?"

"Sir, I met with this sergeant, Amy Anderson, last night. She seems quite sincere. Roy's verified her credentials. We were at Union Station, and she pointed out two guys who were following her. They looked like former military. Could be special-ops guys. That would probably mean White House involvement.

"I walked her out of the station. Sure enough, one of 'em followed us. Sir, this is pretty serious."

"And you think Parker's involved?"

"Can't see any other way that a new finding would come out right now accusing Bolivia of running drugs."

"Jacobs talked to Parker. He denied running a test in Africa."

"From what I hear, but *not* Bolivia." Fred paused, sensing Jackson's apprehension. "Look at it this way. Let's say we put the provision in. Appropriations bills are only in effect for a year. So if we pass the bill and the president signs it, Parker won't be able to interfere in any elections for a year. If the intelligence community thinks it's so important for them to conduct a real test, they can come before Congress next year and explain why."

"I don't know, Fred." Jackson sighed. "I mean, everything you're saying makes sense. But you heard Mannington at markup. He didn't want to tie Parker's hands with the NSA. This would be everybody." He shook his head. "Jesus Christ. This really is a mess. I gotta talk to Jacobs."

"Understood. But you're probably gonna finish the bill when you meet with Chairman Jones and the others at 2:00. There's only three issues left. This one, the bailout of Charlie Harkins's shipyard, and cigarette sales on bases."

"Christ, what a lineup. We can't agree to cigarettes or Lackland and Colbert will lynch us. Liz is gonna go crazy, and Jones is gonna insist on having it. Bailing out that shipyard is flat-out wrong. But how we gonna convince the House of that? And this turd is gonna explode in our face no matter what we do. Remind me why I wanted to be chairman again?"

"Yes, sir. We just left you the easy ones." Fred grinned.

"Yeah, thanks a lot, friend. But, seriously, you've done a great job. There must've been a thousand issues out there. You solved most of them in a week."

"Not me, sir, your staff. And the House staff too. They're pros, sir. They know their stuff, and they get it done. Just like you wanted."

"Well, we owe you. And despite what you're saying, I know the staff wouldn't have gotten it done without your leadership."

"Thank you, sir."

Chapter Fifty-Two

Harris Ward stood on the gray-green marble floor in the hallway of the Dirksen Senate Office Building, outside the defense sub-committee's offices. It was early, but he figured he'd better get a jump on the day, especially after missing the morning deadline for the day's printed version. Sara was furious and had demanded he post a story online by noon.

It was 9:00 a.m., and he still didn't have anything.

One of them had to be coming to work soon. Two youngish women headed his way. The first was a little chubby, with light-brown hair. She looked familiar, and the way she reacted when she saw him made him pretty sure she knew who he was. He smiled as she approached. "Roxy?"

She snorted. "You got the wrong gal, pal. That's her back there." She pointed her thumb over her shoulder and opened the locked office door. Harris thanked her as she disappeared into the subcommittee's suite of offices.

"Good morning. I'm Harris Ward from *Roll Call*. Are you Roxy?" Harris smiled as the thin woman approached.

Roxy stopped, a shocked expression on her face. She cleared her throat and nodded. "Yes?" Her eyes darted back and forth.

"Listen. Can I ask you a few questions about conference?"

"We can't talk about conference until it's over. We're not done," she snapped at him, then continued walking toward the subcommittee offices.

"From what I hear, you're getting close. Can you tell me what's not done yet?"

"No. Can't talk about it." She reached the locked door and searched her pockets for her key.

"I understand you work on shipbuilding projects. Did the conferees close the Charleston Marine bailout provision?"

"I'm sorry. I can't talk about it." She couldn't find her key and knocked on the door.

"I heard you got into a fight with Congressman Harkins. Can you talk about that?"

She spun toward Harris, eyes wide. "I don't know who told you that, but it's not true." Her voice rose with each word.

"Congressman Harkins didn't blame you for his problems with the navy? So, my source was wrong? Is it also not true that Chairman Jackson called Harkins after the meeting to tell him he'd give him his bailout?"

He was fishing here. But maybe she'd bite. From the look on her face, it was pretty clear he was right about Harkins's accusation.

Roxy opened her mouth. Out of the corner of his eye, Harris saw a door open down the hallway, by the vault. Chairman Jackson came out and started walking away from them.

Holy cow. What was he doing here this early? And coming from the subcommittee's secure meeting room? Fred Hendricks stood in the doorway, so it was a good bet their conversation was about elections.

"Mr. Chairman!" Harris hollered down the hall. He thanked Roxy quickly and jogged toward the chairman. "Senator Jackson!"

Jackson stopped and looked around.

Harris caught up to him. "Good morning, sir. Harris Ward from *Roll Call*. Can I ask you a couple questions?"

"I'm late for an appointment," Jackson growled, frowning.

"I'll walk with you as I talk. Has the House agreed to the Senate's provision on election rigging?"

"Haven't decided."

"Is that why you were meeting with Fred Hendricks this morning?"

Jackson's head jerked noticeably. He turned toward the reporter. "Listen, Ward. I don't have time to chat right now. The issue's open."

"But why? I don't understand why the House Democrats wouldn't just accept it. Is the White House pressuring you to drop it?"

Jackson gave him a quizzical look and quickened his pace. Harris matched the chairman's tempo. He was pretty fast for an old guy.

"Senator, why would the White House have a problem with the provision? Jacobs said President Parker denied he was rigging elections."

"Listen, Ward. There's more to this than meets the eye. Besides, it's classified. I've got nothing else to say. You'll know soon enough."

Chapter Fifty-Three

Amy's head still ached, but not as badly as before. Her mouth was dry, so she lifted the empty water glass to her lips in hopes of getting an elusive drop or two. Nothing. She groaned. *I gotta get out of bed. Wonder what time it is?*

She got up, covering her naked breasts with one forearm and hand, and stuck her head out the bedroom door. "Fred? Hello? Anyone here?"

She closed the door and started to get dressed in clothes she didn't remember taking off. But Fred's note said nothing had happened. She rubbed her cheeks. Her face wasn't raw as if it had been scratched by a guy's stubble, and she wasn't sore like she'd made love. Seemed he was telling the truth. Thank God.

Amy walked into the living room. A bedspread and pillow sat on opposite ends of the couch, and the pillow had a clear indentation in it, like someone had slept on it. *What a relief.*

Filtered sunlight streamed through a small, curtained window over the kitchen door, highlighting a glass in the sink. She filled it with water and drank it down. The least she could do was wash the glass to thank him for rescuing her.

She searched under the sink for dish soap and spotted the popcorn bag in the trash. Oh yeah, he said he'd make popcorn.

That was the last thing she remembered. *God, I'm hungry.*

Amy placed the clean glass on a paper towel on the countertop to dry. OK. Time to go.

Taking a deep breath, she opened the front door an inch. She peeked out and up the three stairs toward the street. A white sedan was parked half a block away, with two guys in it facing the apartment. Oh shoot. Those had to be the same guys. She looked the other way. A man was sitting in a black Suburban down the block on the other side of the street.

Jiminy Christmas. They're everywhere. Her hands started to shake as she eased the door shut. What was she gonna do? Wait. The kitchen door.

She ran to the kitchen and peeked through the curtain. It was hard to see if anyone was up the stairs outside. But she could make out a small parking lot. At least no cars were there. She'd have to sneak out and hope that they weren't waiting there too. The lock looked the same as the one on the front door. It'd probably lock if she closed it, like Fred had said.

Christ. Well, they knew she was here, so she couldn't stay. Fred said they wouldn't arrest her. But there were two cars now, so she wasn't sure. They probably had someone posted at her apartment too. Where was her purse? She found it on a chair in the living room and pulled out her phone.

Wait a second. Maybe that's how they'd found her. She'd leave it here. That would give her a head start. But she only had $150. She'd need more cash.

Crap. Looked like she was going back to Union Station.

Chapter Fifty-Four

Harris sat on an overstuffed chair in one corner of the Senate press gallery, cradling his laptop. The other seats on the matching couch and chairs were empty. Only a couple of the office staff roamed around. The Senate wasn't coming into session for another hour. *Wonder what Jackson meant when he said I'd know soon enough? I still don't have a story. Sara's gonna kill me.*

His cell phone buzzed in his pocket, and he pulled it out. "Hello?"

"Ward?"

"Yeah, who's this?"

"Max Welsh, from the Bureau."

"Mr. Welsh. What a pleasant surprise. What's up?"

"I probably shouldn't be talking to you, but what the hell." His voice came out as a growl. "Remember that NSA election thing?"

"Yeah. You said you didn't know anything about it." Harris dropped his laptop on the chair. He stepped into one of the gallery's anachronistic phone booths and shut the folding glass doors.

"I didn't. But we got tasked by the White House real late last night to find a female sergeant who'd gone missing."

"What's that got to do with the NSA and elections?"

"Well, the army's got some guys sitting on her. They told me she's suspected of leaking classified info about election rigging. So I thought of you."

"She works for the NSA?"

"No, that's just it. She's at Belvoir, assigned to INSCOM—ya know, the Army Intelligence Command. She works for General McNeal. He runs INSCOM, but he's also deputy at NSA. But the thing is"—Welsh lowered his voice—"the army guys said she's been meeting Senate staff. And I tracked her phone to a town house on Capitol Hill a couple hours ago. Get this. It belongs to a Senate staffer named Fred Hendricks."

Holy cow! So that's what the chairman was being briefed on. "That's very interesting." Harris struggled to keep his voice calm. "But what's INSCOM got to do with the NSA rigging elections?"

"Hell if I know. But I figured I'd give you a call, since she was meeting with a staffer and knows something about election rigging. I'll probably get my ass handed to me. But these bastards haven't done me any favors. Listen. Try and keep my name and the FBI out of it this time."

"Yeah, sure, and thanks for the tip." *I got to find Fred Hendricks or Chairman Jackson. This is getting hot. But first I'm going to take another look at that election-rigging provision.*

Chapter Fifty-Five

Amy grabbed a black ball cap from the closet shelf and crammed her red curls under it, pulling it low. *I hope Fred doesn't mind.* It wasn't much of a disguise, but at least her bright-red hair wouldn't show.

She took a deep breath and eased the back door open, checking the parking area once again. Still no cars. She closed the door warily until she heard the lock click, then hunched over and crept up the back steps. No turning back now. She looked both ways and saw no one. Heading to the left, toward Union Station, she kept a brisk pace down the alley. As she neared Second Street, she faced a gaping open space between the corner of the town house on the alley and the tall office building across the street. No shrubs or trees to hide behind. *Here goes nothing.*

She walked right across the street, staring straight ahead, not daring to look behind. A peek at the reflecting-glass walls of the office building showed no one following her. All clear.

In less than three minutes, she'd made it to Union Station. First stop, new clothes. Then that hair salon she'd noticed last night. She checked out each of the stores she passed between the side entrance to the station and the women's clothing shop. Sunglasses there, backpack there, new phone at that kiosk. That should do it.

At the clothing store, she tried on a light-blue blouse, black denim slacks, and flats that all miraculously fit. She carried them out to the service desk. "Hi. Could you hold these for me for an hour? I'm late for a hair appointment, and I need to find an ATM machine for cash. Is there one around?" She gave the sales clerk a big smile. The clerk gave her directions to an ATM and agreed to hold the items.

OK. Hair. She walked into the Gorgeous One Salon and smiled at the skinny middle-aged man behind the counter. "Hi. I don't have an appointment, but I'd like to get my hair cut. Would someone be able to help me?"

Without raising his head, he gazed at her through lowered eyebrows. "So you think you can just dance into my *salon* and we drop everything? Maybe you should go to the *barbershop* down the street." A thick, foreign accent accompanied his persnickety tone.

Amy lost her smile. Her eyes widened and started to fill with tears. "I'm sorry. That's not what I think at all. But I need to get my hair cut. Now. Please, isn't there someone who can help me? I promise it won't take long." She wiped a tear from her cheek.

"Our stylists are very busy."

"But I need help. Some men are chasing me." She sobbed as she spoke, unable to control her pent-up emotions any longer.

"Please, *mademoiselle*, don't cry. But we are very busy."

"I have nowhere else to turn. They might be outside right now. There were two cars parked outside with men in them waiting for me when I left the apartment this morning. They've been following me for days. I had to sneak out the back door. I need help." The tears were flowing uncontrollably now.

"*D'accord*. Um, OK. Stop the tears. *Moi*, I, Guillaume, will cut your hair." He looked up, staring at her hair. "But I'm not sure what good it will do. Your color is very distinct. *Et, très jolie.* Um, very pretty." He offered a kind smile. "Come with me. I must be quick."

She followed him back into the salon. He motioned for her to sit at the sink. "No time to change. I will wrap a towel around the neck."

"Do you have time to dye my hair?"

"Color it? *Non, chérie.* That would be wrong."

"But it's too noticeable. You said so yourself."

"*Oui. D'accord.* I will put on a rinse. Which color? I think black."

"Maybe brunette?" Amy suggested.

"No, must be black. Now, sit. There is no time for chit or chat." He turned on the water.

◆ ◆ ◆

Amy looked in the mirror. Her curls were only a half-inch long, and they were black. *Oh my God.* Tears welled up.

"Please, *ange*, do not cry. It will grow." He gave her a small smile and patted her shoulder.

She nodded at the dark-haired girl staring back and took a deep breath.

"Now, follow me out," Guillaume demanded.

Amy pulled a credit card out of her purse. "You've really helped me, but could you please, please, please do me another favor? Can you wait while I get cash from the ATM machine around the corner? I don't want to charge anything in case these men can track my credit card. I don't want them to know I came here. Here, you can hold onto my card." Her hand shook as she handed it to him. "It will only take me a minute. Please?"

He sighed. "*D'accord, ange.* But hurry"—he looked at the credit card—"Miss Amy Anderson. I have a client coming any minute."

She hugged him. "Is there a back door?"

He rolled his eyes, shook his head in resignation, and pointed her in the right direction. She ran out the door.

Once she used the debit card, she might only have a few minutes before they came looking for her. She'd have to be quick.

She checked her balance and withdrew one thousand dollars—the bank limit and nearly her entire life savings. She ran to the salon and paid Guillaume in cash.

"*Bon chance*, Amy." He waved.

She blew him a kiss as she ran out the door. Then she was off to pick up the new outfit. She changed into her new clothes, hurried to the phone kiosk, and purchased a burner phone. Fifteen minutes later, she ran to the sporting goods store and grabbed a black backpack and a pair of oversized sunglasses that covered nearly half her face.

Pulling on Fred's black cap, she rushed over to the Travelers Aid desk and asked if there were any youth hostels nearby. Maybe she could pay cash there. She'd already spent more than four hundred dollars. They suggested a place about two miles away on Pennsylvania Avenue. She'd walk.

As she turned to leave, she saw several men in dark suits standing near the exits. Oh boy. They'd called in reinforcements. This was getting serious. Hopefully, she'd done enough to fool them. They couldn't check every tourist exiting the station.

With her head held high, she walked straight through Union

Station and to the front door. Glancing to the side, she spied a man in a dark suit standing near the doorway. He was looking at two pictures of a young woman with red hair. In the first, the girl was wearing an air force uniform. In the other, she sat at a bar wearing a green blouse and white skirt. Amy shivered as she recognized herself in the photos but forced herself to appear relaxed.

Doesn't look a thing like me. She smiled a sheepish grin and walked through the large doors and out into the hot, humid DC sunshine.

Chapter Fifty-Six

The four elected officials huddled at one corner of the table box in H-140, in the Capitol. Jeff and Fred sat against the wall behind Boyer and Jackson. The two House staffers, Al Kittenger and Jennifer Burns, stood behind their bosses. No one else was in the room.

"So, that's the whole story." Jackson frowned and looked first at Chairman Jones and then at Chalmers, the ranking minority.

"And you're sure about this, Sam?" Chalmers's body was visibly twitching, as if he were a squirrel facing a big old tomcat. Jones sat with a shit-eating grin. Boyer scowled, probably still pissed that Jackson had thrown her staffer, Marjory, out of the room. This discussion was classified at a level Marjory wasn't cleared for.

"'Fraid so, Larry. My guys verified that NSA was planning to attack . . ." He looked back at Fred. "Who was it again in Africa?"

"Mauritania, sir."

"Right, but Kaye Schmidt's amendment on intel smoked them out. They cancelled it. So they turned to the army and Bolivia."

"And this guy, Edison, his factory," Chairman Jones snapped. "You think that's why Parker's doing this?"

"Can't say for sure, Mr. Chairman. That's the best we can

figure. But we know Bolivia's election is Sunday. Unless we do something, the army will make sure the incumbent president isn't reelected."

"Now ain't that the damnedest thing." Jones shook his head while tapping his cane against the table.

"Then we're all agreed?" Jackson looked around.

Jones beamed. Chalmers grimaced. Boyer glared at Jackson.

"Good. Now, Woody," Jackson said, "you know Liz and I are with you on cigarettes, but we can't accept the House provision."

"I knew it." Liz Boyer slammed an open hand on the table. "You promised me we'd take the House provision."

"That's before you had the stupidity to bring it up on the Senate floor, Liz, and got your ass handed to you. No way we can take it now." Jackson sneered at his minority colleague.

Chairman Jones pounded his cane on the carpeted floor. "That's all well and good, Senator, but I'm afraid the House is gonna insist on our provision."

"You can insist all you want. But if Liz and I take this back, we won't get ten senators to sign the conference report. The bill's dead."

"And how would you know that, Senator?" Jones asked, raising his eyebrows. "Did you poll your conferees?"

"Don't need to, Mr. Chairman. Colbert and Lackland both want this killed. Big Tobacco isn't happy about the provision. It won't play well in either Virginia or Carolina. My guys have told me they won't sign. Without Lackland's support, we won't have a majority of Senate conferees. You probably weren't watching the Senate when Liz raised this issue. But let me tell you this—once Lackland and Colbert put the word out they were gonna kill this provision, no one came to her defense. Isn't that right, Liz?"

"There's some truth to that," Boyer muttered just loudly enough for the others to hear.

"So, it's up to you, Mr. Chairman," Jackson said evenly. "You want a bill? This provision's gotta come out. Besides, I can't go back to my fellow Republicans and tie the president's hands on elections *and* screw Big Tobacco. They'll run me out of the Senate. And I'm sure you got at least a dozen Republican colleagues, Larry, who feel the same way about cigarettes."

"I knew you'd betray me, you bastard," Boyer spat.

"Hell, Liz, think what you want. But I'm saving your job. You know as well as I do, if this provision goes in, Lackland's gonna strip you of your position on defense." He shot her a sly grin. "You should be thanking me." He turned back toward Chairman Jones.

"So, what's it gonna be, Mr. Chairman? You recede on the provision, or we call the conference quits?"

Jones looked down at his notes. "Hmmph. Let me see. Whadya think about Charlie's shipyard? The navy is screwing with him. They need that seventy-five million to fix the yard."

"C'mon, Woody, you know as well as I do that Charlie's looking for a bailout. FEMA already gave them thirty-five million. We go along with this and we'll be bailing out big defense companies every time they lose money on a contract. We don't wanna do this. Do we? Larry? Liz?"

"For once, my chairman is right." She frowned at the others. "No, we don't want to do this. It's outrageous. Those bastards are trying to steal us blind. Might as well pull the Brinks truck up and start loading the gold right out of Fort Knox."

"Now, wait a second, Liz." Chalmers's head bobbed with each word. "Charleston Marine's a fine shipyard. That storm set them back ten years. They're losing their shirts. Charlie's right: the navy's screwing them. We should do this. Aren't I right, Woody?"

"The way I see it"—Chairman Jones pounded his cane—"you senators want the House to recede on every damn provision in this conference." He waved his free hand at the two senators. "Now, that just ain't fair. Like the navy ain't being fair to Charlie's folks." He slapped the table with his open hand.

Jackson raised his hands in surrender. "OK. How about this? We put the seventy-five million in the bill, only for Charleston Marine."

"What? You're gonna cave on this outrage, Jackson?" Liz Boyer blasted.

"Just listen," Jackson growled back. He paused for a second, staring at his Senate colleague. "We put the money in. We say it can only be used for the shipyard—"

"Outrageous!" Liz hollered.

Jackson raised his hand to the side, his palm up, as if signaling her to stop. He kept his attention on Chairman Jones. "Like I said—the money goes in, but we leave it up to the Navy Secretary to decide if he'll spend it."

"What good does that do, Sam?" Chalmers pleaded.

Jackson looked at each of his colleagues in turn. "We put the money in. The only thing they can spend it on is Charleston Marine. But the Secretary doesn't have to spend it."

That did it. Liz Boyer had had enough.

These old farts were about to give millions of dollars away. She couldn't take any more of this baloney.

"Of all the stupid ideas." Liz nearly spat in Jackson's direction. "We waste seventy-five million because you three don't have the balls to tell Charlie Harkins to go to hell."

"Now, that's enough, Senator Boyer." Jones slammed his hand on the table again. "Why are you being such a bitch, Elizabeth? Your chairman's just trying to do what's right for the Senate."

Boyer leaned back from the table. Her anger faded, overtaken by the shock of such harsh words from Chairman Jones, her old friend and mentor. She swallowed.

"If it's OK with Larry, the House can accept the Senate's offer." Jones looked at Boyer sternly, then focused on his House colleague.

"Really, Mr. Chairman?" Chalmers moaned. "You're going to tell Charlie no?"

"It's not *no*, Larry," Jackson argued. "We're putting the money in. If Charlie, or you, or Woody can convince the navy to spend the money, Charlie gets it. He can go back to his shipyard and tell them the money's in the bill. Let's just put a little burden on the shipyard to prove they deserve more funds. And look at it this way. The navy can either invest seventy-five million in this shipyard, which will help them build navy ships, or say no. Then the money goes back to the Treasury. So we're not wasting it, Liz." He paused. "It's a good offer, Larry. Take it."

Chalmers looked at Jones, who nodded, and then back at Jackson. "I got to say, Senator, you drive a hard bargain."

Liz Boyer watched the interplay. She was feeling a new emotion, and she struggled to interpret it. It wasn't anger. It wasn't the shock of being upbraided. It wasn't even resignation.

It was as if the light bulb had finally gone on. Jackson had played this perfectly. He was right. They couldn't accept the cigarette ban. Lackland would kill her. Jackson had given the House a provision to bail out a shipyard, but the burden to resolve the issue was on the shipyard and the navy. And he had shocked them all with the outright ban on election rigging. She let out a big sigh.

Jackson looked over at her with a quizzical expression. She returned a thin smile.

"So, Mr. Chairman, I think we're done." Jackson looked around. No one objected. "Then, one last thing. No one should be talking to anyone about any of this, but particularly this election provision." He leaned in toward his colleagues. "Listen, I have to tell Jacobs. So, this is what I'm going to tell him." He leaned closer to Jones and Chalmers and whispered. Boyer craned her neck to hear.

Chapter Fifty-Seven

"First, I want to say, great job, everybody." Fred acknowledged each staff member, one by one, with a nod. "Jackson's pleased. I told him you're all pros. That's why it went so smoothly. Where are we on the Statement of the Managers, Roxy? Oh, and for your information, Judy, we call the report language that explains what's in the bill 'the statement.' The bill itself is called a 'conference report.'"

Judy smiled at him and nodded. She sat in her usual spot on the couch, between Roy and Bernie.

"The House has sent the final version over." Roxy surveyed the group sitting in Fred's office. "We've reviewed it and are about ready to send it back."

"Yeah," Fred added, "about those last provisions, if anyone asks about them, just say you don't know. Or tell them they have to wait till the conference report comes out. Jackson and the other members agreed we're not to talk about them." He looked around the room. "To anyone."

"Then we're done," Roxy piped up. "What about the conference report? We sent it to them a couple hours ago. And the final changes went in within the last ten minutes."

"Al told me they're doing a final review now. He said they'd be ready to read it out beginning around six thirty tonight. So that gives us a little more than an hour. Get something to eat. Call your families. Tell 'em it's gonna be a long night. My guess is Al will want to read every word, being as how we put the paperwork together so fast."

A collective groan went up from the staff.

"Hey." Fred held up a hand. "We're writing law tonight. We can't make mistakes. The best thing we can do is all sit around that table and read every last word. Once it gets filed, screwups can't be changed without another act of Congress."

"So, what's the plan on going final?" Roxy looked at the boss.

"It's gonna take us at least eight hours to read, maybe longer. Best case, we finish by 4:00 a.m. Their subcommittee members get a little time to review it in the morning." Fred took a breath. "So, it oughta be posted on the House website by two or so tomorrow afternoon. My guess is they'll take it up on Tuesday when the House is back in session. We should follow right after them."

Fred glanced around the room. He saw a lot of bloodshot eyes with bags under them. "Listen, I already said this, but you've all done great. I mean it. The chairman's quite pleased. This conference, with all its strange blowups and crazy provisions, has been wild. Twenty-four hours from now, we'll be sitting here drinking champagne and retelling conference stories. But we gotta bust through one more night." He paused and tapped his desk with both hands. "OK. I got a quick errand to run. I'll be back in forty-five minutes or so. In the meantime, grab some caffeine and get yourselves ready for a long night."

Fred stepped into Schneider's liquor store three blocks from his apartment. He asked the attendant, "What do I need to make a Negroni?"

"Good gin, Campari, and decent sweet vermouth. And an orange peel if you got one."

"Thanks."

Fred collected the booze and headed to his apartment. *This is silly. I mean, I can't imagine she's still there, and if she is, the last thing she probably wants is another drink. But at least she'll see I made an attempt to make her feel welcome.*

As he approached the apartment, he scanned the street for any occupied vehicles. There were none. He opened the door, a touch of enthusiasm in his voice.

"Hello? Anybody here?" He looked around. His shoulders sagged. No one was there. *So how silly do you feel now?*

He placed the booze on the kitchen counter, saw the washed glass, and smiled. But her phone sat on the counter. She forgot her phone? Most people her age never even put them down.

Or maybe she'd left it on purpose. She was a techie, after all. Perhaps she thought they'd tracked her here. But Fred hadn't seen any sign of them. Whatever. She was gone. Dollars to doughnuts, she'd be coming back at some point. No way she'd leave her phone here forever. He perked up a little.

Maybe the Negroni fixins were a good idea after all. He looked at his watch. Shit. He had to go. No way he could be late for readout.

Chapter Fifty-Eight

Harris Ward was camped out at the entrance to H-140 in the Capitol. He'd gotten a tip that conference had ended. The professional staff of the House and Senate defense subcommittees would review the final text of the conference agreement here later that evening.

He'd spent the day trying to track down Chairman Jackson with no luck. He finally walked over to the House side of the Capitol, hoping to get someone to talk to him. None of the staff would tell him anything.

He let out a long sigh, but it didn't tamp down his anger and frustration. He contemplated pulling up the story on the undemocratic process that he'd drafted a few days before and adding a blast against the staff for their collective lack of cooperation. But he knew that would only make matters worse in the long run, drying up tips on appropriations even more. Besides, the real catch was Fred Hendricks. Where the hell was he?

A gaggle of staffers rushed down the hallway from the Senate side of the Capitol. Roxy and the other girl he'd talked to that morning were among them. Roxy glared at him, while the other girl smiled. He approached them and looked around. Fred

Hendricks wasn't with them. Weird. "Can anyone tell me where I might find Fred Hendricks?"

The staff laughed. Harris was dumbfounded as they shuffled past.

Roxy's colleague twirled around, walking backward. "We're all wondering the same thing, Mr. *Roll Call*."

"Where's Fred? Where's Fred?" Roxy squealed in a high-pitched voice, sounding a lot like the committee's Republican staff director. The staff howled.

"Now what?" Fred Hendricks growled as he approached from the other direction, the elevator door closing behind him.

"Fred's here," a dark-haired man called out, an unmistakable hint of relief in his voice. The staff waited outside the door to H-140, looking in Fred's direction.

"We were starting to worry, boss." Roxy took a couple steps toward Fred.

Harris Ward said, "Fred, I need to speak with you. It's very important."

"No time, Harris. We're a little late for readout. Besides, we're under strict orders not to talk about conference."

That does it. They've ignored me all day. Not one of them will talk to me. Now, they're gonna pay. "This isn't about conference."

Fred paused for a second. "What?"

"I want to know about the enlisted woman who spent last night at your house on F Street."

Roxy's eyes almost popped out of her head as her mouth fell open. The dark-haired man squinted at the boss. The other woman—the brash one—let out a loud whoop.

Fred jerked up. He looked at his staff, who were all staring at him. "OK, everyone. This doesn't concern you. Go inside and get set up. Tell Al I'll be there in a second."

He turned to Harris as the door closed behind the staff. "All right, Harris. What do you want to know?" Fred's eyes were burning, his nostrils flaring.

Oh crap. That's what I get for losing my temper. He's furious. I embarrassed him in front of his staff. Nice going, Harris. How do I get out of this mess?

"Thanks for taking time. Listen, Fred, I'm sorry about that. But I gotta get a story, and no one'll talk to me. I'm not interested in who you're sleeping with."

"I'm not sleeping with anyone, you stupid bastard. But how the hell am I gonna convince my staff of that?"

"Yeah, sorry. But I need to know why you've got an army enlisted woman staying at your place. I know it has something to do with the NSA and elections. That provision in your bill."

"What?" Fred's mouth dropped open, and he cocked his head as if feigning both ignorance and outrage.

"I got a tip from the FBI that they're following an army enlisted woman who's talking about the NSA and elections."

Fred's head tilted back, and he sneered. "Don't know anything about any army enlisted woman, Harris."

"So, you're denying that you're meeting with a female army soldier about the rigging of foreign elections."

Fred's face was stony. "You don't know what you're talking about. But, yes, I can categorically deny meeting with any army soldiers about anything having to do with elections." He paused, stared into Harris's eyes, and then continued, "You need to drop this. Take my advice. Drop it. Listen. I'm under strict orders not to talk about conference. But on deep background, I can tell you we dumped the provision banning cigarette sales on military bases. There. You got a scoop. Go write a fucking story on how the Senate wants soldiers to die of cancer. Have a good time."

"But I got a source who's telling me—"

"I don't give a damn about your source. Now, I've got ten hours of reading to do, and you're making me late. There are about twenty-five other staff you're inconveniencing. You think that's gonna help you get stories in the future?"

Fred headed into the House hearing room, leaving Harris Ward alone in the hallway.

If that don't beat all. Harris tapped his foot. *He denied it to my face. But the FBI confirmed they tracked her to his house. This is getting like Alice in Wonderland, curiouser and curiouser.*

Chapter Fifty-Nine

Amy Anderson had walked out of Union Station without anyone recognizing her. A blast of hot, moist air greeted her. Typical DC summer weather. She headed southeast on Massachusetts Avenue. Her black backpack was a furnace, causing her blouse to stick to her skin within minutes.

She stopped at a little Japanese restaurant that was open early for lunch, and refueled. Its air conditioning a welcome relief.

She had a vague notion of where she was heading—a youth hostel at Tenth and Pennsylvania SE. As she walked, her confidence grew that she'd slipped her tail. As long as she didn't link to the internet or use plastic, she hoped she'd remain unfound.

She thumbed the new phone in her back pocket, yearning to call Rachel, or anyone. Tell them what she was going through. But her resolve was strong. The phone was only in case of emergency. The only precaution she'd taken over lunch was to put Rachel on her speed dial and add Fred's email address as a contact. That way, if someone were about to apprehend her, she could blast out a note to Fred or maybe reach Rachel before they grabbed her and carried her off to some dark hole.

It was only 1:00 p.m. when she arrived at the hostel after stopping for an iced latte at a coffee shop. "Hi! I know it's early, but could I check in now?"

"Sorry, we don't open until three." The skinny young man smiled from where he stood behind the counter that bore a large welcome sign. He lowered his angular face to return to his book.

"But I don't have anywhere to go, and I'm really tired."

"Look, you can't come in. No one's allowed upstairs during the day. Sorry." He didn't smile that time before returning to his reading.

What am I gonna do now? Amy headed back out to the street. She was still recovering from her hangover, but the caffeine and Japanese food had helped. It was getting hotter, and the humidity was creeping even higher. She had to find some place to hide out until check-in.

She walked down Pennsylvania Avenue toward the Capitol, having seen a Starbucks that direction. Across the street, she spotted a public library. *Perfect. Maybe I can use a computer anonymously there.*

A blast of cool air greeted her as she opened the bright-red library door. The frigid air came as a welcome relief. Once inside, she approached the desk. "Excuse me, do you have computers people can use?"

The gray-haired African-American woman behind the desk nodded. "All you need is your library card. But I'm afraid the computers are all being used right now, dear."

"Oh, shucks. I don't think I have my library card with me, anyway. Out of curiosity, how long can people use them?"

"We have a three-hour limit, but you can check them back out if no one else is waiting."

"OK, thanks."

Amy meandered through the stacks. Her main goal was to stay out of sight and out of the Washington heat. She saw a young boy, about eight, sitting in front of a computer. But he was playing a video game on a handheld device.

"Hey, if you're not using your computer, could I borrow it for a few minutes?"

"Why don'cha get your own, lady?"

"Oh, they're all being used. Whaddya think?"

"Nuh-uh. I got to write a report on this black dude named George Washington. Something to do with peanuts. He was a carver, too."

"But you're not using it. You're playing a game."

"Yeah, but that's 'cause every time I search for him, all I get is this white guy with gray hair in a blue uniform."

"Hmm. How long does your report have to be?"

"Three paragraphs, about peanuts."

"I think you mean George Washington Carver. Tell you what. If I write your three paragraphs while you play your game, would you let me use your computer until you go home?"

"Really, you'd do that?"

"Sure. Whaddya say?"

"Go for it, lady." He motioned with his head to the computer. "But, you do my report first. Deal?"

"Deal." Amy sat down across the table from the boy. "What's your name?"

"Clarence Brown."

"OK, Clarence Brown. It'll take me about five minutes, then I get to use it, right?"

"Right."

"How do you print?"

"You just hit *print*, and it comes out by Mrs. Nelson at the front desk."

Amy logged onto Google and checked out George Washington Carver. She had three paragraphs done in no time. She read the words to Clarence. He told her to make a couple changes because he didn't know some of the words she'd used. Then "Clarence Brown" started her search.

Amy spent the rest of the afternoon with Clarence. She even learned how to play Fortnite while Clarence took a short break.

Clarence switched off the computer at five and headed home. Amy went to check in at the hostel. She told the same desk clerk that she'd lost her credit card but would pay cash. At first, he refused. But when she told him she'd pay for three nights up front and doubled the $33 rate, he agreed.

She ate dinner at a Chipotle a few blocks away. Her curiosity was ramping up. She hailed a cab outside the restaurant and had the driver take her to her apartment in northern Virginia. As they approached, she lowered her head so she could barely peek out the window. She spied a white sedan in the parking lot with two guys inside.

She told the driver she'd changed her mind and wanted him to take her back to DC. As they neared the Capitol, she had him detour past Fred's house, where she, once again, scrunched down in the seat. There were no lights on at Fred's and, to her surprise, no car with guys waiting outside. *Jiminy, I guess Fred's still working. Too bad I don't have a key. Then again, maybe not. I don't want to wear out my welcome.*

She told the driver to drop her at Tenth and Penn SE. She figured she was safe as long as she didn't go home or get on the internet under her own name. Clarence Brown wouldn't be discovered as Amy Anderson.

Chapter Sixty

"Sorry, I got to tell you this, Mr. President, but they lost her." Steve Simpson sat in his office in the White House, holding a cell phone and grimacing. His other hand pressed against his forehead.

"What the hell, Steve?" the president yelled through the phone. "How could they lose her? She's just a stupid non-com. She can't be smart enough to fool the FBI."

"The Bureau's saying she's off the grid. And since she's worked for the NSA, she probably knows exactly what to do. It looks like her phone is still at the staffer's house, but they're positive she isn't. She used a debit card at Union Station around 11:00 a.m. The FBI sent a dozen special agents there within five minutes of when the transaction posted. The agents covered every door, but she slipped away. They used facial recognition technology to check all the cameras at the train station and Metro. They're pretty sure she didn't climb aboard any trains or subway cars. She's still in DC."

"So she's on foot."

"We can't be sure. She could've taken a taxi. But we ran her photo by the taxi companies. No one reported picking up a fare at Union Station that matched her description. So yeah, their bet is she's still in the area. But even so, it's like looking for a needle in a haystack, sir."

"Jesus Christ, Steve, what do we do now?"

"So, good news is she can't do any more damage. We think it's pretty clear she knows she's being followed and is keeping a low profile. It's only a matter of time before she pops up somewhere. Besides, if she fails to report to work on Sunday, she's AWOL. Then she's in a heap of trouble. McNeal thinks she'll show up."

"Maybe we ought to forget her," Parker muttered. "By the time we find her, it'll be too late to undo the damage. Didn't you tell me the conference committee finished?"

"That's what we're hearing. We haven't approached Jackson or the other conferees directly. But word is they'll be giving us a copy of the bill sometime tomorrow."

"I don't care. We're going ahead with the test. I want my factory back."

Simpson clenched his free hand into a fist. "You might need to put a little pressure on McNeal, sir. I think the best approach is to assure him you won't sign the bill if it ties your hands."

"Tell him he better do it if he wants that fourth star."

"I'll relay the message."

"And why the hell isn't there a real golf course here? You'd think with all the money the military has they'd at least have a fucking golf course for the presidential retreat. One fucking hole. Jesus Christ. That's fucking ridiculous."

Simpson closed his eyes, sighed, and stared at his phone.

Chapter Sixty-One

The bleary-eyed staff were seated at the table where the conferees had deliberated in the preceding days. The two House clerks and a few staff members took one side. The Senate held the other. Both House and Senate staffs spilled onto the two adjacent sides in more of a hodgepodge of who sat where.

In the center on the House side, Al Kittenger read the typed-up text of the bill aloud. There were six identical copies. Three were being reviewed by House staff and three by the Senate. One member of the minority staff from each chamber had a copy. If anyone found a typo or other error, the six staffers would pencil the change in their copies.

One staffer from each chamber held a computer printout. It listed each dollar amount provided in the bill. Their job was to make sure that the numbers Al read matched the ones on the computer table.

Six other staff had copies of the Statement of the Managers, three per side. Reading aloud of the statement and conference report went back and forth by appropriation account. Careful attention was paid to the statement. But the intensity did not match the scrutiny of each letter and punctuation mark in the conference report.

On Fred's right, Jeff Leary reviewed the Senate minority copy of the conference report. Fred monitored the changes by looking over Jeff's shoulder as they were called out by Al.

To Fred's left, Roxy read the Statement of the Managers. Fred kept an eye on that as well. He also followed along on his annotated copy of the conference notes to make sure that the final bill language mirrored his own notes. That was his time-tested method of triple-checking the proceedings.

Periodically, Al would need a break. Instead of pausing, one of the other House staffers would continue reading the nearly three-hundred-page document.

By 4:00 a.m., they had completed the task. The Senate staff departed with two copies. The remaining four were for the House, including the one that would be voted on in the House and Senate and become law.

"I can't believe you do this every year." Judy yawned as she slunk along the deserted Capitol hallway with the other Senate staff.

Roxy yawned in response. "For some reason, the House is always ready to start readout late at night. But the truth is, once the members reach an agreement, they want us to get the document prepared and filed quickly, before someone tries to change it."

"What do you mean?"

"I'm too tired to explain." She looked at an openly disappointed Judy and released a big sigh. "You're here to learn. OK. Because we're defense appropriations, we're always gonna get done. Lots of bills don't have that luxury. They get hung up in the House or Senate, and have no chance of ever getting enacted. So, committee chairmen get this idea: 'Hey let's attach our bill to DoD. Then we'll skate through.'"

"That's what they mean by a *rider*, no?"

Roxy nodded. "Yeah, although nowadays the press calls all kinds of things riders." She yawned again. "Anyway, every conference somebody's got something they want to get attached. Most get kicked to the curb, but shit happens. And if that legislation is really smelly, we get tainted with their stink. Hell, even a defense appropriations bill can get bollixed up because some piece of crap gets added."

"But how could they add something?"

"Two things. First, all you need to file a completed conference agreement is for a majority of each House's conferees to sign the document. So, if you got your signatures, you're done, regardless of what's included. But most important, things get added, basically, 'cause the Speaker and the Senate majority leader say so. They want something put in or changed, ninety-nine times out of a hundred, it's going to happen."

Fred was leading the staff procession back toward their offices. He turned around to face the group. "OK. I know we've worked all night, but we're not done. Go home if you want. Take a shower. Eat breakfast. Whatever suits you. But I need you back here no later than 10:00 a.m. Be ready to answer questions from the conferees' staffers, but no one else, until we get word that the bill has been filed."

Roxy glanced at Judy, who looked like she was in disbelief. "Hey, we're done. But like I said, until the bill is filed, somebody could still try to change it."

Chapter Sixty-Two

The ringtone exploded in Fred's head, but it wasn't until the third burst that he recognized what was attacking him. Oh God. Who could be calling? His phone was sitting on the back of the couch, right above his head. He grabbed it and mumbled, "Hello?"

No one responded. What the hell? He looked at the phone and groaned. The alarm. He'd set it for 8:30. Guess he'd gotten his three hours. Now that he knew what it sounded like, he'd make a note to find something a little less bracing. Then he smiled. Nah, he was retiring. Soon, he wouldn't need an alarm. But today he did. Couldn't be late, especially after he'd told his staff to be there by ten.

Fred rolled off the couch and stumbled into the bathroom for a quick shave and shower. He was out the door by nine and stopped at a coffee shop a block from the Senate Hart Office Building to order an extra-large coffee. This would kill his stomach, but he had to power through today.

By nine thirty, he was at the Senate, wandering through the staff offices. Desks were piled high with papers and littered with coffee cups, pizza boxes, soda bottles, and the telltale accordion folders. It didn't look as bad as if a bomb had exploded, but close.

He found Leonard asleep, his long legs propped up on his desk and his suit jacket a makeshift pillow. *He's gonna be sore when he wakes up.*

Fred sat down at his desk and heard the outer door open. Roy Peterson walked in, carrying a large coffee.

"Hey, Roy."

Roy wore the same clothes he'd had on yesterday. "Morning, sir."

"Never seen you with coffee before. How you feeling?"

"I'm fine." He yawned. "Tired. And no, I don't usually drink coffee, but my stomach wasn't ready for another Coke. I must have had a six-pack last night. Think that's the only way I stayed awake."

"Yeah, readouts are tough. I caught a lot of folks nodding off, especially those who weren't the readers. Hey, ya know, I never got to thank you for getting the scoop on the election crap."

Roy gave him a slight smile.

"Yeah, and I know what you're thinking." Fred rolled his eyes. *Thanks a lot, Harris, for giving my staff the wrong impression.* "It didn't happen. The truth is Amy recognized two guys from Belvoir. She was convinced she was being followed. Looked like a couple ex-special forces guys to me. And sure enough, when we were leaving, they followed us. We ran to my house to get away. I wanted to call her a cab, but she was afraid to go home. So she slept in my bed, and I slept on the couch. It was all innocent."

He spoke as if begging Roy to believe him. "Somehow the press found out she was there. Leads me to think the White House is actively surveilling her. Must have pinged her phone. Either they got a warrant, or it was an illegal tap. Anyway, she left sometime yesterday. She's supposed to show up for work Sunday. With the provision in the conference report, I imagine they'll be pulling the plug on the beta test."

"How come *Roll Call* didn't do a story? All Ward wrote about was cigarettes."

"I think I convinced him his tip was flawed. He was talking NSA, Africa, and an army woman. Since none of those were right, I was able to deny his story."

Roy took another sip of his coffee. "You can bet when he sees the language he'll know something was up."

"Yeah, but it'll blow over once the test gets cancelled."

Fred looked up as he heard a couple of the office doors open down the hall. "Looks like the others are arriving. You get any sleep?"

"I dunno. Maybe a couple hours. I'll be alright. This coffee's already sending shock waves through my system."

"OK. Go sit by your phone and answer questions. And thanks again about getting the ball rolling on this election crap. If we hadn't acted, it coulda been real bad."

Roy stood a little taller and walked out, a huge grin on his face.

Chapter Sixty-Three

Amy waved at Mrs. Nelson when she entered the library and thought she detected a look of surprise. *I wonder if it's because I'm back after spending all afternoon here yesterday, or that I'm wearing the same clothes.*

After roaming the library without success, she went over to the desk.

"Excuse me, but do you know where I can find a copy of Thoreau's *Civil Disobedience*?"

Mrs. Nelson chuckled. "Are you trying to find an excuse for writing Clarence's essay yesterday?"

Amy's mouth fell open. "Sorry?" she sputtered.

"You can't fool me. I see Clarence in here most every day. When I read that report, I knew he didn't write it. Now what'd you go and do that for? That child needs to do his own homework instead of playing that silly game. How else is he gonna learn a thing?"

Amy's shoulders slumped. "Yeah, you're right. But he wasn't using his computer, and all the others were checked out. And I needed one."

"Since I've never seen you here before, I'm betting you don't live around here and probably don't have a DC library card." Mrs.

Nelson gave Amy the once-over. "And I'm betting there's more to this story, but that's no never mind."

Amy nodded. A tear started to well up.

"But if you're interested in reading a great work like *Civil Disobedience,* I'm gonna forget what you did for that boy. You can find it right over there." Mrs. Nelson pointed out where the nonfiction titles were located. "We close at five thirty today. But that book's not long. You need anything else?"

"Do you have a copy of the Uniform Code of Military Justice?"

"Say what?" A curious expression overtook the librarian's face. "You're gonna read Thoreau and you want a copy of the UCMJ? You'll find it over there." She pointed to the reference section. "But you better think long and hard if you're thinking about disobeying a military order."

Amy's eyes widened, and her jaw dropped. "Now, why would you say that?"

"Just putting two and two together, dear. My husband's a judge advocate, an army lawyer, you know. So I hear this kind of thing." She gave Amy a stern look. "You best be careful."

Amy thanked her and slumped off to find the works. She plopped down on a comfortable couch with a copy of *Civil Disobedience.*

After a couple of hours, Mrs. Nelson walked over to her. "Since I'm guessing you're gonna be here awhile, I brought you a couple other things you might want to read, by Gandhi and Martin Luther King." She placed two books next to Amy, smiled, and returned to the front desk.

Chapter Sixty-Four

"Al, good to hear from you," Fred said into the phone while seated at his desk. "Seeing that it's past noon, I'm guessing you filed. Right?"

"Unfortunately, not. We got a problem, Fred."

"What? Why?" Fred's forehead crinkled. "Is the House objecting?"

"Not here, man. It's your guys. I just got off the phone with the Speaker's office. They said your majority leader talked to Speaker Martinez. Told her not to file. Said the Senate objects to our language on elections."

"What? He can't do that."

"C'mon, Fred. You know as well as I do if the leaders balk, we're in a world of hurt."

Fred sat staring at the wall, shaking his head. "God damn it, Al. I had no idea. Must be my fucking full committee. That motherfucker. Jackson saved Colbert on cigarettes, and Colbert turns around and fucks us on this. What'll we do now?"

"Sounds like it's the White House, Fred, not Marty. The president's chief of staff also called Martinez. She told him to pound sand. But she's a little more sensitive to Leader Jacobs's complaint. So, what I suggested to her staff was to go back to Jacobs and inform the good senator of a couple things. First, if the White House has seen the language, the press probably has it. And second, if they dump it now, there's gonna be a lotta 'splainin' to do. And all the House is gonna say is 'Ask the Senate.'"

"Yeah, that's good."

"Look, we've got the official papers. We've got the signatures. We're not about to roll over on this. Martinez is giving Jacobs the courtesy of realizing that even he can't stop this from happening. Besides, as she supposedly told him, what's the big deal? The White House says they aren't interfering. Methinks thou doth protest too much."

"You got that right. At least with the provision in, we surely stopped them in their tracks."

"I hope so, Fred. But that election's Sunday. And this bill won't be law until it passes and the asshole-in-chief downtown signs it. Are you confident that Parker won't order them to go ahead anyway?"

"Jesus Christ, Al, you could be right." Fred rubbed his temple with his free hand. "But we've both worked with the military for a long time. Do you really think they'd carry out the order?"

"Hard to think they would. But I'd also guess some White House lawyer is gonna make a strong case of why they have to. And, Fred"—Al's tone was more serious—"since no one bothered to clue you in, you might want to keep your head down. After all, it's pretty widely known you're the guy who fingered them downtown."

Oh shit. He was probably right. *And, dear God, poor Amy. She could really be in the soup when she reports to work on Sunday.*

Fred hung up the phone as Roxy popped her head in. "Sounds like you were talking to Al. Are we filed?"

"Nope." Fred shook his head. "Leader's office is complaining about the election provision."

"Really? Why?"

"I can't say I know for sure. And what I do know, I can't share."

"Jesus, what a mess. I can't believe Jacobs would screw us over this provision, which everyone swears doesn't do a darn thing."

"Yeah, well, all I can tell you is we're hung up right now. Al's pretty sure this is just a Kabuki dance. He still thinks we're gonna file, but they're giving the leader some time to realize he can't stop this one. We'll see."

"I guess we keep the champagne on ice a little longer, huh? See how it plays out."

"Yeah, not much choice. Too bad Jackson's on a plane to Spokane. He could probably push it over the finish line if he were here."

Chapter Sixty-Five

Harris Ward thanked his source for calling as he climbed the white marble steps inside the Capitol.

"Who's complaining?" He paused on the landing. "Uh-huh . . . any idea why the majority leader's office is trying to kill it? OK. Thanks. And again, I really appreciate the call."

He clicked off his cell. If Jacobs was complaining about the election provision, it had to be for the White House. The provision passed the Senate. Jacobs obviously didn't have a problem with it. So, despite all the denials, it still pointed back to Parker. Perhaps Max Welsh had more information about the army gal under FBI surveillance.

Harris placed a call. "Hi, this is Harris Ward. I'm looking for Max Welsh. Is he available?"

"I'm sorry, Mr. Ward. Mr. Welsh no longer works here," a woman's voice responded.

Harris almost dropped the phone. What the heck? "I'm sorry. Did you say Max Welsh no longer works for the FBI?"

"Oh, no, sir. He still works for the Bureau, but not here. He accepted a transfer to the field office in Birmingham, Alabama."

"But I just talked to him a couple days ago. He didn't mention a transfer."

"Oh, are you a friend of his? It came up pretty quick. All I know is when I got to work yesterday, my supervisor said Mr. Welsh no longer worked here. He transferred to Birmingham. Now, why that man would want to leave headquarters to go to Birmingham," she said with a laugh, "I sure don't understand. But I guess these things happen."

Yeah, Harris mused, *things like this happen when you piss off the big boss, but he doesn't have enough evidence to fire you and can't allow the truth to come out.*

"I'll be darned. Would you happen to have a number for him in Birmingham?"

"No, sir, I don't. You'd have to talk with Public Affairs, unless he's a relative. Are you a cousin or something?"

Lying to the FBI was never a good idea. "Ah, no. Just a friend. Thanks for your help."

"No problem. I always liked Max. I hope he likes Alabama." She laughed again as she hung up the phone.

Finally a story. But it didn't add up. Why would the White House let the ban pass only to object now? Unless . . . they changed the provision. Harris decided to call the leader's office and see what they had to say for themselves. Max had said that gal worked for the army. Maybe it wasn't the NSA after all. Harris needed the actual language. Needed to see if they were really changing it.

Chapter Sixty-Six

"Mr. President, I assume you're calling from a secure phone. Is that correct?"

"Of course I am, Simpson. I'm at fucking Camp David. You think this is a pay phone or something?"

"Of course, sir. Just needed to make sure." Steve Simpson braced himself. "Sir, I'm awfully sorry, but I need you back at the White House."

"What the fuck, Steve. Why?"

"It doesn't look like Jacobs can kill the provision. Word is the press might have gotten wind of it. Jacobs's staff called. I tried to tap dance my way around why we needed them to kill it. Threw out the executive-privilege claim. Told them they can't tie your hands. But, bottom line, the Democrats are threatening to tell the world that the White House killed this thing. If something were to leak before Sunday's event . . . well . . ."

"So what? It's not law until I sign the bill."

"Yes, sir. But it's McNeal. He's balking. He heard that Congress is going to pass a complete ban on beta testing SWEET REVENGE. He wants to pull the plug on Sunday."

"Didn't you tell him the lawyers said we're good to go?"

"I did. But that wasn't enough. He's questioning the legality anyway." Simpson took a deep breath.

"But it was Congress who demanded we create this program. How can testing it be illegal?"

"Sir, you're exactly right. But McNeal's worried. He has to answer to Congress, and particularly the appropriators. They control his budget. He can't afford to piss them off. He knows they're gonna pass a complete ban. This isn't like the language in the intel bill. It's not easy to get around."

"But we're doing it under the authorities in my finding on counter-narcotics. It has nothing to do with intel."

"Yes, sir, but the appropriators control counter-drugs and intel, and McNeal's agency."

"I control his agency, too. I'm the fucking president."

"Yes, sir, but you don't *really* control his budget—that's the appropriators."

"God damn it! This is all Jackson's fault. That motherfucker is gonna pay for this. You tell Jacobs that Jackson's got to go."

"OK, sir. I will. But no matter which way McNeal turns, he can't find a loophole to carry out the test."

"But our lawyers!"

"Yes, sir. But he's consulted DoD lawyers. They said, absent a direct order from you, Mr. President—as commander in chief— he'd be skating on thin ice if he conducted the test."

"Tell him I motherfucking ordered it."

"Yes, sir, I did. He wants you to issue the order to him—to his face."

"What a fuckhead. No way he's getting that fourth star now, Steve."

"I understand, sir. In the meantime, I directed General McNeal to give us a copy of the software tools."

"What the hell good is that gonna do?"

"Probably nothing. But if McNeal flakes on you, I'd at least like to have some kind of backup plan."

"God damn it. All right, Steve. Order up Marine One. I can helo back this afternoon." He sighed. "I guess it's alright. There's only one fucking hole here anyway." He paused for a second. "Hey, get me on Burning Tree tomorrow. Make it in the morning. Before it gets too hot. I don't want to have them renaming it 'Burning Parker.' Heh-heh."

"Yes, sir, Mr. President." Simpson hung up the phone and groaned. He slouched in his chair. *And I've got five more years of this, assuming he wins again.*

Chapter Sixty-Seven

Two champagne corks popped simultaneously, and loud whoops erupted in Fred's office. It was only 2:00 p.m., but it was Friday, the Senate was out of session, and, most importantly, the bill was filed.

Roy sank into the couch and let himself relax.

"Je-sus Christ!" Mindy hollered. "It's a fuckin' bill." She clinked Roxy's glass, her smile as wide as the Mississippi.

"We did it, boss." Roxy toasted Fred with her glass raised.

Fred sat with his feet resting on his desk and raised his glass back at her. "And thank God. I was starting to worry when Al said Jacobs balked." He released a huge sigh. "Just glad it's over with."

"So, what was the holdup?" Leonard slouched in his chair, stretching his long legs under the coffee table and crossing them at the ankle.

"That stupid provision on elections, of course." Roxy shook her head. "I mean, it screwed us up in committee, almost did on the floor, and finally in conference. And why? For a provision that everybody swears doesn't do a damn thing." She squinted in Fred's direction, scowling.

Fred's face was blank. "Yeah, well, I can't say why, but the hero of that whole shitty affair was Mr. Peterson." He raised his glass in Roy's direction. "The country owes him a debt of gratitude."

"Say what?" Roxy screeched.

Roy beamed.

"That's right." Fred paused, a faraway look on his face. "And a gal who did the right thing even though it could put her in jeopardy."

"From where I sit," Mindy said, "I think Chairman Jackson's the hero. He carved up the House, and Boyer too. It's tough to go into conference when they got a dozen guys staring at you. But it's particularly hard when your minority counterpart ain't no help. In fact, hell, she was a hindrance."

Fred smiled. "You're right about that, Mindy. So, Jeff, what's Boyer saying now that it's over?"

Jeff Leary took a big gulp of champagne and shook his head. "It's the damnedest thing. She bitched, moaned—hell, she screamed. And yet somehow, when it was all over, she thanked me. She said I did a good job. I almost fell out of my chair. And, get this, she even told me, and I quote, 'Jackson did a pretty good job.'"

"Holy shit!" Roxy shouted. "Who believes that?"

Jeff nodded. "Un-effing-believable."

"Somebody must've swapped out her meds." Mindy snorted.

The staff let out a deafening roar.

"Hey, Stevie Guy," Fred called out. "Pop another bottle. I think we're just getting started."

Roy stood up. "I'll be right back."

Roxy followed him out. "So, Peterson," she called.

"Yeah, Fowler?" Roy sneered.

"If Fred says you're a hero, then you're OK by me. Why don't you let me get you a glass of champagne?" Roxy's voice had a sweet, almost maternal tone.

"There you go. Still busting my chops. You know I don't drink."

"Not even a glass?" She tilted her head. "We're celebrating getting this dog done, finally."

"I don't drink," Roy snapped, unable to keep the anger from welling up inside him.

"OK, forget it. Let me buy you a Coke. Like I said, if Fred's on your side, that's good enough for me. Peace?" She offered her hand.

Roy stared at her for a second. Could she be serious? "OK, deal." He shook her hand. "But I don't need another Coke. I haven't recovered from yesterday's six-pack. Only way I made it through readout."

Roxy sat on the corner of Mindy's desk. "Yeah, readout's a killer." She paused. "So, it looks like you and I are gonna have to work together for a while. What do you say we try and get along?"

"OK by me."

"I promise not to hassle you about your drinking. Maybe you can stop treating Mindy and me like a couple-a whores."

"I never meant to—"

"I know. But just the same." She leaned over, grabbed a bottle of water out of Mindy's refrigerator, and tossed it to Roy.

He sat down at his desk across from Mindy's. "Thanks."

"You know, it would help if we knew why you refuse to drink with us."

"It's a long story."

"I got nowhere to go. Fred's got another three or four bottles to open. This party isn't breaking up any time soon." She grinned.

He took a deep breath. "Here's the short version. Not something I'm proud of. I was a cadet, West Point. I had a habit of drinking . . . a lot. So, a couple of us got fake IDs and hit New York. This guy, Jimmy Baldwin, and I were doing shots in a Brooklyn bar. We got hassled by some locals who were anti-military. Bush had just invaded Iraq. That wasn't popular with these guys. Anyway, a fight started. I busted a guy's jaw. Cops came. I got arrested and tossed out of the academy."

"Holy moly. That's awful."

"Yeah, I still wanted to join the army, but the active guys wouldn't take me. Finally, I got accepted into Norfolk State's National Guard ROTC program on probation, assuming I kept a clean record. But I had to pay my own way.

"Julie agreed to marry me if I stopped drinking. So we got married. She quit nursing school so I could go to Norfolk. And I haven't had a drink since. Probably the best thing that's ever happened to me." He took a big sip of water. "But it does make things like today tough when everybody's whooping it up."

Something like understanding crossed Roxy's face. "Yeah, I get that. Well." She stood up and walked over to Roy's desk. "Cheers." She clinked her glass against his plastic water bottle. "No matter what you're drinking, we're celebrating today. And you're the hero. C'mon, let's go join the party."

Roy stood up and smiled. "Thanks. It means a lot, coming from you. Especially with your relationship to the boss."

Fred looked up with a sagacious expression as they walked back into his office.

Chapter Sixty-Eight

Three-Star General Mac McNeal paced in the hallway outside the Oval Office.

They couldn't be serious. Simpson had to be bullshitting. No way the president would order an attack on Bolivia's election now. Not with Congress poised to ban all testing of offensive cyber actions in any foreign election. It was political suicide.

And, holy cripes, we'd get crucified.

McNeal's hands trembled. His aide-de-camp wore a concerned look that McNeal imagined mirrored his own, so he forced a smile. "I'll be going in alone, Stan. Same as usual."

"Yes, sir."

"I doubt it'll be a long conversation. You should be able to make it to your daughter's volleyball match. That starts at seven, right?"

"Yes, sir, but don't worry about me. Whatever you need, sir. I'm here for you."

"Thanks."

The door opened, and Steve Simpson beckoned McNeal into the Oval Office. McNeal glanced at the major, smiled, and raised his eyebrows. Then he turned and walked in. *Here goes nothing.*

"General, Steve tells me you've got a problem." President Parker sat at his desk.

"A problem, sir? No. I explained it to Mr. Simpson. Our lawyers are saying we can't carry out the operation."

"Heh-heh." President Parker nodded and twisted his head toward Simpson, who stood slightly behind him. "What was it that FDR supposedly told his Navy Secretary, Steve? 'You can get a new lawyer, or I can get a new secretary.' Something like that, right?"

Steve Simpson frowned. "Yes, sir, something to that effect."

McNeal's stomach knotted up.

"You see, General, it doesn't really matter what your lawyer says, because I'm ordering you to carry out the operation. Got that? Is that good enough for you? Is that why you had me dragged back to DC? So you could hear me order you directly?" By the time he'd finished, Parker was nearly shouting. His face had turned red, and the veins in his neck and temples pulsed.

"Mr. President," McNeal said, forcing himself to remain externally calm despite his racing heart. "I've taken an oath to defend the United States Constitution and to execute the orders of the commander in chief. I intend to fulfill my oath. But, sir, I beg you. Don't make us carry out this attack. Their president was lawfully elected. Their election system is one of the cleaner ones in Latin America. The—"

"She's a narco-terrorist. Haven't you read the latest intel on the socialist bitch? She not only nationalized American companies, she's in bed with the drug dealers. Isn't that enough to knock her off?"

"Mr. President, with all due respect, I've read the intercepts regarding her brother and the drug cartel. There isn't much there that suggests that Simona Corazon is involved."

"Don't be a fool, General. Of course she's involved. She's probably skimming the profits off for her own retirement fund. Now. Did you understand my direct order?"

"Yes, Mr. President."

"Good. Get the hell out of my office."

General McNeal saluted. He stood ramrod straight, the muscles in his neck taut, then spun on his heels and marched out.

Chapter Sixty-Nine

"Sara? It's Harris." He paused as his editor mumbled a whispered hello. "Hey, I pulled up *Roll Call* on my computer, and I can't find my story. What's going on?" Harris sat on the couch in his living room, holding his laptop, fast-forwarding through the early morning weekend news on TV with the sound muted.

"Good morning, Harris," she muttered through the line. "For future reference, I think six is a little early to be calling on a Saturday. Unless there's an emergency." She finished her sentence with a yawn.

"It might not be an emergency, but it's certainly a problem. I can't find my story."

"And you won't." She sighed. "We pulled it."

"What? Why? This is a big fucking deal." *I gotta watch my language.* "I mean, quoting a former vice president, that is. But seriously, why would you kill my story? The White House is planning to steal an election."

"Harris. It's a great story. Problem is you haven't corroborated one fact."

"What do you mean?" Harris pushed aside his laptop and stood, gripping his cell phone. "I get an anonymous tip that the White House is going to rig an election in Africa. The vice chairman of the Senate Intelligence Committee denies it." His voice started to rise. "Then she offers an amendment on the Senate floor— jumping her chairman, I might add—on a bipartisan bill."

"That's old news, Harris."

"Let me finish." He paused, fearing a protest, but none came. "Jacobs kills that bill because the White House tells him to. So the appropriators pick up the same language. By that time, Jacobs realizes he's boxed in. He can't kill the defense appropriations bill. I mean, he has no explanation for why he would. Unless the White House *is* planning to screw some country."

He took a deep breath. Hearing no dissent, he continued, "But the defense conferees change the language. They ban anyone in government influencing any election. So Jacobs balks again. Why? Because the White House must've demanded it. Now that's a story, Sara! And it reinforces what Max Welsh from the FBI told me. The army was going to carry out the attack, not the NSA. Jackson was tipped off by the army gal. That's why the language was changed. Sara, this is huge!"

Harris took a breath and regained his composure. "I'm sorry for yelling, but c'mon, it's Parker. We know what he's capable of. Look what he did to Mitsunaga. He tried to ruin that American hero's life. And why? To enhance his presidential aspirations. You don't think he'd do this?"

"It's not about what I think." Her voice softened. "I think Parker's a liar and a cheat. But the American people elected him. And what was the mainstay of his campaign? Fake news by the media. He convinced America that we wronged him in the mess with Mitsunaga. So, if I'm going to publish a story accusing him of impeachable crimes, I'm going to make sure the facts line up. I'm sorry to say yours don't."

Harris fumed. "But my source at the FBI—"

"You mean the guy who's no longer taking your calls."

"They transferred him."

"You don't know that." Sara's tone was reproachful. She sighed. "He could be avoiding you. And even if he was onto something, when you tried to corroborate that story, the staffer, what was his name?"

"Fred Hendricks."

"Yeah, that guy. He categorically denied everything the FBI source claimed. Isn't that right?" She was getting worked up again.

"Yes, but—"

"No, Harris. No buts. Let's say it's all true. And, oh by the way, we checked with Jacobs about trying to kill the provision coming out of conference. His people denied it. Hell, we even tried to get the Speaker's staff to confirm your story. They said, 'We've got nothing for you on that.'" She sighed again. "I'm sorry, Harris. You're a great reporter, but there are just too many holes in this one. I'm not going to be accused of fake news again." She hesitated a moment. "Not unless I've got the smoking gun in my hand. You've got the gun, Harris, but no smoke. I'm sorry."

Harris hung up the phone and collapsed onto his couch. *I can't believe it. Parker's going to get away with it. All I can do now is watch to see if some African dictator loses his election.*

He jerked straight up. Wait a second . . . what was it Hendricks had said—there was no army woman. So maybe he was lying about her. Wouldn't be the first time some guy lied about a girl he was sleeping with. He'd said it wasn't the NSA—but Harris knew it was the army. And he'd claimed it wasn't Africa.

That had to be it! Somewhere other than Africa, the army was going to rig an election. But the bill language stopped them.

Or did it?

Chapter Seventy

The massive white stallion pranced down the center of the street, clip-clopping over the cobblestones in rhythmic perfection. The silver decorations on the gleaming black leather saddle reflected the sunlight, sending starbursts through the crowd with each step.

The rider sat straight. She wore leather slacks tucked into matching boots. Her crisp, white cotton blouse was open at the neck. A long red scarf draped down her back, tugged by every gust of wind. Her thick black hair was tightly braided and adorned with small yellow-and-red flowers. She smiled broadly. The color of her lips matched her scarf, a stark contrast to her alabaster complexion. One hand waved to the crowd; the other grasped the horse's reins.

Two silver-helmeted motorcycle riders, wearing ornate costumes in the red, yellow, and green colors of the Bolivian flag, flanked her. A troop of dancers in bright fabric, accented with gold and festooned with copper bells, sashayed behind.

"Bo-lí-var! Bo-lí-var! Bo-lí-var!" the crowd, standing ten deep, chanted. She led the powerful horse through the streets of Sucre up to Freedom House, where Simón Bolívar had declared independence. She dismounted and waved to the thousands assembled in the compact park across from Freedom House. Then she bounded through the crowd to a small gazebo in the center and bounced up its steps.

The gazebo wasn't high enough for her to be seen by all, so she climbed up on a bench as she pumped her fist in time with the chanting crowd. She still couldn't see over the throng. So she grabbed ahold of a verdigris pole attached to a metal railing at the edge of the gazebo and hoisted herself up. Now she had a commanding view of the sea of people.

Gripping the pole with her right hand, she raised her left to silence the crowd. The chanting continued. Someone handed her a bullhorn.

"Thank you." Her voice echoed through the plaza and down the side streets. The thousands assembled all around her cheered wildly. She raised the bullhorn again. "Thank you, my fellow Bolivians. I love you all." A deafening roar swelled through the plaza. "Thank you for coming today to join me at this sacred site, the birthplace of Bolivia. Thanks also to our past heroes for giving us the freedom that we cherish. But my friends, I must warn you, there are those who want to deny us our freedom. They want to welcome the colonialists back. We can never"—she screamed the last words at the top of her lungs—"never let this happen!"

The *Bo-lí-var* chant struck up again.

Simona encouraged the voices, punching the air with her bullhorn. Then she spoke again. "I want to thank you for electing me so many years ago. I have fought for you every day to keep the colonialists at bay. And if you vote for me tomorrow, I will continue that fight every day that I am your president." The cheering started up, but she continued, "I will fight to stop the bankers and the *yanqui* industrialists from taking our country from you, the people." She raised her voice even louder. "The proud, strong, beautiful people of Bolivia! A country given its freedom right here nearly two hundred years ago by the great liberator, Simón Bolívar!"

A thunderous *hoorah* rippled through the massive crowd.

"I, Simona B., will carry on the liberator's legacy. Vote for me tomorrow, my friends. Make sure all your neighbors vote. The future of our country depends on you. We can either return to being a captive colony, or we can safeguard our freedom, our democracy, and our liberty. The choice is yours, my friends."

Booming praise resounded again. After a moment, she raised her bullhorn. "Thank you for coming today and for your support. I love you all. May God bless each and every one of you and your families! And may God bless our great, *free* nation! Thank you!"

She passed down the bullhorn, let go of the pole, and waved both hands as she jumped down onto the bench and then the gazebo floor. With a face flushed from the excitement, she hugged her brother, who stood next to her. "Isn't this fantastic, Miguel?"

"They love you, Simona. It was a great speech." He motioned with his head off to the side where a row of television cameras were positioned. "And you see that? The media captured the whole thing—the crowd, the overwhelming support, and your every word. This will play on everyone's TV tonight, Simona. Your words, your truth, your honesty, integrity, and strength will be in every living room in Bolivia." He looked deeply into her eyes as he held onto her shoulders. "And tomorrow, my beautiful sister, you'll be reelected easily."

She beamed at him. Together, they left the gazebo. Her staff pushed the well-wishers back to clear a path. Simona waved and shook hands as they made their way through the adoring crowd.

When they reached the street, she climbed into a waiting

black sedan. Desdemona sat in the front seat of the car. "Madame President, I have great news. The final polls are out. They have you ahead of Montoya by more than twenty-five points. The election is yours." She smiled at the president. "I hope you get a good night's sleep. Tomorrow night you can accept the country's mandate with clear eyes and a calm demeanor."

"Thank you, Desdemona. I will try. And thank you for all you've done."

Chapter Seventy-One

Amy glanced at the new librarian standing at the front desk. Perhaps Mrs. Nelson had Saturdays off. She eyed the clock on the wall.

It was only five, a half hour before the library closed. But Amy was as ready as she was gonna be. *I sure wish I had someone to talk to about all this.* She stood up, placed several books on the rack to be returned to the stacks, yawned, and grabbed her open backpack. She spied her phone and considered calling Rachel, but it was better not to have to sacrifice another phone if they were still tracking her.

Outside, the heat and humidity weren't as miserable as they'd been the previous couple days. She walked back to the hostel to check in.

She opened the door and smiled at the dark-haired young man with pleasant features. "Hey, Pat. I'm surprised to see you. Figured you'd be off today. I wanted to make sure I was all set for tonight."

He put down his book. "Hey, Amy. I work almost every day, especially on weekends when I don't have class."

"You're a student?"

"Yeah. I'm at Georgetown's School of Foreign Service. I want to work for the State Department."

"Wow. Good for you. No wonder you're always reading." She paused for a second. Maybe he'd be a good person to ask about civil disobedience. "I've spent the last few days boning up on civil disobedience and whether it's ever lawful for the military to disobey an order."

Pat chuckled. "Why you doing that?"

Amy looked at him. *Should I tell him? Nah, I can't. Maybe a little. He might know something. He's at Georgetown. He must be smart.* "Oh, it's nothing really. But is that something you know anything about? I mean, I've read Thoreau and Gandhi, and even a little about Martin Luther King."

"But none of those are military," he said. "The military has different rules."

"I know. But I also read about an army lieutenant who carried out orders to kill civilians in Vietnam. He went to jail. They said he shouldn't have carried out those orders because they were against the law. Unconstitutional." She gave him a curious look. "I mean, how's someone supposed to know when an order's illegal? I don't think it's fair."

"You're probably right. And, if I remember correctly, in that case, the guy's commanding officer didn't get in much trouble, even though he ordered it. Crazy. But seriously, why are you looking into this?" He wrinkled his forehead. "Are you in some kind of trouble?"

"No, not really. And I can't talk about it. I'm in the air force, and the stuff's classified."

"Wow. That's kinda scary. What are you gonna do?"

"I don't know. It seems to me I should do the right thing, but I could go to jail for a long time. I just don't know."

"I wish I could help."

Amy perked up a little. "There is one thing you could do for me. See, I left my phone at a friend's house, and my cousin doesn't know where I am. Do you think I could borrow your phone to call her? She lives in DC, but she's been out of town. I wanted to see if she got back yet. She might be able to help me."

"Sure." He picked up his cell from the counter and handed it to her.

Amy dialed Rachel's home phone. A cheery voice answered.

"Rachel, it's Amy. You're home!" Amy blurted out in excitement.

"I'm sorry. I can't come to the phone right now. Please leave a message after the tone."

Amy's shoulders slumped. She clicked off the phone, handed it back to Pat, and forced a smile. "It was her answering machine. I guess she's still not back."

"Why don't you call her cell?" He offered his phone back.

Amy shook her head. "Rachel doesn't have one. She says they're too easy to tap, and people can track your whereabouts."

"Wow. She sounds a little paranoid."

"Yeah, maybe. But she works in intel, so maybe she's onto something."

"Really?" Pat glanced down at his phone. He looked back at Amy. "Suit yourself."

"Hey, now that I know you're here and I've got a room, I'm gonna run out and grab a bite. I'll see you later."

"OK. Have fun."

Amy walked out and saw an opening in the traffic on Pennsylvania Avenue. She dashed across the street. *I think I'll go back to Chipotle. A burrito sounds good.*

As she reached the corner of Ninth and Penn, sirens came blaring from both directions. Sounded like fire trucks. *I hope everything's OK.*

A black SUV with flashing headlights raced past her down Pennsylvania. It stopped on Tenth Street by the hostel. Another matching vehicle approached from the other direction.

Oh shit.

Amy ducked to the left down Ninth Street. She pulled her cap down low over her dark hair. *Stay calm. Don't run. They don't know what you look like.* They must have been sitting on Rachel's phone. The Little Pearl restaurant sat just ahead. She quickened her pace and popped in. More sirens could be heard heading her way. She tried to smile as she entered the white building through the bright-blue door and held up one finger when she spied a waiter. "Do you have a table for one?"

"Sure. Would you like to sit in the garden?"

Amy resisted the urge to scream, *No!* She shook her head and took a deep breath. "It's still a little warm for me; I'll sit inside, if that's OK."

She looked around and saw a table in the corner away from the door and windows. "How 'bout over there?"

"Suit yourself. You're our first customer this evening."

"Thanks." Amy took her seat. *What am I gonna do now? I can't go back to the hostel.* She sobbed once and wiped her eyes. She released another deep breath and focused on the menu. *Oh no, it's one of those fancy fixed-price places. At least there's a cheeseburger option.*

The waiter had gone out to the patio and walked back in. "Something big must be going on. I saw about eight SUVs with flashing lights out there." He smiled at her. "I mean, it's DC. I read there are something like twenty-eight different police forces in the city. You'd think there wouldn't be any crime here." He chuckled.

"Yeah, we should be so lucky." Amy's heart was pounding.

He pulled out a pen and pad of paper. "Anyway, those guys sure are some serious-looking dudes. All in black suits." He shook his head and poised the pen. "What can I get for you?"

All she could muster was, "Cheeseburger."

Amy finished her cheeseburger and paid. The sirens had long since ended. But she couldn't be sure there weren't still black-suited agents around the corner. The restaurant was starting to fill up quickly. She asked the waiter to call a cab for her and sweet-talked him into keeping an eye out while she went to the ladies' room.

When she came out, the cab was waiting. She thanked the waiter and rushed out the door, looking straight ahead. She didn't run, but walked as quickly as she could, jumped into the cab, and slouched in the seat.

At least I've got a plan.

Chapter Seventy-Two

"Sir, you're not going to believe this, but the air force non-com slipped through our fingers once again. At least we know where she's been. It's a youth hostel on Pennsylvania Avenue. If she comes back, the Bureau will nab her." Steve Simpson gripped the cell and held it away from his ear as if expecting a blast.

"What? I told you to stop following her. She's already fucked us. What more can she do?" Parker barked.

"Yes, sir, you did." Simpson paused for a second. "I guess the FBI garbled the message. Anyway, she's still in town. A desk clerk at the hostel let her use his phone. He described her as having short dark hair. I'm guessing she dyed it. But the clerk didn't know where she'd gone. She's pretty clever, sir."

"So what? Who cares?"

Simpson took a deep breath. "Sir, I'm worried about McNeal. He didn't sound all that convinced. We really need him to co-operate."

"What about your backup plan to have our staff do it?"

"I think they could. It's pretty straightforward. But I checked with the lawyers. They said this isn't like Iran-Contra in the 1980s, when Congress hadn't prohibited the NSC staff from acting. In this legislation, sir, there's no loophole allowing the White House to run the operation. I guess the appropriators learned something in thirty-five years." He chuckled but stopped abruptly.

"Every time I talk to you, Simpson, all you have is bad news," Parker growled. "I don't want you calling again unless you've got something good to tell me. Do you fucking understand?"

"Yes, sir." Simpson's voice was little more than an exhausted whisper.

Chapter Seventy-Three

Darkness was rapidly approaching. As the sun set, the river took on a deep-green appearance, and the soft breeze only caused a few ripples. Fred Hendricks was lying on the deck of his docked sailboat, trying to repair his emergency motor. Appropriate to the eighty-degree temperature, he wore tan shorts that accentuated the small love handles at his waist and no shirt, revealing his farmer's tan.

The telltale crunch of gravel signaled the arrival of a car on his long, winding driveway. He looked up to see the flicker of headlights bouncing along the rough road, and he threw on his red curly-*W* Nationals T-shirt and stood up gingerly, wary of his aching back. Who the hell could that be?

A dark taxicab pulled up behind his beat-up truck. The passenger door opened on the far side. A shadow of a person wearing a black hat stepped out. What the heck?

He quickened his pace across the thirty yards of grass between the dock and the driveway, limping a little as his sciatic nerve acted up, a result of contorting his body for the last several hours on his boat deck.

"Hey," he shouted in the direction of the taxi driver. By the cab's interior light, he caught a glimpse of an older, balding Middle

Eastern man with a gray mustache. "You got the wrong address, buddy. This is private property. You can't drop somebody here."

The driver smiled and waved as he accelerated in reverse down the winding driveway. His headlights cast flickering light in the darkness.

Fred could only see the passenger's silhouette. Walking closer, he could make out that a woman stood in his driveway. The fleeting light revealed her *I Heart DC* T-shirt, black jeans, and backpack, but not her face.

Fred kept walking straight toward her. "I'm sorry, but there must be some mistake. Who are you?"

"It's Amy Anderson, Mr. Hendricks."

"What?"

She slouched her shoulders and stifled a sob. "Amy, sir. I'm sorry, but I got nowhere else to go." She stepped a little closer, and he took her in.

"Amy? You—you changed your hair."

He approached her and started to reach out but fought the urge to hug her.

"I'm sorry. Men in dark suits have been chasing me for days. I dyed my hair, and I've been hiding out at the DC Public Library and sleeping at a youth hostel. But this afternoon, I used this guy's phone at the hostel to try and call my cousin. Five minutes later, the area was swarming with black SUVs. I barely got away. I didn't know where else to go. You were my only hope."

"How'd you find me?"

She perked up. "Oh, that was easy. How many Fred Hendrickses do you think own a cabin on the Patuxent? I used the library's computer. I found property-tax records and other stuff. It's all on the internet. I had the taxi drive by your town house, and it didn't look like you were there, so I took a chance and had him drive here. It cost me a hundred dollars, but . . ." She paused and blinked back tears. "After they found me at the hostel, I didn't know where else to go."

"Oh dear. Are you OK?" He looked at her with concern. He couldn't help staring at her hair for a few seconds before scanning the rest of her. Her figure was accentuated by the tight T-shirt and black jeans. It brought back memories of her naked body lying on his bed.

He jerked his head up and let out a deep sigh. *What am I gonna do with her?* "Are you hungry? I don't have much chow, except a couple leftover burgers."

"No, thanks. I evaded the cops by ducking into a restaurant and ate while I figured out what to do."

"OK, let me wash up a little. I've been working on my boat. Why don't you have a seat?" He motioned to the Adirondack chairs facing the river. "Can I get you something to drink? A beer or something?"

"I'd love a beer, thanks."

Fred opened the screen door and stepped inside. It banged shut behind him. The noise must have startled Amy, who let out a surprised yelp.

He changed into a clean shirt, put on his Top-Siders, and grabbed two beers. He brought them out in the dwindling light and offered one to Amy.

She smiled. "Budweiser. This wasn't what you gave me to drink that night, was it?"

He twitched a little at her question. "Yeah, I have to apologize for the boilermaker. I should've realized that might go straight to your head after a couple Negronis on an empty stomach. That was pretty stupid."

"Not your fault. I know you were trying to help." She took a big swig of beer.

Fred eased himself into the chair next to her. "So, we finished the bill. We put language in so you can't do the test."

"That's fantastic." Amy's face was gleeful. "Thank you. I didn't know what I was gonna do. I have to be at work at seven tomorrow or I'll be AWOL and headed to jail. So I don't have a choice. But if they forced me to run the test, well, I just didn't know." She took another long drink. "I spent the last three days reading about civil disobedience and when it's OK to ignore a direct order from a superior. I'm so confused. I mean, if you disobey a lawful order, you get in trouble. But if you obey an unlawful order, you can get into trouble too. It just doesn't seem fair. And how am I supposed to know if the order is lawful? I mean, I think it's wrong to interfere in Bolivia's election. But is the president allowed to order us to do it anyway? It's just all so confusing, Mr. Hendricks."

"Fred," he purred.

"Fred." She looked into his eyes.

"Yeah, it's tough, Amy. But the good news is you shouldn't have to worry about it. The law's crystal clear. They can't interfere." He let out a heavy sigh. "I mean, technically it's not law yet. Congress still has to approve it, and the president has to sign it. So I guess it's a gray area. But there's a lot of legal precedent on legislative intent. And it's real clear that the legislative intent is that they can't do the test."

He took a long swig of beer and continued, "And, in my experience, the military's pretty good at following the law. They ignore our report language guidance all the time, but that's not law. But when Congress writes a law, with really clear intent—and, like I said, this language is crystal clear—the Pentagon almost always follows it. So, you shouldn't have to worry."

He paused for a second and looked her over one more time. "But I don't have room for you to stay here. I don't have a couch, and my back can't take sleeping on the floor or in a chair, especially after working on my boat all day."

"But you have to let me stay," Amy whimpered. "I have to sleep tonight. I've got to be fresh in the morning. I can sleep anywhere. Even in this wooden chair, if you give me a blanket and pillow."

"Well, it gets pretty cold at night here, but there's a comfortable chair inside. How are you gonna get to work in the morning? And don't you need a uniform?"

"Do you think I can get a taxi to pick me up at 5:00 a.m.? It'll cost me another hundred dollars. And I'll have to sneak into my apartment to change, but it's the only choice I have."

"You can't count on a taxi showing up here. Tell you what. If you're serious about sleeping in the chair, I'll drive you in the morning."

"Really? You'd do that for me?"

"Sure. I wake up early most of the time, anyway. It's Sunday. The bill's done. I've got nothing else to do. If I'm tired, I can take a nap at the town house later. Yeah, I'll drive you."

"You're wonderful." Amy jumped out of her chair and gave Fred a big hug and a kiss on the cheek. Before letting go, she whispered in his ear, "You're my knight in shining armor, Mister Fred." She kissed him again on the cheek and sat back down.

Fred was startled but energized. He stood up. "Hey, I'm gonna grab another beer. You want one?"

"Sure. Got any of the kind you had at your apartment, that flying squirrel something or other?"

"Nah, just Bud. It's leftover from a party I had with my staff here a couple weeks ago."

"That's fine." She let out a long, contented sigh. "This is the first time I've felt relaxed since I spotted those two guys at the bar."

Fred walked inside to grab more beers. When he came back out, a hint of the moon had started to creep over the horizon. He handed Amy a beer and sat down.

"It's beautiful here. And that water looks so inviting. It must feel great. Especially on a hot day." She leaned forward in her seat and stretched, as if releasing the tension from her body.

"Yeah. This is a pretty special place. The river's fun to swim in all the time—in the summer, that is. Too damn cold by late fall."

"Oh, I'd love to go for a swim. Can we?"

Fred cocked his head. "Did you bring a suit?" He shook his head and chuckled. "I don't have one that'd fit you."

"No, Fred." Her lips curved into a smile. "Skinny-dipping. We're in the country. It's dark. No one can see us."

Fred's mouth fell open. "Well, yeah, but . . ."

"I mean, you'll see a little bit." She stood up and opened her arms wide, facing him. "But are you really going to tell me you're going to see something new?"

He wrinkled his brow. "Of course I've seen naked women before . . ."

"No, silly. I mean *this* naked woman." She tilted her head and put her hands on her hips. "C'mon. You're not seriously going to say you didn't see me when I took my clothes off in your bedroom, are you?"

"Didn't you see my note? I told you nothing happened," he stammered.

"Now, don't you lie to me, Fred Hendricks."

She folded her arms and looked at him with an accusing grin.

"Well, um . . ."

"Yeah, I thought so." She laughed.

He smiled and shrugged his shoulders. "So, what gave me away?"

"Let's see. There's no way I could've unbuttoned my skirt the way I was feeling. And, oh yeah, my clothes were all neatly folded on the chair. I would've left them in a pile on the floor. And . . ." She paused for a second. "I have this vague recollection of falling and being caught by two strong hands." She pointed to her rib cage, right below each breast. "Now, since I know you're a gentleman, why don't you get us some towels for when we get out?"

He jumped out of his chair. "Be right back." He hurried toward the cabin. His back felt great.

A minute later, Fred returned with a large pale-blue towel around his waist. He threw her a similar green one.

She caught it. "Green. My favorite color." She kicked off her shoes and wiggled out of her black jeans. Then she looked at him. "Are you staring at me?" She winked.

"Sorry. I didn't really mean to."

"Uh-huh." She turned around and lifted her T-shirt over her head and took off running. "Last one in's a rotten egg!" she hollered as she ran.

Fred followed the T-shirt, bra, and panties trail on the ground. He could barely see her as she jumped off the dock and grabbed her knees. "Cannonball!" she screamed at the top of her lungs right before she hit the water.

Fred reached the dock, dropped the towel, and hopped in. The water was cold but refreshing. It gripped his muscles. He felt the blood rushing to his fingertips and toes. *This is wonderful. Who would believe it?*

They swam around and splashed each other for a few minutes as the moon rose. Amy was nearer the shore, and Fred noticed her hair almost looked red again.

He swam close to her. "Your hair!" Without thinking, he ran his fingers through it. "It looks red again."

"Oh, is it? That's great. The guy told me it was just a rinse and that it'd come out when I washed it. I've been keeping my head out of the shower the last couple days to make sure I kept up the disguise. I forgot about it tonight. I guess it doesn't matter, since I'm going to work in the morning."

Fred pulled his hand from her hair, but Amy caught it and placed his palm against her cheek. She kissed it and swam away backward toward the dock. "You're a nice man, Fred. If it weren't for you, I don't know what would've happened to me." She took one more stroke and reached the ladder at the dock. "I think I'm ready to get out. Could you turn around while I climb?" She gave him a half-serious smirk. "It's not my best side."

He laughed and turned around. She climbed out, and in the quiet, he could hear the rustle of the towel as she dried off.

"OK. It's fine now," she called.

Fred swam to the ladder. He started to climb out as Amy walked in the direction of the cabin, her towel covering her. He grabbed the blue towel he'd left next to the ladder and wrapped it around his waist. "Ya know. That felt great. Really invigorating."

"I love to skinny-dip," she yelled over her shoulder. "But it's not the kind of thing I get to do a lot. It just feels so real to be swimming naked in a cold river."

She continued toward the Adirondack chairs, picking up her clothes as she went.

"It's getting a little cold out here, Amy. What say we go inside?"

She nodded and followed him through the swinging screen door. The kitchen had yellow walls, oak cabinets, and a laminate countertop. It seemed pretty rustic, with an old stove, fridge, and sink. Fred was just thankful everything looked clean. No piles of dirty dishes anywhere. No mess to apologize for. He led her into the living room.

She plopped down in a comfortable, overstuffed chair. "I think I can sleep right here."

Fred checked his watch. "Well, it's already nine o'clock. You probably ought to sleep pretty soon if we're gonna get up at 4:30 a.m. There won't be any traffic on Sunday morning, but it'll take at least ninety minutes to get to Belvoir."

"Yeah, and I have to stop by my house to get a uniform first." She lifted up one corner of her towel, exposing most of her thigh. "Can't report for duty wearing a towel."

Fred's heart thumped at the glimpse of more exposed flesh. He shook his head. "No," he sighed, "you sure can't." He turned toward the bedroom. "Listen, I'm sorry about the chair, but it's the best I can do. I'll get you a blanket and a pillow."

Amy curled up in the chair.

"I'll set my alarm for 4:30 a.m. and wake you up," he hollered and walked back in. "The bathroom's right over there." He pointed toward a doorway off the living room. "If you need something, wake me up." He tossed her a pillow and blanket.

"Thanks. I'm fine just like this." She pulled the blanket over her.

"You gonna sleep in the towel?"

"Yeah, why not? I don't have pajamas."

"I could give you a T-shirt or something."

"No, I'm fine. The towel's soft. It feels nice."

"Suit yourself." He flipped off the lights and walked into the bedroom. He closed the door partway. *What a night. What a sweet young woman. She makes me feel ten years younger. Too bad that still makes me old enough to be her father.* He pulled off the towel, threw it onto a chair, and slipped into bed naked.

Fred was lying on his back, drifting off to sleep, when he felt the bed move. Startled, he opened his eyes and caught Amy smiling at him.

"I can't go to sleep. Can I sleep here?" she asked.

Fred's body jolted awake. "Yeah, I guess so. You sure?"

She nodded. He closed his eyes, and she eased over next to him.

"Fred," she whispered. "You've been wonderful. But this whole experience has been so awful. I'm still scared. Could you put your arm around me? I need a little comforting."

"OK." He reached out and slipped his arm under her bare back. She rested her head on his shoulder and put one hand on his chest. Slowly, she ran her fingers through his hair.

"You're in great shape," she murmured as she stroked his belly. She lowered her hand and gasped. She whispered in his ear, "And ready."

Fred's breath caught.

She giggled. "I'm ready too. Is this OK?"

"Oh, yeah."

Amy rolled on top of him and eased herself down.

"It's perfect," he growled softly.

Chapter Seventy-Four

Fred reached over to the nightstand and silenced the blaring alarm on his cell phone. *Oh, Lordy. I got to change that ringtone.* He felt an arm wrapped around his chest.

"Good morning, Mister Fred," Amy mumbled in his ear. "Thank you for a wonderful night. I haven't slept that well in ages." She nibbled his ear and rolled to the far side of the bed. She reached down, picked up her towel, and covered herself as she walked into the living room.

Fred got dressed and walked out of the bedroom. Amy stood by the door, clothed and carrying her backpack. She smiled.

Fred grinned, sheepish. "You ready?"

Amy sighed. "I guess so."

"Hey, you shouldn't have anything to worry about. Like I said, they won't dare do a test now."

"I hope you're right." She took a deep breath and walked out the door.

Fred locked the door behind them. "There's a 7-Eleven not too far from here. We can grab some coffee. I don't keep the stuff in the house. I'm not supposed to drink much of it. But getting up at four thirty seems like a pretty good excuse." He jumped into the truck and started it up.

Amy got in, and he backed down the driveway and onto the street.

Fred glanced over at her. *I wonder what she's thinking. Should I say something about last night? It was wonderful, but it doesn't make any sense. I mean, it's crazy. She's a beautiful young woman; I'm a broken-down old fart. I didn't take advantage of her, but maybe that's what she's thinking.*

The truck pulled into the 7-Eleven. Fred got two large coffees for them and Amy added a bagel to the tab.

Back in the truck, they sat in silence. Fred glanced at Amy every now and then. She seemed upset. Was she regretting last night? Maybe she realized what a mistake it was. Or maybe it was about work and not him at all. Should he ask her what was bothering her? Maybe he didn't want to know.

Traffic was light. The sun was coming up as they reached I-495, the Beltway, where he'd turn toward Belvoir.

Amy finally spoke up. "Hey, do you think we'd have time to drive by your apartment? If there's nobody staked out there, I'd like to pick up my phone. If that's OK."

"Sure. We've made good time. We're plenty early." He paused. *Should I keep the conversation going?* "With all that coffee, I could use a head call. Hey, what does the air force call a bathroom? I mean, it's head in the navy and latrine in the army."

Amy shrugged. "Bathroom or latrine, I guess. And please don't mention it again. That coffee is hitting me too." She smiled.

Fred punched the accelerator and sped into DC.

Amy scrunched down as the truck neared Fred's town house.

"No guys sitting in black SUVs or white sedans," he said cheerfully. "Looks like they gave up trying to find you."

Amy perked up in her seat. "Gee, that would be great."

Fred pulled into the small parking lot behind his house, and Amy's face seemed a little paler.

"You OK?" he asked as they got out of the car.

"Yeah, seeing this place brings back a lot of scary memories."

"You should be fine now." Fred unlocked the back door.

Amy pushed past him. "I really got to go. I'll be quick."

"Be my guest." Fred looked around the apartment. He folded the blanket on the couch and placed the pillow on top of it.

Amy came out of the bathroom and released a deep breath. "OK, I feel a lot better now." She cracked a grin as Fred rushed in to relieve himself.

When Fred came out, she was staring at her phone. She'd picked it off the kitchen counter, but it didn't look like she'd turned it on. "Everything alright?" he asked.

"Yeah, but I'm not going to tempt fate. Who knows if they're still tracking me?"

"We better keep moving. You don't want to be late."

Amy looked around. She noticed the gin, Campari, and vermouth sitting on the counter. "You've got the makings for Negronis," she said with surprise. "Did you get that for me?"

Fred shrugged.

Amy gave him a half hug. "You're such a sweet man, Mister Fred. I can't believe any woman would ever divorce you."

Fred ignored the comment. "Hey, we got to go." He opened the door and followed Amy out to the truck.

Chapter Seventy-Five

"Ernie. Wake up. I see something."

The driver of the white sedan yawned. "What time is it, Burt?" He opened his eyes and squinted as the sun peeked over the top of the three-story apartment building. The collar of his white shirt was open, and his tie hung loosely around his neck.

"A little after six. See that truck parked by the stairs?"

He held up his hand to block the sunlight. "Yeah."

"The guy driving looks familiar. Did we see him with her at the bar in DC?"

"Maybe. Is she with him?"

"Dunno. Someone got out and dashed up the stairs."

"You better take some pictures."

Burt lifted the camera with the telephoto lens and focused. "Yeah, pretty sure that's him. Betcha a week's pay it was our girlie who jumped outta the truck and zoomed inside."

"Get your mic up. See if we can catch some convo. Why is she showing her face now? I mean, we're done with this case in about an hour."

"Do you think she's been hanging out with him all this time?"

Ernie yawned again. "Nah. The Bureau guys locked onto him for a couple days. They said he was at work almost the entire time. The feebs were a little nervous tailing him, though, since he works for Congress. Pretty sure he hadn't done anything."

"Well, she hasn't really done anything, either, Ernie. We caught her talking to that staffer, but headquarters says he's got all the tickets for this shit. And if this is the same guy from the bar, he's the other guy's boss. I mean, why are we still sitting on her, anyway? The FBI went home hours ago. They were the hot and heavy ones. We're just supposed to keep tabs on who she's talking to. Granted, since we ain't seen her for three days, we can't be sure who she talked to. But if it's her with this guy, hell, why do we care?"

"Look, our job is to sit on her. Watch her. Since she's back, assuming it's her, that's what we're going to do. And if she heads back to Belvoir after this, then we're done. She's INSCOM's problem."

"You better start the car. Someone's coming."

Amy ran down the stairs, carrying her uniform, and jumped into the truck. "OK, Fred, go."

Fred pulled onto the street and gestured with his head. "I think those guys in that white sedan figured out who we are. They've been pointing a camera at me. But they haven't pulled out guns and tried to arrest me. And the other thing—there's no sign of the black SUVs. I'd say that's all good news."

"Please hurry."

Fred glanced at Amy as she tugged her T-shirt over her head and undid her bra.

She looked at him. "Fred, are you peeking? Keep your eyes on the road." She threw on a conservative, white cotton bra and slipped into her air force blouse.

"Yes, ma'am." Fred smiled.

Amy slid her jeans and panties off. Fred looked over at her again.

"Stop peeking, Fred." Amy couldn't completely suppress a giggle. "Why, you're just a dirty old man."

"Guilty as charged, Amy. Guilty as charged." Fred frowned a little and stared at the road.

Completing the makeover, Amy slipped on her black pumps as they pulled into the Fort Belvoir gate. As they approached the security guard, she flashed her badge and shouted, "Hello." Then she directed Fred to the INSCOM building.

"Listen, Amy, before you go." Fred gazed straight ahead, watching the road as he spoke. "You know, last night was wonderful. And you're a special person. You're gorgeous, smart, and brave—"

"Fred, don't—"

"Just let me finish, OK?" He paused. "Now, you've got your whole life ahead of you. So, I mean, I don't know what you're thinking. I don't want to sound presumptuous, but whatever it is, to be frank, you shouldn't be wasting your time with me. I'm old enough to be your grandfather. Hell, I'm retiring soon. Maybe this month. I don't know yet. You need to find some smart, good-looking young guy who'll love you and treat you with respect. Not this broken-down, old warhorse." Fred blinked a little and tried to smile, still focusing on the road.

Amy sat staring at him. The truck pulled up to INSCOM headquarters, and she shook her head and sighed. "Oh, Fred." She opened the truck door and grabbed the backpack stuffed with her clothes. "Here goes nothing. Wish me luck."

She jumped out, slamming the door behind her.

Chapter Seventy-Six

Maine Senator Demands Investigation

Standing in front of a nearly completed navy destroyer in a Maine shipyard, Senator Margaret Johnson, a Republican from Maine, blasted the conferees on a defense appropriations bill for bailing out a South Carolina shipyard. A blistering report in the Washington Post *exposed the language buried deep in the five-hundred-page compromise legislation. "As chairman of the seapower subcommittee," Johnson said, "I can assure you the Senate Armed Services Committee intends to get to the bottom of this outrage. We will receive testimony from the navy in an emergency hearing on Monday."*

A navy spokesman welcomed the hearing and the chance for the Navy Secretary to testify on the issue. Johnson, who has announced she will stand for reelection next year, faces a serious challenge from the sitting governor, Steve Chase.

An Appropriations Committee source informed Roll Call *that the criticism was a misunderstanding. The source stipulated that the language does not mandate that the Secretary award any funds to the shipyard. Furthermore, the source noted, the Secretary of the Navy is prohibited under federal acquisition regulations from paying any amount unless the navy determines it's justified.*

A careful reading of the language by Roll Call *finds some ambiguity in the provision. The language in question states that:*

Up to $75,000,000 shall be available to the Secretary of the Navy only for Charleston Marine shipyard for damages due to Hurricane Donald.

While payment to the shipyard is authorized, it's unclear who determines how much should be provided. Roll Call *reached out to Senator Johnson for further clarification on the issue. She was unavailable.*

The seapower subcommittee hearing is scheduled for 3:00 p.m. Monday afternoon.

Harris Ward shook his head and slammed his laptop shut. The President of the United States was trying to overthrow some country's government, and all he was allowed to write was a puff piece about the sea turtle trying to protect herself from extinction.

Only one thing to be done now. Keep an eye on today's news for strange election results.

Chapter Seventy-Seven

Amy turned the knob and walked through the office door. *No one's here. What the heck?* She looked at the clock. It was nearly seven. Where was everybody? She threw her backpack under her desk and switched on her computer. Had they cancelled the test and told everyone not to report? She looked up. The light was on in Major Whitehall's office. He'd tell her what was going on.

She knocked on the doorjamb. "Good morning, sir. Where is everybody?"

"Sergeant Anderson! It's about time. Where the hell have you been? I don't know what you're up to, but you're in deep shit." He frowned. "The others are getting set up in the ops center. But General McNeal wants to see you."

Oh boy. They're already in the vault. Looks like Fred was wrong. We're actually going through with it. She followed the major out the door and down the long hallway through the nearly deserted one-story building. They reached the corner office suite. *Stay calm. Tell my story. If they're going to lock me up at Fort Leavenworth, so be it. I'm doing the right thing.*

An army major, sitting outside of the general's private office, stood and saluted when they walked in. "The general's waiting Major . . . Sergeant." He glared at Amy.

Whitehall nodded and led Amy in. General McNeal sat behind a huge wooden desk. Pictures of the general with military officials and other dignitaries lined the walls.

Amy glanced around, noticing the couch and chairs, which looked brand-new. Brass floor lamps. A bronze rodeo-cowboy sculpture on a stand held one corner. On a credenza behind the general, a multi-tiered rack displayed dozens of military challenge coins. A three-star army flag occupied another corner. She and the major stood at attention in the center of the office.

General McNeal stood up and returned their salutes. He commanded the room with his size and stern demeanor as he walked around his desk. "At ease. Thank you, Major. I'll speak to Sergeant Anderson alone."

Major Whitehall nodded. "Sir, we're all set to begin the test."

McNeal looked pensive. "Very good, Major, but hold off for now."

"Yes, sir." Whitehall turned to leave, closing the door behind him.

"So, Sergeant Anderson, counterintelligence tells me you've been meeting with congressional staff. They claim you released information about project SWEET REVENGE. Is that correct?"

"Yes, sir, but I can explain."

"Please do."

"Sir, I think it's illegal and immoral for us to be rigging an election in a democratic country. Sir, the Constitution says—"

"Hold it right there, Sergeant. This isn't about the test. This is about you going around channels and talking to Congress. Who gave you the authority to brief congressional staffers about this test? This is Sensitive Compartmented Information. No one authorized you to brief Congress."

"No, sir, they didn't. But the two men I spoke to are both cleared to receive this information."

"Not from you!" McNeal shouted. Amy flinched and looked down. "You're not authorized to speak to anyone."

Amy looked back up, her heart pounding. She took a deep breath to calm herself. "Sir, with all due respect, the whistleblower statute, Section 1034 of Title 10, says talking to a member of Congress is legal, sir."

"So you're an expert on military law now, are you, Sergeant?" McNeal growled.

"No, sir. I didn't mean that. But I've spent the last three days reading military history, the Universal Code of Military Justice, and writings on civil disobedience, sir." Her heart was still banging in her chest, but she wasn't scared. "It's clear that any serviceman or woman is allowed to brief Congress when they suspect an unlawful act is taking place. It's also clear, sir, that a member of the uniformed services is forbidden from following an unlawful order."

"And what makes this unlawful? Because you say it is?"

"Congress just passed a law saying so, General."

"What you're referring to isn't law yet. Congress hasn't passed it. And, more importantly, the president hasn't signed it." His voice boomed.

"Yes, sir, but the legislative intent is clear." *That's what Fred told me.*

"The President of the United States ordered me to carry out the test. I'd say that trumps a piece of language that isn't law yet."

"Yes, sir. I understand. But it's a dilemma, sir. The president's order could be unconstitutional. If so, then neither of us, sir, is allowed to follow it." She paused and looked at the general, who didn't seem so tall or as imposing as he had a minute before. "I mean, sir, the president is asking us to fix an election. I don't know how that can be anything but wrong. Sir?"

General McNeal sighed. He circled the desk and plopped back in his chair. "Listen, I've got my doubts about this test. But an order's an order. And this wasn't from some flunky White House staffer or newly minted four-star. This is the President of the United States. Who are we to question the president? He was selected by the American people to make these kinds of decisions."

"Sir, we've taken an oath to protect and defend the Constitution. Not the president."

"Yeah, I know." He sighed again and stared at his flag. "OK, Sergeant, you're dismissed." He sounded tired. "But I'm not done with you."

"Yes, sir. But the test, sir?"

"Get out. That's an order." He paused, smiled, and added in a softer tone, "And a God-damned lawful one, too."

As Amy nodded and left, she overheard the general say, "Stan, get me the White House."

Chapter Seventy-Eight

"Madame President, the polling places have finally closed. The exit polls show a twenty-point lead for you. Because of large crowds, many polls stayed open an extra hour. It looks like everyone in the country voted."

"Even the young people?"

"Especially them." Desdemona beamed.

"Thank you, Desdemona. Can you ask my brother to come in?"

"I'm sorry, ma'am. He's not here. He said he had an errand to run but would be back in time to celebrate your victory." She smiled. "The results should start coming in any minute."

Simona nodded. "OK, I guess all we can do now is wait."

"Jonas, what do we know?" Presidential candidate Carlos Montoya sat at his desk, his face haggard.

Jonas stood in the doorway. "Our poll watchers are starting to report in. It doesn't look good. You might eke out a slight plurality here in Santa Cruz. But all reports are that President Corazon will sweep the rest of the country."

"Should we head to the hotel, greet my supporters, and concede?"

"No, sir, not yet. The results are being tabulated in La Paz. You can't concede until we have an accurate count. But, frankly, it'd take a miracle at this point."

"Miracles are for priests and witch doctors, Jonas, not bankers."

◆ ◆ ◆

Amy sat at the computer terminal in her office. *It's been a long day.* She sighed. *I guess I should see what they're reporting about Bolivia.*

She connected to the internet and began her search. She found the election returns online and scanned the results. *I don't believe this. It's not possible. What could've happened? I got to tell Fred. Where did I put his email address?*

◆ ◆ ◆

"What do we know, Steve?"

"It's still early, Mr. President." Steve Simpson let out a heavy sigh. "But it looks like what we expected."

"OK." Parker yawned. "Wake me up when the final results are in. I want to call and congratulate the president."

"Yes, sir."

◆ ◆ ◆

Harris Ward turned off his TV and flipped on his computer. *Who held elections today?*

He searched releases from AP and Reuters. Nothing about African elections. *I thought Mauritania was supposed to be voting this weekend?* "I'll be damned."

He read aloud. "They cancelled the election. The dictator-for-life declared it a waste of money. Hah. Nothing to interfere with there." *Who else is voting? Bolivia. What's going on there?* He clicked on the latest story from South America.

"Holy cow!"

Chapter Seventy-Nine

"Is this Sergeant Anderson?"

The gravelly voice sounded familiar, but Amy couldn't quite place it. "Yes, this is she."

"Amy, it's Fred. How are you? I read your email this morning. What the hell happened?"

She let out a long sigh. "I don't know. It doesn't make any sense. It's impossible."

"Why do you say that?"

"Because Montoya beat Corazon."

"Well, I'll be. You ran the test after all."

"No, Fred! We didn't do anything. We were ordered to stand down. We spent the day writing an after-action report on the, um, whole issue." She paused for a second. "I can't say much more on an open phone line. Can you go secure?"

"No, I'm still at the apartment. Getting ready to head to the office. My chairman's looking for me. But you're saying she should've won, because . . . well, you know."

"Exactly! She was so far ahead it didn't look like anything could stop her. But Montoya won!"

"Amy, are you being pressured by, um, anyone?"

"*No!* Fred, Major Whitehall told us General McNeal called the president yesterday morning and resigned his commission. That was right after he ordered us to stand down. Major Whitehall kept us working all day, but not on that."

Fred was quiet on the other end of the line. Finally, he said, "OK. Let's think this through. How hard would it have been for someone else to do this? Like the White House staff, or something."

"If they've got some techies, some geek hackers like me, it wouldn't be a problem at all. The key is the tool to get into the database. Once you've got that, it's a snap. But doesn't your law prevent anyone from doing it?"

"Well, yeah, pretty much. We tried to cover all our bases. I think we did. But it's not really law yet. Like we talked about. So I guess somebody could have. Anyway, what about you? Are you OK?"

"I'm fine. Relieved. But I'm still under investigation for leaking info. Major Whitehall is furious with me for going around channels. Best case, I'll get a slap on the wrist. Worst, I'll be emailing from Kansas. Fort Leavenworth."

"Jesus, I'm sorry. But remember, you did the right thing. I know that's not much consolation now, but it's true."

"I guess. But it doesn't look like we stopped it. It was all for naught." She released a despondent sigh.

"Regardless, the country owes you a big thank-you. Listen, I'm late for work. I'll keep my fingers crossed that all you get is that slap on the wrist. And one last thing . . ."

Amy perked up. "Yeah?" An expectant tone rose in her voice.

"Maybe it wasn't rigged. The polls could've been wrong. But whatever happened, it wasn't your fault. So, um, take care." Fred hung up.

Chapter Eighty

She opened one eye to a pitch-black room. She sat up, rubbing her eyes and trying to focus, but her head felt like someone was pounding on it with a hammer. "Oh my God." She groaned and glanced around. "Where am I?" A familiar luminescent light told her it was nine o'clock.

Simona, you fool, you're in your own bed. She stared at the bank of windows. The heavy shades had been lowered. Blackout curtains blocked nearly every speck of light.

Her eyes widened as reality dawned on her. She fell back against her pillow. *I can't get up. I'm not ready to face anyone.* How could she lose . . . to a *banker*? What would she do now? She felt alone. Where was Miguel? He hadn't even come to her victory celebration last night. She scoffed. Some victory.

The cacophony of cars honking and people screaming and hollering rose up from the street three stories below. *Dios mío,* what was all that noise? She eased out of bed, her white cotton nightgown draping to the floor. Her dark hair fell loosely over her shoulders. *Why can't they be quiet? It's like they're trying to kill me.*

A loud rapping exploded on her door, adding to her misery. She groaned again. "Quiet." She spoke barely above a whisper. The pounding on the door—and in her head—continued.

"Madame President!" She recognized the voice of her campaign assistant, Desdemona, hollering at the door. *Can't that stupid girl be quiet? I'm going to fire her.*

"Madame President, wake up! It's Miguel." The voice sounded strained, almost as if Desdemona were crying.

"I'm coming." This time Simona managed to be a little louder. "Stop knocking." She held her head in both hands. The rapping stopped. Simona took a deep breath and opened the door a crack. In a fatigued but bitter voice, she demanded, "Why are you waking me up, you stupid girl?"

"I'm sorry." The girl sobbed. "I'm sorry, but it's Miguel. He's downstairs, on the street."

"What? What nonsense is this?" Simona snapped, more pain flaring in her head.

"His body's on the street. They dumped it and drove away."

Simona's blood froze to ice. "What? Who?" She ran to the window, tore open the curtains, and lifted the shade over her head. A crowd of people circled around the body of a dark-haired man dressed in a black suit, lying facedown on the street. It almost looked like . . .

No. Impossible. Ambulance sirens blared, adding to her misery. "Who is that?"

Desdemona bawled. "It's Miguel!"

"It can't be." Desdemona was wrong. She had to be wrong.

The medical technicians turned the body over, and Simona saw him. Miguel. Her *hermanito.*

She took a step back and collapsed. Desdemona grabbed her before she hit the floor. "Noooooo." Simona let out an anguished scream. The blood drained from her face. Her eyes glazed over.

She sat on the floor and rocked back and forth as tears streamed down her cheeks. "No, no, no. Miguelito, Miguelito, Miguelito, Miguelito. No." Her sobs racked her as though she were having a seizure.

Suddenly, she stopped swaying and wiped her eyes. "Desdemona, my robe. Hurry."

Desdemona dashed to the closet and grabbed an ornate red-and-gold robe. She helped Simona to her feet and then to don the robe.

Simona headed downstairs. "Come. We must go to him. Maybe there's still a chance."

As the doors to the palace opened, the crowd parted. Corazon hurried down the cold stone steps in her bare feet and rushed to her brother. She felt faint as she saw him up close, his pale face, his vacant eyes.

He was gone.

She gripped Desdemona's arm for support. "What happened?" she demanded.

"Madame President." The white-haired medical technician kneeling on the ground next to Miguel's body bowed his head. "It looks like a drug overdose."

"What? Impossible. My brother doesn't use drugs. You're wrong."

"I'm sorry, ma'am." The technician's hands shook. "But the marks on his arms, and his pupils, his skin, and lips, it's pretty clear. It's an overdose."

"It can't be. Miguel would never . . ."

"Yes, Madame President." He took a deep breath. "But with the, um, outcome last night, I'm sure he was very despondent. Could it be suicide?" He looked down at Miguel and shook his head. "There's no sign of foul play. An autopsy will tell us for sure.

But with my twenty-five years of experience, I can say he exhibits all the signs of a drug overdose."

"No, I won't have it. My brother would never." Her voice cracked as she spoke. Her shoulders drooped, and her knees started to wobble.

Desdemona grabbed her from behind. "Please, Madame President. Let me take you inside. There's nothing for you to do here. Please. Stop torturing yourself."

Corazon nodded. She turned around and started toward the palace. As she approached the entrance, her Uncle Rodrigo appeared in the doorway.

"Tío!" she called through her sobs. "It's Miguel. They think it was suicide. Why would he do that? Now I'm alone. Now, of all days. He's not here to help, to give me strength, to encourage me to continue to fight. What am I going to do, Tío?" Fresh tears streamed down her face. "You were right. The people rejected me for Montoya. I should have listened to you."

Rodrigo reached out to embrace her. She fell into his arms.

"No, Simonetta," he said, his words choked, "you must not think like that. You have been a great president. Sometimes these things happen. I am so sorry about everything. But about Miguel, there is something you must know."

"What?" She tried to pull away. "Was Miguel using drugs?"

"No, my dear child, never." He swallowed. "But in order to raise money to train the factory workers, he borrowed from the drug cartel."

"What? Why?" Her heart pounded. This was all too much to process.

Her uncle released a heavy sigh. "He said it was the only way to get you the money you needed. He thought it would be safe. I warned him. But he didn't think they would ever harm him, since you were president."

"But now, since . . . oh my God, Rodrigo! It's all my fault."

"No, Simonetta. Miguel knew what he was doing, and why. It is tragic what happened, but you cannot blame yourself. You did what you thought best for your people. If you want to blame someone, blame his killer, Fernando Roca."

The ice in her veins turned to heat. She stood up straight and extricated herself from her uncle's embrace. *Fernando Roca, is it? That murderer will pay dearly.* "He will rot in hell."

An aide walked up to them. "Excuse me, Madame President. Carlos Montoya is on the phone."

"Now?" she snapped. "I'm not talking to him. Tell him to go away."

"Simona, please, you must not do that. You must take his call. He is the president-elect now," Rodrigo pleaded.

"No. He must respect my brother's death. Not now. Not to-day. Maybe tomorrow."

"Please, my darling niece. It is your duty. You must put your grief behind you."

"What does he want?" She glowered.

The aide shrugged. "He says it's urgent."

Chapter Eighty-One

As instructed, Fred Hendricks knocked on the door to the office on the southwest corner of the first floor of the Dirksen building.

"Yeah?" growled a muffled voice from inside. "That you, Fred? Come on in."

Fred popped his head through the door. Sam Jackson sat in the far corner, behind a plain mahogany writing table piled high with papers. Out the window to the chairman's left, Fred could see the façade of the Senate's Russell Building. An office building stood on his right. Bustling traffic rumbled along on the street corner below.

It was an odd location for the powerful former chairman of the Appropriations Committee. Because of his many years in the Senate, Jackson had his choice of dozens of fancier offices with sweeping views and two-story ceilings. Instead, he'd chosen this fairly modest suite located on the hallway adjacent to the appropriations subcommittees' offices.

Story was a former chairman had seated the entire Appropriations Committee staff on that hallway and that the offices used to be interconnected so the old chairman could walk the length of the building from his corner office through all the staff offices without ever emerging into the public corridor. Some said he'd used it as a way to sneak past pesky reporters and others who waited outside his door to pounce on him.

Without moving, Jackson called out through an open interior door. "Betsy, hold my calls and shut the door, please. I need to talk to Fred."

Then Jackson turned back to Fred. "Come sit down." He motioned to a straight-backed wooden chair next to him.

"Yes, sir. How are you? You're here pretty early for a Monday."

"Yeah, I had breakfast with Jake."

"Oh. How's the majority leader?"

"That's just it, Fred. He's pissed."

"Why? I thought things were going fairly well."

"It's Parker, that God-damned idiot. This election thing."

"I thought Jacobs approved the language."

"He did. But you see, I, um, actually told him the House Democrats insisted we cover the whole government. Then the White House told him it was all my fault." He grimaced and continued, "Parker demanded that Jacobs strip me of my chairmanship."

"What? That's outrageous. The White House denied they were doing anything wrong." Fred fumed. "Sir, I talked to that sergeant again." He lowered his voice and leaned closer to Jackson. "She told me the army refused to run the test. But something's fishy. The candidate the White House wanted, the guy who was way behind, he won anyway.

"The sergeant told me that almost anyone who had the right tools could have interfered. That means the White House staff could've done it. Like Iran-Contra. And since the bill hasn't passed yet—"

Jackson signaled time-out with his hands. "I know all about the election. But the White House denied interfering. Jacobs talked to the Director of National Intelligence, the Secretary of Defense, *and* the president's National Security Advisor. They all denied any involvement. They didn't do it, Fred."

"Sir, but it's Parker. You know you can't trust him."

"Fred, I just told you," Jackson barked. "They didn't do it. It's not just Parker. You know I don't trust that asshole. The problem is that now Jake doesn't trust me!" He paused for a second. "We screwed this up."

"But he can't strip you of your chairmanship."

"Yes, he can. But he doesn't want to." He shrugged his shoulders. "But he told me I've got to make some changes." He shook his head slowly and frowned. Then he cocked his head and looked at Fred. "Why didn't you tell me you were sleeping with that gal? You can't let your johnson interfere in work stuff, Fred. You know that."

"What? No, sir, it wasn't like that."

"Jacobs was told the FBI tracked her sleeping at your place near Union Station. That's not what you told me."

"No, sir, not exactly. But it's not what you're thinking. The poor girl is new in town. She was afraid to go home. And why was the FBI tracking her if the White House is innocent? Anyway, she didn't have anywhere to go, so I let her sleep at my place. I slept on the couch. That's the God's honest truth, sir."

"Yeah, alright. But you should've told me. Anyway, like I said." He released a heavy sigh.

"Sir, before you say anything, I want you to know I'm planning to retire."

"What? Jesus, Fred, you don't have to do that. We can—"

Fred signaled time-out back at his chairman with a smile. "I started the paperwork several months ago. Working for you has been a pleasure. I really appreciate the opportunity to be your defense clerk. But I've been working for the Senate for nearly forty years. I'm tired. Averaging about a buck ninety-five an hour at this point. I'll make almost as much being retired as I do working. Working for you has been terrific, but candidly, it's time to go."

"Are you sure? We can move you back to Lackland's staff. I know I could arrange that."

"Nah. What the hell would I do? They've already got a mil-con clerk. And no way I'd want them to bump Jeff Leary from defense. Hell, sir, you couldn't pay me enough to work for Liz Boyer. Not in this or any other lifetime."

Jackson chuckled. "You're not going to believe this. But after conference, she sent me a bottle of Napa Valley wine."

"You're shitting me!" Fred yelled, then covered his mouth. "Oh, sorry."

Jackson waved him off. "Yep. And a thank-you note."

Fred laughed. "That's unbelievable." He shook his head. "Come to think of it, Jeff said she thanked him after conference too." He stopped for a moment as if deep in thought. "You think she's starting to figure this stuff out?"

"We can only hope. You know as well as I do, we try to do things in a bipartisan way on our committee. Maybe it finally dawned on her."

"I think Chairman Jones yelling at her might've helped."

Jackson smirked. "He really lit into her. That 'bitch' comment probably hit close to home. I mean, she's got to know most folks call her Lizbitch."

"If the shoe fits, sir." Fred smirked.

"Yeah, now Fred, you're sure you want to retire?"

"Absolutely, sir. Forty years is a long time."

"You going to work downtown? Hell, you can probably make a million bucks a year or something."

"Nah. Not me, sir. I got plenty of money and not much to spend it on, except a leaky sailboat."

"You better figure something out. Are you a golfer?"

"Never was much interested."

"Hell, Fred. You're going to be bored out of your skull with nothing to do."

"We'll see." Fred paused for a second. "So, you're going to need a replacement. You've got a fine staff here. If you want a guy with a military background, Roy Peterson's a National Guard captain. He's solid. But my advice is pick Roxy Fowler. She's my right hand. I brought her over from milcon. So, she might be tainted as a Democrat, but she's the best we got."

"Where'd you find her?"

"Get this. I was speaking about the defense budget at George Washington University. She's in the audience waving her hand. I finally call on her. She stands up and says something like, 'Isn't the use of advance procurement a violation of the full-funding principle in navy shipbuilding? And, moreover, isn't the whole use of multiyear procurement a violation of the Constitution, which stipulates we can only maintain and equip an army for no more than two years?'"

Fred let his mouth fall open, and then he smiled. "I tell you, Senator, I nearly keeled over. She was a junior, so I arranged an internship for her in Lackland's office. When she graduated, I got them to bring her on the committee, on milcon, with me."

"That's quite a story. Sounds like a real appropriator."

"Absolutely. She's still young. But, hell sir, no younger than half the subcommittee clerks you've hired over the years. She's as smart as your last guy. And she works as hard as anybody."

Fred took a breath. "Or maybe you want to go outside. Get somebody new. Just about anybody in the business would give their eyeteeth to be your defense clerk. And I'm not just saying this, sir, but especially for you. It's been an honor."

"Thank you, Fred. You're a good friend. And you did a hell of a job this year. I don't know when I ever had such a smooth-running process. From markup all the way through conference."

"That's nice of you to say, sir, even if I know it's not true." He chuckled. "I mean, we wouldn't be having this conversation if things were that smooth." He paused and held up his hands. "But I'd still be retiring, if you're wondering. It's time."

"Understood. So, you think this Roxy Fowler is something special?"

"I do, sir. She's the best."

"Get her on my schedule for tomorrow, or whenever's right for you. I assume you want to tell your folks what you're planning."

"Thanks, sir. I'm ready to go now. I can clean out my office and be gone by Friday."

"Then Friday it is. You need me to sign something or—"

"It's all taken care of. I'll let Roxy know to get on your schedule in the next couple days."

"All right, old friend. We'll miss you."

"I'll miss you, too, sir." Fred stood and moved toward the door.

"Hey," Jackson called out.

Fred turned back to the chairman. "Yes, sir?"

"Like I said, you better think of something. You can't just walk away from all this, or you're going to be bored stiff."

Fred shrugged his shoulders and left.

Chapter Eighty-Two

"Mr. President. What a great day. I can't thank you enough."

"Heh-heh. I think we should be thanking each other, Hans. I mean, you're guaranteeing me New Mexico, right?" Parker sat with his feet up, his hands crossed behind his head, talking to the phone on his desk. He glanced over at Steve Simpson with a satisfied smirk.

"Absolutely, sir."

"Tell you what. If I win New Mexico, you'll have a spot on the podium at my inauguration."

"Thank you, Mr. President. I'd be honored."

"Now. You got your factory back yet? I told Montoya he better keep his promise. He said he would."

"I placed a call to his office this morning. They said he's real busy, which is to be expected, but that he'd call me. I'm hoping to hear back soon."

"He did tell me you might have to work out a deal." Parker cracked his knuckles.

"What?" Hans Edison snapped. "What kind of deal?"

"Beats me, Hans. Just telling you what he said." Parker chuckled. "But you know he's a banker, not some dumb socialist princess. I'm betting he's going to want some payback."

"Hrumph. We'll see about that."

"Tell you what, my friend. I think you should be grateful that you're getting it back." Parker sat up straight and glared at the phone. Steve Simpson, standing by the president's side, nodded.

"Yes, sir. You're right. Can't lose sight of the big picture. Ya know, on that other thing. I got to say, as a tech guy, that was pretty clever. You might not know this, but I spent my early years playing around with software."

"I know, dating apps, right?" Parker replied impatiently.

"Among other things. Anyway, that was pretty ingenious. The way you could change—"

Steve Simpson frantically waved his arms at the president.

Parker nodded and cut Edison off. "Let's forget about that, shall we? Just remember, though, my folks are the best. You never want to be on the other side. Heh-heh."

"Yes, sir."

Parker heard a distant voice on the phone. "Who's that talking?" he asked.

"Sorry, sir. I just got word the Bolivian president is on the other line. I better not keep him waiting. Thanks for everything. Goodbye."

Steve Simpson hung up the phone, shaking his head. "That was close, sir."

"Yeah, yeah. What time am I teeing off?"

Chapter Eighty-Three

The president and president-elect were seated on matching blue-and-gold upholstered armchairs, which rested on lemon-yellow Persian carpet. The two of them remained alone in the huge room. He leaned forward, his hands clasped together as if in prayer. She sat rigid. Her face was pale, her lips painted in muted-red gloss and her dark eyes vacant. The long-sleeved black dress she wore brushed the floor.

His eyes scanned the cream-colored room, tracing the gold-leaf accents around the windows and on sconces in each corner. Searching for something to say, he began, "My, this is a beautiful room."

"Already measuring the drapes, are you, Montoya?"

"Oh, no, Madame President," Montoya stammered. "That's not what I meant at all." He cleared his throat. "First, I want to say how sorry I was to hear about your brother. It must be quite a loss for you."

Corazon gasped but quickly regained her composure. "Thank you. Is that why you insisted on coming to see me . . . to offer condolences? His body's not even cold." Her tone grew harsher and louder with each word.

"Oh, no. It's not that at all," Montoya apologized.

"So you did come to measure the drapes. You're really something, *Mr. President.*" Corazon spat out the words.

Montoya leaned back, gripping the chair's arms, and told himself to remain calm. She was suffering twin losses and overwhelming disappointment. But he couldn't control his feelings. "No, Madame President. You're wrong!" His voice was brusque. "I'm here to inform you that a great injustice has been done." He took a deep breath. "My staff has uncovered some . . . improprieties in the election."

Corazon scoffed. "Not only do you come on the same day my only brother has been killed, but you accuse me of cheating. What's wrong with you? Have you no shame? Are you planning to lock me up and tell the masses I betrayed them? Let me tell you something, Montoya. You won't get away with it. The people love me. You might've snookered them into voting for you. But once you and your capitalist cronies start to rape the country, they'll turn on you. And I'll be vindicated!" She stood and pointed to the door. "Get out!"

He jumped from his seat. His hands shook, and his voice raged. "No! No, Madame President. You're completely wrong. I'm not accusing you of cheating. I'm saying you won the election. The votes were miscounted."

"What! What are you talking about?"

"Please, ma'am, sit." He motioned to her with an outstretched arm.

Slowly, she sat.

He glared at her. "First off, you have me all wrong. I'm not some money-grubbing opportunist who ran for president to steal from our country," he bellowed, waving his arms. Then he stopped himself and took another calming breath. "I oppose some of your policies, particularly nationalizing the lithium and electric-vehicle facilities. I know your decisions were well meaning, but they're wrong for the country."

"Fine. What do you mean by 'the votes were miscounted'?"

He sat back down, nodding slowly, deep in thought. After a moment, he said, "As a candidate, I thought I should make sure that no one played any games with the voting. So I dispatched fifty of my people to oversee the vote in dozens of precincts. My people watched to make sure everything was done right, no funny stuff."

He stared at the president. "When my staff counted the votes in the precincts, it was clear you'd won. But when the results were announced, and you lost, we knew something was wrong. My principal analyst told me there must've been mistakes in the totals. He quickly compared our data to the official election results. He found that, precinct by precinct, I was given your votes, and you were given mine."

"How is that possible?" she said in an accusatory voice. She tilted her head and pursed her lips.

He sat quietly for a moment and whistled under his breath. *How much should I tell her?* At length, he said, "We believe the election computers malfunctioned and somehow reversed the vote. In our review, we found no sign that any of this was intentional."

"Why should I believe you?" Skepticism laced her voice.

"Because I'm telling you I lost!" he snapped. "What possible motive could I have for lying? I'm giving you a chance to regain your presidency. I'm doing what's right by Bolivia. Can't you see that?"

Corazon squinted at Montoya. Finally, she exhaled. "Yes, I suppose so. Why are you doing this? You could be president. Who would know other than your own staff?"

"Madame President, I'm following the will of the people. I could not assume the presidency in good conscience knowing that the people had voted for you. Look. I never really wanted to be president. I just wanted you to stop pursuing policies that are wrong for the country."

She paused for a long time, and then smiled. "Mr. Montoya, I believe I've underestimated you. What do we do now?"

"If you will allow me, ma'am, I have an idea."

Chapter Eighty-Four

"Congratulations, Mr. Hendricks."

"Thanks, Judy."

"Have you thought about what you're going to do next?" Judy hollered over the din in the Dirksen hearing room.

Fred chuckled and shook his head. "Nope."

"Are you gonna find a new job? I hear you could make a lot of money."

"Nah. I don't need more money, Judy."

"Oh. Aren't you lucky?" She laughed. "Maybe you'll do some volunteer work."

Fred scoffed. "Nah, not my thing."

"Travel?"

"I've traveled all over the world for work. I don't lust to wander anymore." He winked at her. "I'm just going to take it easy."

"Oh. I guess that sounds nice." Judy scrunched her nose. "Don't you think you'll get bored?"

"Could be, Judy. Could be."

"Hey, boss!" Roxy shouted. She was holding three bottles of champagne, one in her right hand and two tucked under her left arm. "Grab a glass. The chairman's coming to offer a toast."

Fred spotted Jackson making his way through the crowd. The

chairman appeared puzzled as he scanned the many faces in the room. His head bobbed when he spotted Fred.

Mindy handed the chairman a glass, and Roxy scurried across the room to pour. Mindy and Stevie Guy opened the other bottles and began pouring sips for the forty-odd people gathered in the hearing room.

Roy whistled loudly, and the conversations ceased.

Jackson surveyed the room. "I won't take a lot of time. But I wanted to stop by and take a moment to recognize a great career. To thank Fred for his long service to the country, the Senate, and this committee." He paused, and a few people clapped. "Fred, you said that forty years is a long time. Well, that's a fact. Aren't many who stay around here that long—certainly not us politicians." He chuckled, and the audience followed suit. "But seriously, you've served this committee with distinction. For myself, I have to say what a great job you did this year." He reached up and patted Fred on the shoulder, and turned to face the crowd.

"Now, I want you all to know I tried to get Fred to stay. Isn't that right, Fred?"

Fred nodded.

"But he told me that forty years is long enough. And who could argue with that? Fred, I've enjoyed working with you, and I wish you all the best in retirement. I know you'll find something to do that holds your interest. And if you ever get bored, we're still here. Aren't we?" He raised his glass. "So, don't be a stranger. The door's open if you change your mind. And thanks again."

The staff applauded. Jackson waved, took one small sip of the champagne, and clinked glasses with Fred.

Fred raised his hand to quiet the crowd. "I'll just say a thing or two. First, thank you, Mr. Chairman, for stopping by. And to the rest of you here, thanks for your friendship over the years. We've had a good ride, sir. But, Mr. Chairman, I think it's time you found a new horse. It's truly been an honor to work for the Senate, for this committee, but especially for you, Mr. Chairman. Truly an honor. So, thanks everyone for coming. Drink up and have fun."

Jackson shook Fred's hand and walked out of the room.

Roxy approached Fred. "Good speech. Nice the chairman came."

"Yeah, he's a good guy. I think you're going to get to know him a little better." He gave her a sly grin. "Let me tell you. He's a straight shooter. Just don't try to BS him. If you don't know the answer to something, say so. And then promise to find out." He paused. "Yeah, and make sure you almost always know the answer." He grinned again.

"I'm supposed to meet with him tomorrow. What should I tell him?"

Fred laughed. "He's a politician, Roxy. He'll do most of the talking. Just be yourself. You know this stuff as well as anybody. He'll see you're smart and knowledgeable. That's all it'll take. You'll see. You got nothing to worry about."

Roxy shook her head. "I can't believe you're leaving. I'm not sure we'll survive without you."

"Ah, you'll be fine. No one's indispensable around here."

"Maybe, but you're pretty damn close." She drummed her fingernails against her champagne glass.

"Thanks for saying so. But you'll see. By the time the budget comes up next February, nobody will be saying, 'Gee, we miss Fred. What are we going to do?'"

"I don't know about that."

"Trust me. Somebody always steps up. This time, that's likely you. You'll do fine."

"I hope you're right." She sighed, a faraway look in her eyes. "I'm not sure I'm ready yet."

"You are. Just remember—he's the chairman. A lot of outsiders see the staff making decisions and misunderstand how the process works. You weren't elected. Your job is to do what *he* thinks is right, not what *you* think. Sometimes staff forget that, and then the door hits them on the way out. You keep that in mind, and you'll do fine."

"Thanks." She took a sip of champagne. "Question . . . on a new subject. What really happened with that election provision? I saw the election results in Bolivia. Were we screwing around there? I mean, it sure looks like it."

"Not much I can talk about. You don't have all those clearances yet. I mean, you probably will in a week or so, but . . . here's what I can say: everyone in the executive branch is denying any US government involvement."

"You think they're lying?"

"One thing I've learned over the years is it's awful hard to do something in this town without someone finding out. If you've got SecDef, DNI, and the White House *all* denying it, it's hard to think they did anything. Am I suspicious? Well, it's Parker, so hell yes. But everything leads me to say I guess the polls in Bolivia were wrong." He drained his champagne. "But take it from me—this is something you've got to keep your eye on when you take over. The whole issue needs better oversight. Roy's doing a great job watching NSA, but things can get complicated."

He put his glass down on the dais. "Now, I know you and Roy have had your problems, but he's pretty good."

Roxy held up her hand. "Save it, boss. Roy and I worked it out. Hell, if you say he's a hero, that's good enough for me. And even from my vantage point, I could see he knows his shit."

"That's good. You'll need him. But even with his help, you're gonna find there's a lot of players out there besides the NSA. I think you'll see what I mean when you get briefed up on all this stuff. And a hell of a lot of it lands right on your shoulders."

"Jesus, boss."

"You'll be fine, Roxy. Just something to keep in the back of your mind."

They stood in companionable silence until she asked, "So, what *are* you going to do?"

"As little as possible." He chuckled.

Roxy trained a stern gaze on him.

"It's been a long climb. I'm glad I got a chance to be the defense clerk for Jackson. But I'm tired of long days, lost weekends, lost holidays. I plan to sail, fish, sleep, read a little, and that's it."

"Don't you think you'll get bored? You'll miss the excitement and everything."

"Oh, I'm sure there's things I'll miss. You all, of course. But nah, I'm ready."

Mindy leaned in. "Hell, I'd retire tomorrow if they'd pay me. What the hell do I want to work for?" She drained her beer and crushed her can. "Gotta get me another. Want to make sure I get my money's worth."

Fred and Roxy laughed.

Chapter Eighty-Five

"Good morning, Mr. President, what a surprise!"

Hans Edison leaned back in his ergonomic chair and rested his feet on his Lucite desktop. He gazed at the three Monet paintings of water lilies that hung on his light-blue walls. To his left, through floor-to-ceiling windows, Pacific Ocean waves crashed on a rocky coastline beneath brilliant sunshine.

"Edison, what the fuck did you do?"

"I'm sorry, Mr. President. What's this about?" Edison motioned to a nearby assistant, who looked dumbfounded.

"Montoya. Didn't you talk to him a couple days ago?" Parker yelled.

"Yes, sir, right after I last spoke to you." He laughed. "You were right. He drives a hard bargain. But my folks convinced me I'm a lot better off getting my factory back, even if I have to share profits with the Bolivian government. I guess it's a win-win. I can't thank you enough." Edison paused, the phone wrenched between his shoulder and ear.

"What'd you tell him?"

Edison made eye contact with his assistant. "I told him he had a deal. What else would I have done? I'm sorry, Mr. President. Is that a problem?"

"Not about the factory, you idiot. I don't give a fuck about your stupid factory. About the election."

Edison put his feet on the floor, leaned forward in his chair, and lowered his voice. "Nothing about the election, sir. Why are you asking?"

"Because Montoya's stepping down. He's abdicating, if that's the right word. The socialist bitch is still president."

Edison's eyes widened. "You're kidding. I had no idea. Why's he doing that?"

"Because he's an idiot. What'd you tell him?" Parker bellowed.

Edison imagined the president standing in the Oval Office. His face crimson. His lips quivering. Spittle forming at the corners of his mouth. He tried to erase the image as he sat, shaking his head. "Mr. President, I can assure you I said nothing about the election. But even so, why would he step down?"

"How the hell do I know? He said their election computer had a glitch. The results were bollixed up. He said Corazon actually won."

"A glitch?" Edison grimaced. "Jesus Christ. I don't like the sound of that. I hope this doesn't throw a monkey wrench in our negotiations."

"You and your fucking factory. Can't you see this is bigger than that?"

"Yes, sir, I guess so. At least I've got a contract."

"All I've got to say to you, Edison, is you sure better hope that's the last we hear about this. I got you your factory. Now you better get me New Mexico. Is that clear?"

"Absolutely, Mr. President. Loud and clear." Edison shook his head as the president hung up. "Jesus Christ, that man's one step away from certifiably nuts." He looked at his assistant. "Tell me again why I'm supporting him."

Chapter Eighty-Six

"Sara, what do you mean I don't have a story? The election in Bolivia was fixed. Montoya admitted it." Harris stood in his living room, shaking his head and staring at his cell phone. He held the phone back up to his ear.

"Montoya said there was a computer glitch." Sara's exasperated voice came through the speaker. "They found it, and he's stepping down. End of story."

"No. Can't you see? It was Parker," Harris pleaded.

"Harris, how many times do we have to have this conversation? I'm starting to feel like Bill Murray waking up to the radio—and I'm not that fond of 'I Got You Babe.'"

She paused, but Harris didn't laugh at her joke.

Sighing, she continued, "I told you. The White House, the Defense Department, *and* the intelligence community all categorically denied rigging any election. Hell, your sources even denied it."

Harris plopped on his couch. He hunched over, cradling his head in one hand. "I've been thinking about that. Fred Hendricks denied that the NSA was rigging an election in Africa. This wasn't Africa. It was Bolivia. And it wasn't the NSA, it was—"

"Well, it wasn't the army. DoD denied involvement by *any* of their components. That includes the army."

"But it happened, Sara." Harris stood up and paced around his living room.

"Face it. There's nothing here. Bolivia had a computer failure. Shit happens. They're a third-world country. And, oh yeah, you have no source to confirm anything you're alleging."

"That's because all my sources are getting disappeared. General McNeal resigned the same day as my source said they were going to run the test. Max Welsh of the FBI got transferred after he talked to me. And now Fred Hendricks gets fired."

"Not fired. He retired. After they finished the bill, and after working something like forty years. I read the blurb the committee put out."

"Isn't it curious they all got disappeared after getting involved in this mess? Sara, please. I know there's a story here. You've got to let me tell it. I can smell the story. Hell, I can taste it—"

"You need to acquire a new taste. Understand? I've heard enough. Drop it, or you'll 'disappear' like the others. Do I make myself clear?" She hung up.

Harris threw his cell phone against his couch. Un-fucking-believable. Parker was gonna get away with it again!

He flipped on his TV. CNN was reporting from Bolivia. He turned up the volume. There was a picture of the Bolivian palace on the screen. A man in a business suit and a woman dressed in black stood on the balcony, waving to an assembled crowd.

In the upper corner of the split screen, a Hispanic man holding a microphone spoke. "Earlier today, Bolivian citizens were shocked to hear the apparent winner of Sunday's election, Carlos Montoya, declare that a computer malfunction had caused him to receive votes that should have been recorded for his opponent, Simona Corazon. Montoya claimed that Corazon was the rightful victor. Accordingly, he withdrew from the race, and Simona Corazon was declared the winner. Corazon announced that, in the spirit of unity, she had offered Montoya an invitation to serve as her Minister of Finance. He accepted. His first decision was to undo the nationalization of the lithium and auto industries."

Harris turned off the TV. "Jesus Christ. I wonder if Parker was involved in that too."

Chapter Eighty-Seven

Fred eased himself down onto his Adirondack chair in the shade. He grabbed the T-shirt lying next to it and wiped the sweat off his face and chest. Then he took a big swig from a can of Budweiser, and stared at the river.

A humid haze hung over the water. The sky was cloudy gray. He checked his watch—two thirty. It was Saturday. Maybe the Nats game was on TV. He glanced at his boat on the river, tied up to his rickety dock, and resolved to get that motor working or die trying. But not right now. He closed his eyes and leaned back against the wooden chair. "God, it's hot." *We could sure use some rain to break this heat.*

The crunch of gravel in the driveway alerted him to a vehicle. He stood up and walked toward the cabin. Who the hell could that be?

A blue sedan crawled up the driveway. The driver's window rolled down. A young blonde woman smiled at him.

He shook his head at her. "I'm sorry. I think you're at the wrong house," he hollered as he limped toward the car.

The vehicle pulled up behind his truck, and the passenger door swung open.

"Hey, Fred."

Fred wrinkled his brow. "Amy? What the hell are you doing here?"

"Nice to see you too." She chuckled.

"Did you Uber all the way out here? That's crazy."

"Uber? No. That's my cousin, Rachel. You know, the one who works for the Intelligence Committee."

The driver turned off the engine, got out, and smiled, displaying her perfect teeth.

"She wanted to meet you."

"Hi, Mister Fred," said the blue-eyed, blonde beauty. "I'm Rachel."

Amy strolled around the vehicle, carrying a six-pack of Flying Dog beer. "We came for a swim. I told Rachel about your great swimming hole." She held the beer out, offering it to Fred. "And I brought the good stuff to pay for renting your dock."

"Rent my . . . what?"

"Just kidding. We came to swim. It's so hot."

"The river looks beautiful," Rachel called out as she and Amy headed in that direction.

Fred followed along.

"That's OK, right?" Amy said. "I didn't think you'd mind. And don't worry"—she stopped for a moment and pulled her blouse off her shoulder, exposing a kelly-green strap—"I'm wearing a suit this time." She winked and smiled. "It's just a swim, Mister Fred."

Fred was a few steps behind when Rachel whipped off her T-shirt, exposing a tiny red bikini top that barely covered her ample chest. She quickly dropped her blue shorts. Her bikini bottom, even more revealing than the top, showed an enormous amount of deeply tanned skin.

She hollered, "Last one in's a rotten egg!" She took off toward the river, running right out of her flip-flops, her big brown bottom bouncing along.

"What? No fair." Amy tugged off her blouse without unbuttoning it and dropped her shorts. Her bikini was more modest than her cousin's. "I see you wore the skimpy one, huh, cuz?" she shouted.

"Why not?" Rachel cried. "You said there's no one here except Mister Fred. And I got this new tan to show off."

"Well, like they say—if you got it, flaunt it."

"I'm flaunting, Amy." Rachel reached the dock and leaped into the air with a scream, her arms held up straight above her head. She hit the water and went under. When she came up, her bikini top was around her neck. "Oops."

"Rachel, your top!" Amy screeched.

"I got it." Rachel grinned.

Fred chuckled and drained the last sip of Budweiser. He lowered the can and muttered, "Oh, Lordy. And they said retirement was gonna be boring."

He looked up as Amy reached the dock and leaped into the air, clutching her knees to her chest. At the top of her lungs, she screamed, "Cannonball!"

To The Reader

Shoot the Staff is a tale of how a defense appropriations bill becomes law. Not the *Schoolhouse Rock* version, but like that cartoon, it's fiction. The incidents and characters represent composite sketches. They are a product of the author's imagination, not actual people or events. The excerpts describing DoD counter-drug regulations are the exception. Those were copied from a Joint Chiefs of Staff document.

I wrote this book because, to my knowledge, no one has provided an accurate portrayal of how the appropriations process works and the pivotal role of the staff. But lest the message be misinterpreted, the author believes the most important exchange comes near the end of the story, in which a character is told:

> *"Just remember—he's the chairman. A lot of outsiders see the staff making decisions and misunderstand how the process works. You weren't elected. Your job is to do what he thinks is right, not what you think. Sometimes staff forget that, and then the door hits them on the way out. Keep that in mind, and you'll do fine."*

The book also serves as a warning. Well-meaning legislators write and pass laws which they believe will benefit the nation. But authority in the wrong hands can have unintended and deleterious consequences.

Once again, I am grateful for friends and family who suffer through early drafts and Quill Pen editors who rework my thoughts into this completed project. I alone am responsible for any errors.

About the Author

CJ 'Charlie' Houy is a veteran of Washington DC, having served for thirty years on the staff of the Senate Appropriations Committee. Senators praised him in the *Congressional Record* as "a model of responsible and enlightened public service" and "a consummate expert on defense issues." He is a recipient of several honors and awards, including the Secretary of Defense Medal for Outstanding Public Service. He is also the author of two novels of political intrigue: *Vigilante Politics* (2017), and *Senate Intelligence* (2019). His first novel, *Vigilante Politics*, was listed as one of the "100 Best Politics Books of All Time" by Bookauthority.org. Charlie's novels are available online and in bookstores. He spends his time in the Central Coast community of Pacific Grove, California.